The Transition Witness

Teresa Tsalaky

Published by Visionary Press

ISBN 978-0-9904290-1-2

eBook ISBN 978-0-9904290-0-5

Cover design by DW Designs and Braden Welke

I

Chapter 1

DC-1128 set the pulse monitor to calibration and slid it onto her wrist. She imagined that it merged itself into her flesh, so much was it a part of her. She turned the bracelet a full circle on her wrist, just to remind herself that it was, in fact, an object separate from herself. She had heard of the new technology that could fuse aluminum to living tissue, but it had not yet been perfected. She was close enough to the top of the Consolidate to know such things. That's one reason she had taken this job—to get closer to the inner circle. Now she had the knowledge she needed, if not to defeat it, at least to leave it.

I'm lucky that this doesn't monitor my *pulse,* she thought to herself as she adjusted it to fit snugly.

As she strode through the bright white corridors of the Transitionary, her mind filled with every detail of her plan. One misstep and she would be rendered, melted down to a chemical soup for extraction of anything of value. She vowed to do everything just right, including waiting for the perfect transitioner.

Perhaps this day there would be a transitioner with the spark—one human who preferred the dull monotony of life to the promised ecstasy of death. She knew them from their moment of death. That was her job, after all, to be there for that instant. When a transitioner's breathing slowed to six cycles per minute, his transpod number appeared on her optiscreen. Every time she walked the white hallway toward another transpod, she had to swallow several times to calm a

1

bit of nausea. And every time she walked through the door of a transpod to take over from the transitioner escorts, the same thought came into her head. *You can't leave a task like verifying death to the rank and file.*

Most of them transitioned in the same monotonous manner, their breath surrendering little by little, steadily slowing and receding. That dreary pace of inhale-exhale haunted her day. She heard it in everything—in the back-and-forth swish of her clothes washer, the hum of her flycar's motor, the sound of her pants legs touching each other with every step. In recent years, everything had become breath. If she relaxed her eyes for just a moment, even inanimate objects—the floor, the wall, the transpod's glass—seemed to slightly expand and contract, breathing, breathing, forever breathing.

Inside the transpod, there would come a time when the body simply failed to take another breath, the end heralded by an absence, by what didn't happen. But occasionally, there was a transitioner with the spark.

The first time she saw it, she was green. She had been at her job less than a year and was still telling herself that it was worth the price, that they would die anyway, whether or not she was there to verify it, and that this might allow her to one day save many people from this fate. She was still telling herself those lies on the night that she had her first transitioner with the spark.

Like the others, this transitioner began his descent with the typical steady ebb and flow of breath, each exhale lingering just a moment longer, each inhale more reluctant than the last. But this time, when the pause at the end of the breath extended so long that she knew it was his last, it didn't simply stop. Instead, his eyes flew wide open as his lungs inhaled a rapid gasp.

Those two tiny movements of eyes and breath jolted her like a storm's first thunderclap. She physically jerked back, and in the moment it took to recover her composure, the transitioner's eyelids had fallen shut, and a final sigh was abandoning his chest.

From that night on, she was always ready. In every transpod, she held her body steady and kept her face as blank as fog, bracing herself for the possibility of a spark. And they did come, perhaps one in a thousand. What did she see in that instant, in those eyes as wide as a yawn? Was it awe? Their eyes popped open as if demanding one last glance at the world. But when she looked into them, she saw a different focus. Those eyes did not see her or the transpod at all. And the emotion she interpreted not from the expression around the eyes, but from deep within them. They were not surprised or dazed or afraid. They were wonderstruck.

Chapter 2

Darby sprang from his bed like a cat from a trap. It's not that the knock at the door was so loud, but rather that he knew the potential menace behind it. His heart, softened by sleep, now pounded like a jackhammer as he hurriedly pulled his wool trousers over his pajamas. There would be no need to make himself fully presentable. The messengers of death don't care if your hair is combed.

Darby had been waiting for this day since his Listing. They never tell you exactly when they will come, only that you've been bestowed the honor of making it on the List. The transitions are too numerous to schedule. By law, they must be done between age fifty and fifty-one, but they are not planned on a calendar. The Consolidate simply goes down the List as reliably as a clock's tick.

Other than its start, today would be like any other. Darby would eat grits lightly sprinkled with salt for breakfast, plug into his thought facsimilator for the required morning session, take a thirty-minute lunch break with salt tea and a sandwich, and then force himself to spend one more hour in focused manufacturing mind. At the end of the required six hours, he would unplug, exhausted but able to relax his brain by choosing the recommended two hours of VirtualVision, affectionately dubbed "the fun tunnel" by its addicts. Actually, everyone except Darby called it the fun tunnel. And only Darby called them addicts.

Why did he persist in being so different? He often chided himself for not gaining more control over his thoughts so that he could fit in with others. He spent six hours a day in total focused concentration for his work. Why couldn't he choose to think like everyone else during his free time? He longed for friends, for the warmth of human camaraderie, the security of belonging to a group of one's choosing. But every time he tried to talk to someone, it felt like the place where a stream meets the sea, where the freedom of flowing is suddenly engulfed by a much larger force. He quickly bored of the things other people talked about. And they responded to his ideas with blank looks and polite smiles. More connections lost.

He couldn't remember a day when he hadn't been this way. As a child, his mother had pushed him to play with other children. But he didn't like their games. He wanted to go outside, run like the wind, arms outstretched and screaming like an eagle, then jump down a hill and tumble. That was fun. But other children didn't play outside. They stared hollow-eyed into their fun tunnels where they played with their minds, but not their bodies. His body needed the freedom of a child, and his mother had understood that. Somewhere secret, she had relished his difference. When he begged to go outside and play alone, he could see it in his mother's eyes—fear and hope mingling together like oil in milk.

As a child, he wasn't able to name the contradiction he saw in her eyes. Now, he knew what it was, but he didn't know why.

He'd seen the same look on the day of her Listing. The fear he understood. But what was she hoping for? What was worthwhile enough to leave him behind?

He knew what everyone believed about the transition, how it was as easy as slipping into sleep only to wake into a dream of utter beauty. It was a place where you no longer needed a thought facsimilator and long, hard concentration to create. Here on Earth, it was illegal to own your own thought facsimilator, and the one used for work was tightly monitored. If your mind strayed away from creating the day's product, even for a moment, a sharp zap snapped you back to your task. But there, on the other side of the transition, you could turn your thoughts to your own desires, and your every whim appeared effortlessly and in an instant. At least that's what they said.

Had his mother believed it? Is that why, on the day of her Listing, she seemed genuinely happy as she gave him the only gift he would ever call precious?

She had held it closed in her hand, like a secret. He stretched out his arm to receive it, and she gently unfolded the gift onto his palm, as if it was delicate and needed protection. The two blue stones were smooth and shiny, each with one flat and one rounded surface. The size of sparrow eggs, they seemed to glow from within.

"A day is coming when you will know what to do with these," she had said. "Trust your heart."

But today was the last day of his life, and he still didn't know what to do with her gift.

His palm felt the icy hardness of the doorknob. He said nothing to the men as he gestured them in. Transition takers always looked somber to him, but he knew it was professional emotionlessness they displayed on their faces. One of them handed him the transition notice. He stretched

7

out his arm to receive it. He read the bold type. "Tomorrow, two o'clock p.m."

Chapter 3

The alarm buzzed out its intermittent cadence, mechanical beeps loud enough to command action. Two burly men clad in dark blue ran down the Transitionary's circular corridor past DC-1128, the force of their speed and intent nearly carrying her along with them. She hastened her pace. She liked to get a look at the strugglers, just to make sure she was making the right choice, for it seemed logical to choose someone who showed a willingness to fight. They always seemed to wait until they were in front of the transpod door, and then some instinct kicked in. They hadn't, after all, been shackled, just gently led by their transitioner escorts—those two soothing women with honey eyes and reassurance in their voices.

That's where DC-1128 had started, as a transitioner escort. When she applied to the Consolidate, her trait-matching test had shown she possessed all those motherly mannerisms that would calm even the most frantic fears. Yet she had no children to bestow them upon. She would not bring life into a world that scheduled death like a trip to the dentist.

What other characteristic had the trait test shown that made her compatible for her promotion to transition witness? How could someone with motherly instincts also be callous and detached enough to attend to the murders of thousands of innocents? Coldhearted, contemptuous, cruel. These were the words she used to describe herself.

She could hear the grunts and squawks of men wrestling before the scene came into view. By the time she got there, the noises of exertion had stopped. The blue-clad transition enforcers had the man on the ground, one with a knee on the transitioner's back, the other administering a transdermal. Though the transitioner's face was flushed, he had stopped struggling and was as limp as a doe in a jaguar's mouth.

It confirmed for DC-1128 why she would not choose a man such as this. His fight for life was spur-of-the-moment, and he had given up as soon as the transition enforcers had him pinned to the floor. No, she would not choose one of these strugglers to aid her escape. She needed someone in complete control of his impulses, someone who acted with premeditated precision, someone who would fight to his last breath. And yet, she had no way to know the virtues of her victims. She had only the spark as a yardstick. It would have to be enough.

She did not linger to watch the transition enforcers drag the man into his transpod. She had to maintain an appearance of aloofness, and now her left eyeglass lens was showing the next assignment. She shifted her focus to the optiscreen's message. *Transpod 12, Darby Tate.*

As DC-1128 entered the transpod, she felt goose bumps rise on her arms. Was it just a breeze from the whoosh of the pneumatic door? She had spent so many years placing straightjackets on the flailing arms of her emotions that she no longer knew whether physical feelings were caused by an internal or an external source.

The transpod and everything in it was so white that it all blended together into a flat one-dimensional surface.

Only the pale arms and faces of the two transitioner escorts, poking out from their white smocks, punctuated the void of color. DC-1128 nodded their dismissal, and they flowed past her and out of the transpod like river water flowing around a rock.

The face of the transitioner was as ashen as eggshells and still as the moon. Brown hair framed smooth skin. *Not at all like age fifty,* she thought—no typical hints of gray at the temples or wrinkles under the eyes. As she settled herself by the table, she tried to stop her brain's habit of speculation. Was this one a tailor or trader? A banker or bailiff? A dodecman or doorman? Were there tiny scars on his fingertips or bulging biceps under his shirt? A callous on his earlobe or an ink stain at the corner of his lips? Any of these could be hints—clues to tie him to a life. *No, no, don't,* she reprimanded herself. *He's no one now, no one.*

His breath told a different story. It continued yet, slow but steady. It needed a real being to enter and exit. Otherwise, it would just be the wind whistling through an abandoned building. But this was breath. Breath! That metronome of existence. That element that every living thing exchanges with every other. His breath, her breath. In that tiny room, she was inhaling some of what he exhaled, and he, too, was taking in molecules that had just been a part of her. Yes, they each took one tiny part of her with them, and she felt like she was disappearing bit by bit.

The spark came so fast that she barely had time to stifle a gasp. But she had gone over this moment so many times in her mind that her hand automatically grabbed the transdermal patch from the pocket of her scrubs. Now with focused intention, she slipped it under the sheet with

11

minimal movement and pressed it against the skin of the transitioner's neck.

Would it work as Ari had promised? In a few hours, DC-1128 would be risking her life just to find out. But so had Ari risked his to provide it. And he had asked nothing in return, only that she succeed. "Your freedom is enough for us all," he had said. "We only need hope, and with your freedom, we will finally have that." But she had promised herself that if a person could survive out there, she would come back for them, and Ari knew it without having to ask.

Ari was a Level Three, even higher up in the Consolidate than her Level Four as a transition witness. That's because he was a chemist, and chemicals controlled everything. DC-1128 might be responsible for the matter of death, but what Ari created could control life as well. He made chemicals for people who fainted, chemicals for people whose blood pressure was too high, chemicals for people who are too nervous, chemicals for people who are too shy, chemicals for people looking for bliss, chemicals for people who had made it onto the List.

"Better Living Through Chemistry." That's what the framed print hanging behind Ari's desk said. It was black and white but yellowed. In it, a woman with coiffed hair and an apron bent daintily over a dishwasher and poured a powdered cleanser into it. Her face gleamed with happiness. Inset in the upper right corner was a picture of a man in a lab coat pouring a vial of liquid into a flask. This was the one print Ari owned from the time before the dodecahedrons were built, and he cherished it. Not because he agreed with its message. No, he had seen that chemicals helped the Consolidate hold its power. And it was not because he loved antiquity. He was more concerned about the future than the past. Rather, he cherished it because it was his promise—his vow to himself—that he would one day use his skills for the benefit of all, not for the Consolidate. He had taken the first step toward fulfilling his promise by creating the transdermal cryopatch for DC-1128.

Why she insisted on using her Directory of the Consolidate employee identification number rather than her name he couldn't fathom. He had planned to someday ask her. Little did he know that as of this moment, he would lose the chance. At the end of her shift, DC-1128 would not leave the Transitionary for home. Instead, she would descend into its bowels, to the morgue and the rendering plant—the one place where no one bothered to monitor an opening in the dodec.

Chapter 4

DC-1128 began her practiced breaths, the ones that Gemini had taught her to reduce her heart rate and keep her face from flushing. There must be nothing that could give her away, not even sudden color in her cheeks. *Three counts in. Breathe. Three counts out. Relax. Four counts in. Breathe. Four counts out. Relax.* Back to three counts, then four, and three, then four. Slow and deep. Controlled and calm. *Thank you, Gemi,* she thought, as she felt her heart slowing to a more normal pace.

She grabbed the transitioner's forearm, the pulse monitor on her wrist resting on his pulse point. It emitted its low tone, confirmation that his heart had stopped pumping blood.

Just as this transitioner's veins carried vital nutrients from one point to another, so the veins of the Consolidate carried the various manufacturing materials from one city to another through long tunnels stretching from dodecahedron to dodecahedron. One of these would be her escape route. She and her transitioner would travel through it like two blood cells amid the renderings.

Her transitioner. What was this sudden sense of ownership? This total stranger, already beginning to grow cold—how their fates had suddenly become inseparable. Would he mind that she had hijacked his death? Would he cooperate? Would he even wake up?

Stop it, she reprimanded herself. *Don't think about that. Stay focused. Focus! I need to prepare. It's today.* After all of the

15

hours of meticulous mental rehearsal, and in spite of her daily and diligent practice of Gemini's breathing technique, DC-1128 still felt giddy and distracted. But as she exited the transpod, she remembered to not look back.

Chapter 5

At four-fifty p.m., DC-1128 slipped into her office, ten minutes before her shift was to end, and pulled the small backpack from under her desk. It felt too heavy for the few items it held—a second set of transporter coveralls, two UV cloaks, R-fifty thinsulate, a fire orb, a pound of protein powder, and of course the particle-beam pistol. If she had to use it, at least she would finally be killing honestly, with a purpose.

Though she had never been able to practice with it, she had held it in her hand for hours, going over the movements in her mind—safety off, depress trigger, release and reload. She had ten seconds of sustained beam to hit her target before the gun required its five-second recharge. She had thoroughly studied its construction and operation, its capabilities and weaknesses. "Cuts through aluminum but not steel," the tutorial had said. And how did it cut a human? Right in half, she imagined.

She had also studied the natural world, memorizing all the available information she could download to her optiscreen, and so she felt prepared for that as well. She quietly recited the knowledge that mattered most. "Wood burns. Roots nourish. Branches shelter. Leaves heal." The words had become her mantra, her way of reigniting her courage when it started to falter. *My life depends on a tree*, she thought wryly as she cinched her pack. And she truly believed it. The gun she might need for minutes against a few humans. But the much bigger antagonist lay outside the dodec's walls. There were no people out there to worry about. But the fierce winds and sudden floods and flash freezes—those would be the daunting foes.

That the natural world would be both scourge and savior, both menace and sustainer, was a strangely soothing concept to DC-1128. Something seemed right about it. It did not force the reconciliation of opposites that was so common in her protected world. It let one thing be two things, both at once. It let contradiction exist.

She slipped the pulse monitor off her wrist and into her top desk drawer, zipped up the front of her brown coveralls and hoisted the backpack over her shoulders. She pulled the cap down low over her forehead, hoping none of her Transitionary colleagues would recognize her face underneath it. But who actually looked at each other in those sterile hallways? The guilty avoid direct gazes, even those of their co-conspirators. And it required only half a glance to see what needs to be known—the brown coveralls that signify a transporter or the blue uniform of a transition enforcer. White was for the escorts, and black was reserved for the verifiers of death. Each of these colors had roots in some distant past, had meanings she wasn't familiar with.

But all she needed to know today was that brown would be her temporary identity, would get her past the rendering plant and into a transport. It wouldn't work for the morgue. For that, she would have to take her chances, get in and out while no one noticed.

She opened her office door a crack to make sure the hallway was clear and then slipped into it, her brown disguise stark against the white walls. Two white smocks passed. She dared not look to see where their eyes focused.

The ten seconds waiting for the elevator seemed an eternity, and she felt all the thousands of moments of nausea from her years in the transpods combine into a whirlpool in her stomach. Saliva flooded her mouth as she struggled to hold herself in check. *Three counts in. Breathe. Three counts out. Relax.* Relief flowed over her as the elevator doors opened to emptiness. Stepping into an elevator is where it would have been hardest to avoid eye contact. *From here, it's easier,* she lied to herself. And she began her descent.

When the door opened, she would be in an alien world. The beamkey from Orion had gotten her into the elevator, but only her wits would get her through whatever she would find in the rocky depths of the Transitionary.

I must walk with purpose, as if I know where I'm going, she thought, reciting the next detail of her memorized plan.

A ding announced her arrival, and she strode out into the corridor without hesitation. *A river.* She heard the distinct sound of gurgling liquid—a sound made only by water traversing its obstacles. She saw that the walls were indeed rock, and they were damp. *Surely not from water seeping through them, not at this depth,* she thought. *Condensation. Heat meets cold.* She felt the humidity on her skin. Warm air, cold rock. The play of oxygen and opposites.

Her time with Ari had taught her such things. Anything to do with molecules, and Ari was lit with passion. It was so infectious that he could hold her attention talking about the buildup of electron density between nuclei or why sodium sulfate becomes less soluble at high temperatures. "Water is the only liquid that expands as it freezes," he had once announced, as if he was a proud papa bragging about some great accomplishment of his offspring. Details remembered. Something she might need once she got beyond the dodecahedron that covered the city with its protective glass.

Ari is what I need beyond the dodec. That thought had constantly entered her head during her months of preparation, but she knew it was not pragmatic. His knowledge of the elements didn't mean he could control them, so he was no more fit for survival than any man. But most importantly, he worked outside the Transitionary. Of the entire group, only she and Orion had access to the elevator she had just stepped out of. And Orion's head injury had left him with seizures, not fit to face the obstacles on the outside. So it had to be a transitioner. She had no choice.

She could see that the corridor was about to end at a wall with hallways branching in either direction. To pause as if she didn't know where she was going could give her away. She would have to choose a direction in advance. *Left,* her brain said, and she followed the instinct. As soon as she turned the corner, she saw the dim neon of the morgue sign and the brown coveralls of a man walking toward her.

What was the custom here? Did they nod to each other in passing? Did they know each other? Would he see that she did not belong in his world? *Three counts in. Breathe!* She looked him right in the eye and gave a slight smile. He smiled back and passed. *Three counts out. Relax.*

Her hand felt the cool aluminum bar that opened the morgue door. As she pushed it, its heavy clank momentarily pulled her attention from scanning the room through the door's glass window. She finished her scan as she entered the room. *No one. Empty.* Well, not exactly. There were plenty of bodies from that day's take—two long lines of them, silent beneath their sheets. She had verified them all, almost fifty from a single shift. And now they lay there, all together, a mute jury, and she knew their verdict.

Her knees wobbled, and she grabbed the steel edge of the conveyor belt to steady herself. What had she done all these years? And for what? A chance to get outside and be claimed by the elements?

The sounds she heard now quickened her heart so fast that no amount of breathing would slow it. First, a buzzer sounded, and then a clang as gears engaged, and then a nonstop rumble. The conveyor belts had started, and they were taking the bodies—*her transitioner's body*—steadily toward the rendering plant. Soon, the bodies would be dropped into a chemical soup that would make Ari's eyes shine just to think about it.

She ran to the dark openings in the wall that the conveyors disappeared into and began pulling back sheets to search the faces, back and forth between the two conveyors, searching for the one. But death distorts, and how could she be sure when she had seen him only once, had only paid attention for a few seconds after the spark? Brownish hair. Strong jaw. Slight stubble. What could she remember? As each body was engulfed by that awful mouth, she felt her plan unraveling.

Chapter 6

Frantic now, DC-1128 began pulling the sheets all the way off the bodies, no longer caring whether she left a trail of evidence on the floor. Where was he? Where? Had she missed him? Already her mind was going over everything it knew about these dank depths, trying to formulate a new plan. "Transporters work in teams. At Transport Control, they're never alone," Orion had told her. "They must have a room or office somewhere between the morgue and rendering plant where they meet up. You'll want to be careful passing that." Could she simply kidnap one of them and demand a transport as ransom? No, at Level Seven, a transporter's life would be worth nothing to the Consolidate.

There! She knew him first by the transdermal patch, one corner of it visible on the side of his neck. She checked the hair, the face. Yes, this was *her* transitioner. She had found him. She put her forearms under his arms, moving forward with the conveyor as she struggled to lift him. He was heavier than she expected, but her adrenalin was flowing now, sending blood to the places that gave strength, and with one big heave, she was able to move the dead weight, tumbling with him to the floor as the blank spot on the conveyor disappeared into the wall.

She rolled him onto his back and unshouldered her pack. She had put the syringe in its front pocket for easy access, and now she unsheathed the three-inch needle and jabbed it into his chest. A second passed, then another, each an agonizing infinity. He remained still as a corpse. *Breathe, damn it. Breathe!* But the only sound was the conveyor belt droning its monotonous rumble.

Then finally, like a free-diver who has stayed under too long, Darby Tate surfaced with a big gulping breath, his greedy lungs taking in all they could hold. Eyes wide, a look of bewilderment spread across his face. He tried to talk, but all that came out was a cough. He gulped to soothe the rawness in his throat, and the words came out as a harsh whisper. "I saw the sacred ones. They exist."

DC-1128 was too intent on her task to indulge his hallucinations. Already she had his brown coveralls out of the pack. She pulled him up to a sitting position and shook him hard. "Listen, you have to put these on. Do you hear me?"

"Where...?" his question trailed off.

She stared at him intently as if her mere will could command his actions. "There's no time. I'll explain later. But we have to get out of here. Now! Do you understand?"

He nodded as he struggled to shake off the fog. As she helped him stand and pull on the coveralls, she was talking rapidly. "We're in the morgue. I kept you from dying. And now we're going to get out of here. Then you can live as long as you want. We're going to get out through a transport tunnel. We're supposed to be a transporter team. Do you know what that is?"

He could still only whisper. "Yes."

Good. At least a Level Six, she thought. "You may have to be the one to drive. Can you drive?"

"Yes, but..."

"You have to look like you know what you're doing. You have to walk like you know where you're going." She shook him again. "You have to get with it. Do you want to stay alive?"

The smile that visited Darby's face was genuine and broad. He began to chuckle, and the chuckle grew into a laugh.

A crazy man. Great. She grabbed his arm to pull him along as she turned toward the door. "Just follow my lead. And don't say anything.

Follow the sound of the river, she thought as they turned right into the hallway. They passed doors built right into the rock. She understood why the walls weren't sealed and finished. Unnecessary materials meant unnecessary waste. In the world of the dodec, all existing structures were used without alteration whenever possible. Alteration meant waste, and waste had to be minimized.

The sound of water magnified through the natural hallways, and its volume increased as they went, confirming her direction. She glanced at the nameplates on the doors they passed. Mechanical Room, Transport Scheduling, Rendering Plant. And now her stomach turned as she realized the source of the sound she had been following. This was not a river of innocent water, no pristine underground stream, no pure aquifer. This was a lake of dissolved bodies, the place where flesh and bone were separated, dissolved and separated again into their finer constituents.

She heard the sound of a whirlpool and imagined the centrifuge separating one component from the next. From there, the liquids would move into their individual streams to the processing pools to be recombined and solidified. In the closed-loop world of the dodec, everything was recycled.

25

It had to be. Even a few weeks' waste would overwhelm the system.

Carbon, nitrogen, calcium, phosphorous—the human body provided a wealth of materials for the material world. Potassium for fertilizer. Chlorine for cleaning. Sodium for seasoning and for the dodec's glass.

"Most of the mass of the human body is oxygen, but most of the atoms are hydrogen," Ari had told her.

Hydrogen, the fuel that both powered the Consolidate and gave it its power. Control the hydrogen, and you control a person's ability to stay warm, the distance he can travel, the amount of labor required to take care of himself. Control the hydrogen, and you control his life.

Ari had told her that before the dodecahedrons were built, inventors had designed a simple device that used resonance to separate water into its individual molecules, easily making hydrogen on demand, with oxygen as the only byproduct. Because their devices created more energy than they used, they appeared to violate the laws of thermodynamics. But more serious than that, they could violate the Consolidate's hold on the populace. So the Consolidate bought up all the patents, threatened and harassed anyone who tried to make the information public. To assure their control, they made liquid hydrogen as the world's new fuel—something that had to be manufactured, stored and sold. And human bodies were one source of it.

As DC-1128 continued past the rendering plant, she wondered how Ari had known these things. History rewritten by the victors, and this knowledge was contained in no textbook.

An acrid smell assaulted her nostrils, and she automatically covered them. As she passed the door from where it seemed to come, she glanced through its glass window. A trickle of yellow powder fell from a chute into a freight-car box. Sulfur. One more byproduct of the human body. Brimstone. The old religions had used it as a threat—wrath raining down upon any unrepentant populace, carried on God's breath. And what wrath would be visited on this society once God got around to it, she wondered. What fury awaited her on nature's breath?

The hallway was about to end, and she could see that a cavernous room lay beyond it. She pressed herself flat against the wall, one arm forcing her transitioner into position. She looked back. No one else occupied the hallway. She could afford a moment to assess the situation. Peering around the corner, she saw a glass room in the center holding an attendant. Tunnels opened into the walls, the back ends of transport freight cars peeking out from their shadows.

A transporter team stood at a window that opened into the glass booth, and one of the duo seemed to be signing something. At the far left, another brown team was disappearing into the tunnel's black throat. That would have to be it. To wait for a better chance would be too much of a risk. Someone could come down the hallway at any moment. They had to go now, while the attendant was distracted.

DC-1128 grabbed her transitioner with one hand and felt for her particle-beam pistol with the other. She nodded toward the tunnel that the transporter team had just entered.

"Walk confidently," she whispered to him. And they entered the exposed arena of Transport Control.

27

Chapter 7

DC-1128 glanced sideways without turning her head. The transporter team that had been at the glass booth was now walking toward one of the tunnels. Did the man in the booth not see her and her transitioner? Or didn't it matter? Perhaps he did not monitor every transporter team's whereabouts.

It was only two-hundred feet to the tunnel, but if counted in heartbeats, it measured a mile. At least her transitioner was cooperating. He had been mute as a fish and was playing his part beautifully.

DC-1128 kept her eyes forward toward the tunnel into which the two brown-clad men had disappeared. She had to get there before the transport lifted, but her pace must remain steady to not draw attention. She hoped she would not have to use her pistol, but if she did, it would be the last deaths she would ever witness, and she considered it a worthy tradeoff.

She nudged her transitioner to guide him to the right side of the transport until they were in shadow. Inside the transport cab, the team would be making final preparations, entering their destination and checking with Tunnel Control for permission to begin their trip.

DC-1128 whispered into her transitioner's ear, "When I say go, stay low and go in front of the cab to the driver's door. When he gets out, get in. Ready?" Darby Tate nodded. "Go!" she whispered.

As her transitioner scurried to his position, DC-1128's face popped up in the passenger's window, the particle-beam pistol pointed directly at his temple.

"Out," she mouthed, and he automatically raised his hands. "Out! Now!" So tense was the moment that she didn't realize she had shouted.

The man's shaky hand reached down to open the transport cab door, and as he slid out, she had one more command for him. "Down on the ground, arms out!" But she kept her pistol pointed forward at the driver. He didn't shake at all, and for a moment she thought she would have to make good the threat that her pistol posed. Before she was forced to make a decision, he opened his door. She watched as he slowly slid from his seat and onto the cab's sidestep. But what she didn't notice was his hand under the console, pushing a button.

Blaring blasts of sound assaulted her, and she jumped into the cab and scrambled over the seat to find her transitioner. He was already on his way in, and they nearly slammed into each other. As she bounced back to her seat and closed the door, she heard a sound between the intermittent blasts of the alarm. Thundering feet. It sounded as if an entire army was about to descend upon them.

"Drive!" she screamed. But before her transitioner had a chance to even find the throttle, she lifted it up and slammed it forward.

The cab and its freight car rose two inches above their magnetic tracks and lurched forward like a drunkard. A portion of the front fender sliced away and dropped to the ground, victim of a particle beam. She aimed her pistol backward out the window and fired without a target. But now, the bigger threat was not the particle beams behind her, but the closing gate in front, its iron jaw dropping from the ceiling like a deliberate guillotine.

That most basic of human instincts guided Darby Tate's hand to the throttle to pull it back. But DC-1128's intent was stronger. She would rather die here than live a half-life under the dodec, and she forced his hand forward. As the transport careened toward the closing gate, she forgot to breathe.

The screech of iron on steel and shower of sparks blinded her and assailed her eardrums. She threw her arms up in front of her face without thinking. The cab jerked back and forth, nearly breaking free of its magnetic grip. The boxcar hit the wall and exploded into a rain of yellow powder. Brimstone, the element of God's wrath. A spark caught, and the tunnel exploded into blue fire. The force of it pushed the cab forward even faster, but they remained ahead of it, and now it would serve to block their pursuers.

As the distance between them and the wall of blue flame increased, DC-1128 took her first breath in what seemed like minutes. She looked over at her transitioner, expecting to see him frozen like stone, a deer in the headlights. But no, his shoulders were moving up and down like raindrops hitting the pavement. His head was tilted back a bit. And he was laughing. Not a silent chuckle or quiet guffaw, but out-loud laughing.

Crazy man, she thought, and turned her attention to her next task. In minutes, they would hit the first bridge, and she had to get him ready.

"Listen!" she yelled, so forcefully that even the smile left his face. "When I say jump, you have to open the door

31

and jump. Do you trust me?" The smile returned to his face, and his eyes lit with playful mockery.

"This is serious. Will you jump when I tell you, no matter what?" He bit his lip to contain the smile and nodded his consent.

Good boy. Stay with me, just a few minutes more. But they wouldn't have to wait that long, for even now, the tunnel was on an incline, and she could see the small speck of light far beyond. As they sped forward, it grew and grew, a shining eyeball that would soon engulf them. *I didn't know it would be so bright,* she thought as it grew as big as the tunnel itself. *Good thing. He won't see what he's jumping into.* And as the cab burst free from its confinement in the tunnel, she screamed, "Jump!"

Floating. Freedom. The world was only air and light. As Darby fell, a remembrance seared into his brain like a lightning strike, and the all-encompassing peace of it pervaded him. But before he had a chance to catch and hold it, the thunder came. Boom! He slammed the surface like a bullet hitting its target, and the thunder engulfed him. Tumbling, tumbling, the water rolling him over and over. The impact had knocked out his breath, and now he dared not inhale, as only water would enter his lungs. Which way was up? He must find the surface, but he could see only bubbles and blue currents.

I float. Just relax, he told himself, and in mere moments his face had pierced the surface. He gasped a quick breath and held it, prepared for the ongoing onslaught of water. Through the froth, he could see the bobbing green of trees, and between attempts to simply stay afloat, he made his way toward them.

Sticks assaulted him, hundreds of sticks of every size—floating debris pulled from the shore by the most recent flood. A river of sticks. And now he realized the danger. A large branch or log could knock him unconscious. He pushed himself as high above the surface as his arms would propel him, and eyes wide, he looked upstream for any threat. A rock hit his shin, and he knew immediately that the threat lay below as well. Then he noticed the cold. An icy fist of liquid held him in its grip. He doubled his efforts. He had cheated death less than an hour before. He would not let it win now. And with the last bit of strength in his aching arms, he made his way to shore.

Sprawled on the rocks, exhausted and breathing like a bellows, he looked back at the river's roiling surface. DC-1128 was nowhere in sight.

II

Chapter 8

Ari Stockton sat back to admire the pattern of hexahedrons he had drawn. He couldn't leave an electronic trail, so it had to be sketched out by hand, and he thought it was beautiful—hexagons connected by lines and labeled by letters. This one looked like an elephant, he thought, its body made of hexagons all touching each other, its trunk a group of hexagons single file in a curving line, four legs of hexagons dropping down the page. *This is where science becomes art,* he thought, gazing at its pattern. But when he looked at the specific combination of letters—the N's and O's and H's that labeled each hexagon—he had another thought. *This is where men become gods.*

With the knock at the door, he nearly crumpled the page rushing to cover it with a stack on his desk. "Yes," he barked out in his best authoritarian tone.

Gemini waltzed through the door in her lilting manner. To him, she never seemed to walk at all. It was always some magical combination of dancing and floating that carried her from one place to another. Although seventeen, her petite frame seemed more fit for a fairy than a woman, and he imagined gossamer wings at her back.

"Dad, you're working too late again," she said as she came around his desk to kiss his cheek. She always kissed his scars on purpose to show him that he was loved even where it's ugly. They felt like elephant skin beneath her lips.

He glanced at the clock. It was just past seven. If he let his passion for his project subside, he could feel the weariness beneath it. Yes, it was late, but he was nearing a breakthrough. He could feel it. And humanity couldn't wait. *He* couldn't wait. He had perhaps one more year to perfect his formula, a matter of months before he would be on the List.

He had heard that some Level Twos were still alive at fifty-five, even sixty. Had they bargained for an extension, made some offer to the Level Ones so compelling that they would make an exception? He could offer them his formula and perhaps save his own life. Or he could give it to the people and perhaps save them all.

Gemini leaned one hip on his desk and slammed her palm smack over the paper at the top of the stack. "What's more important here than a delicious dinner?" she teased, smiling with eyes that seemed to play hide-and-seek even as they held a steady gaze.

You, my dear Gemi, he thought. *You're more important than all of it, than all the people enclosed by the dodec.* He placed his hand on hers and gave it a little squeeze. "I'll be there in a minute. I promise."

That was all the reassurance she needed, and she waltzed back out of his office, teasing him with a "you better" backwards glance.

The breeze that her movement created felt refreshing, smelled like the ozone they pumped into the dodec on spring days. *O-three.* The words automatically entered his brain. He couldn't help it. For him, everything in the natural world could be diminished down to numbers and letters, and long ago he had stopped trying to keep his mind from making the translation.

He took the paper from the bottom of the stack and slipped it into a thin plastic case. He turned to the yellowed print behind his desk, pulled its frame forward a bit, and slipped the paper into its hiding place. Although the formula wasn't perfected yet, he had put two vials of it in DC-1128's escape pack, along with an explanation of it. He would trade it out for the final formula in time. But if he didn't have time—if the transition takers came for him soon after his Listing, or if DC-1128 made her escape before he had time to perfect it—at least she would have the part of it that would take her beyond the veil—the chemical that would take her to the place where every question was answered before it was asked. The question was, would it bring her back?

Chapter 9

Gemini winced as another pain shot across her lower abdomen. She nearly dropped the cabbocoli just before the table. She could have asked her father for one of his concoctions to ease the pain, but this was a woman's matter—one of the few things she didn't talk to him about.

Once a month, when her menses came, she thought of her mother—that woman whose image expanded and contracted with the whims of memory. The monthly reminder that she could give birth made Gemini long for the one who had birthed her. But her mother had died in the accident when she was just seven.

The accident. When that article—that most common device of grammar—is put before a word, it makes it a life-defining thing. Such a simple word. But it made it not just any accident, but rather *the* accident—the one that had altered her life forever, had changed her father forever.

Her father was such a gentle giant with his fuzzy moustache and curly eyebrows, his stubby fingers and just a bit of a belly. How those fingers could hold the delicate glass of a test tube or a tiny microscope slide, she didn't know. Flasks and beakers and droppers and stirring rods. The world of his work was made of glass. And so was his inner world since her mother's death. Ever since that day, Ari protected Gemini as if she wore a label that said "breakable." She might have rebelled against it, insisted on more freedom, but she knew that when her father obsessed over her safety, he was also protecting the one thing that could break in himself.

She set the ceramic bowl of cabbocoli safely on the table. It was her turn to cook, which meant it would be cold by the time her father pulled up his chair. He was always home by five-thirty on his kitchen duty days, as if cooking on a stove was as fun as brewing a chemical soup over a Bunsen burner. Her turn to cook gave him license to be late, especially in recent months. Whatever his new project was, it held him captive and wouldn't let him go at the end of the day. Fortunately, his office was just two blocks away, and she didn't mind the brief walk past The Remedy Shop and Trinket Village, over the cracking cement and past the coffee vendor—a quick trip to the Division of Chemical Sciences high-rise to remind her father that supper was at seven.

One-hundred and twenty-six chemists worked in his building, but the structure seemed large enough to house a thousand, towering as it did into the city sky. As a child, she thought that if she stood at the very top, she could touch the dodec. But then her father took her there, and the dodec's glass girth was still far off, way up in the sky, separating her from the heavens.

She had once imagined it was this barrier that kept her from her mother, for certainly there had to be something—some object solid and real—that kept her mother from coming back, some boundary that her mother could not cross. But a year after the accident, she learned in school the real purpose of the dodec, and her mother no longer had an excuse. The dodec was there as a shield not only from fierce weather, but also from the deadly sun, that bright eye that burned human tissue, that distant annihilator. Without the protection of the dodec, the sun's unseen rays would penetrate deep into her skin and damage the protein that held it together. She had learned that it could even blind her. And from that learning on, she was thankful for the protection that the Consolidate provided with the dodec's low-emissivity surface and layers of noble gasses between glass.

The sun had gone down now, and the clock read ten past seven. Her father would be coming through the door at any moment. She pulled the meat mash from the oven and set it on a potholder on the table.

"Here I am," she heard him holler down the hallway. "I smell cabbocoli. I *love* cabbocoli!"

His resonant voice traveled the air currents easily, wafting down the hallway like some deep perfume, winding around the corner to the dining room. And there, at a tiny patch under the table, its vibrations found their way into the microphone, where they were converted into electrical impulses and transmitted to the monitoring station.

Chapter 10

The dishes done and their recaps of the day traded, Ari and Gemini settled into their evening routines—Gemini to her room and her homework, and Ari to his tobacco pipe and books. At Level Three, he was rich enough for such a collection. Physical books had not been made since the dodecs were built. Anything that could be electronic was electronic. No paper was wasted. But Ari had scrounged the flea markets and traded in the online shops, and now an eclectic collection of titles sat on the living room shelf, and another stack sat on the floor by his recliner. The one on top was his most recent acquisition. He picked it up and placed it on his lap. He would be gentle with its brittle pages. *The Auschwitz Experiments*, the title said, and he opened it to a random page and read.

> *He introduced himself as Uncle Mengele and offered them sweets. He showed them the playground, painted in colors not otherwise seen in the dull grayness of the camp. The next day, he sewed them together back to back; now they would be not just congenital twins, but conjoined. A few days later, they died of gangrene. It did not matter. They were Gypsies, and in the mind of a Nazi, destined for the ovens.*

Ari took a long draw on his pipe to reflect. He had heard that word before. Nazi. What was it? Some sort of military group, if he remembered correctly. That was it, yes, in one of the two world wars before the World Civil War. And he recalled a symbol associated with them—a symbol that had represented eternity in one of the ancient religions. Why a military group would choose the symbol for eternity he couldn't fathom. And he couldn't imagine anyone sewing two children together. It made modern society seem almost sane.

He wished he knew a history saver with whom to discuss these things, but they were Level Tens and barely made a living, so few and far between that he had never met one.

That's the field he would have gone into if his parents hadn't been so insistent. "The sciences will get you closer to the top," they had said over and over, and he wasn't an independent thinker at that age, so he took their advice. When he discovered his passion for chemistry, he was glad of his choice. And later he learned that textbook history didn't really matter. It had been scrubbed, so even the history savers didn't have accurate information.

He learned the most from old novels. To allow old novels to exist, the Consolidate must have thought them safe—mere things of imagination. But he knew many truths could be hidden in fiction.

A knock at the door pulled him from his reflection. It would be one of The Uptown Group members, there for the Wednesday night session. The door opened to Vostro's towering frame, and he lumbered in like an earthquake, nearly having to duck under the lintel.

"I see you're still indulging," he said, nodding toward Ari's pipe.

"Life is short, may as well enjoy it," Ari said.

"Yours, maybe. I plan to live to a hundred."

"In your dreams," Ari said, and led his friend into the dining room. "A spirit shot, as usual?"

Vostro nodded and took his place at the table. Ari went to the kitchen and returned with a vial of blue liquid. He liked serving his colleagues from the tools of his trade. It was his signature, and it gave him a bit of delight.

As Vostro sipped the biting liquid, he felt his chest warm, and an inward sigh replaced the hard spot that held his stress.

The second knock was Orion. To the degree that Vostro was tall, Orion was scrawny, and they looked like a sideshow next to each other. At only nineteen, Orion might still grow into his skin, Ari thought.

They sat at the table and made small talk, Ari glancing now and then toward the top of the stairs for the light that would signify Gemini's door had opened. She never joined the group, even though at least one member was close to her age. "I'm not much for games," she had explained to her father. "But why didn't you ever invite me?" It was not an accusation but simple curiosity fueling the question. Of course Ari knew the answer, but he couldn't come up with an adequate lie when put on the spot like that. So he had just shrugged and changed the subject.

The wooden game board was now open on the table, each of its twelve indentations holding two black stones. White dice sat in the middle of the board, waiting. After a few minutes, Vostro asked the question on all of their minds. "Where is she?"

DC-1128 was always as prompt as an alarm clock. To miss the weekly meeting could only be the result of one of two things.

"I'll call," Ari said, and pushed twice on his wrist assistant. The universal tone for "not available" sounded, and he hung up with a touch of the screen and looked at the others. "Let's give her a few more minutes."

But they all knew she would not be showing up. She had no family other than the friends she had adopted, and they were all there at the table. She was as cautious as a stray cat with day-to-day matters, so it was unlikely that she herself had a mishap. That left two possibilities. Either she had found the transitioner she was waiting for and was now on the outside, or she had been caught and they might never know her fate.

"We'll need a new courier," Vostro said, breaking the silence. And they all took on the dispassion that was needed for the feat they were planning.

"I go to Old Town once a week for my fitness session, but I never have a reason to be in the Manufacturing District," Orion offered.

Ari glanced at the top of the stairs to make sure his daughter was safe behind her closed door. "I go there now and then for metals, but it may not be often enough when it comes time to act."

They usually had these conversations while playing their game, as if they needed a cover even in the privacy of Ari's home. And in fact, they did. They were hiding their planning from Gemini. Ari had insisted, over Orion's objections, that she never know about their scheme for the overthrow. And so they always talked in quiet voices as they rolled the dice and moved the stones, voices low enough to not be understandable behind Gemini's closed door.

But underneath the table, there was an ear that heard every word. And Ari's worry was less for DC-1128's fate than for his daughter's. How would she bear the loss of the woman who had become like a second mother?

Chapter 11

While the group downstairs played their silly game, Gemini studied her civics. No, not studied, she devoured it. The words of the text were like breath to her, and at only an inch away on her optiscreen, she felt like she could enter them, live inside them, see how the concepts they contained had shaped and shifted the life of society. No other subject had enthralled her like this, and from the first class, she knew this was her destiny. Politics. One day, she would be part of the Consolidate, and the thought of it made her heart dance. She might even meet the Benefactor. She imagined herself shaking his hand, then holding onto it as she looked into his eyes and said a heartfelt thank you for everyone, making him understand the volume of gratitude due him.

This golden dream was the second thing she never shared with her father, and she felt the weight of keeping it a secret. They never talked politics. She simply knew from his offhand remarks how he felt about the government. And just as he had put an invisible label on her saying "breakable," he had put one around his own heart saying "do not crush."

But one day, she would find a way to make him understand, and he would be proud of her accomplishments. She would tell DC-1128 first and get her advice. A woman who went by her Directory of the Consolidate number, who was also a friend of her father's, would know just how it should be presented. For now, she would focus on learning all she could so that she would be prepared to explain the reasons behind her feelings.

This week's assignment was an essay on the World Civil War. "Discuss at least four societal elements that brought it about, and what has changed so that such a conflict can never again befall us," the instructions said.

Gemini could easily name three of the contributing factors—unfettered access to dangerous ideas, diversity of religions, polarization of opinions. She would have to go back and reread the text to find the fourth element. But first, she wanted to get the ideas on paper that were lighting her brain.

"The World Civil War was the best thing that ever happened to society," she began. "Although billions died and many more were injured, it made clear what had to be done to create permanent peace and increased prosperity."

After two more paragraphs, she paused. Something downstairs was distracting her attention. It wasn't a noise, but the lack thereof. Her father and his group often had periods of silence as they concentrated on their game, but the quiet was usually punctuated by periods of muffled conversation. Mostly, she heard Vostro's voice, for it was as loud as he was tall, as if volume was a function of height.

Tonight, the quiet had lasted too long. Gemini decided it was time to be gracious and say hello to her father's friends. But it was more than common courtesy that pulled her off her bed and away from her civics essay. There was something down there she needed even more than politics.

Each week, when she walked down the stairs for her greeting, her father would say her name, as if he was obliged to announce her, and the men at the table would turn and smile. But DC-1128 always stood up, her face brightening like a sunrise. "There's the fairest girl in all the land," she would say—had always said since Gemini was seven—and as Gemini approached the table, DC-1128 would open her arms and enclose Gemini in a hug so warm that it dissolved every hurt she had ever felt. If not for the men sitting there, Gemini would stay there forever.

But this night was different. Before she could even see the table, she felt the absence. As she walked down the stairs, there was no radiant face, no open arms, no beaming proclamation. DC-1128's seat at the table was vacant.

"Where's DC?" she asked, before her foot hit the last step.

"Couldn't make it tonight," her father said. "She had something to attend to."

Gemini could always tell if her father was lying. Even the half of his face made immobile by the ropes of scar tissue would give him away with a little twitch. No, he wasn't lying. But something was not right. She knew it from the knot in her stomach that turned solid as a rock. She knew it from the void in her chest that felt as empty as that chair. And for the first time since the accident, she knew the prescience of doom.

Chapter 12

DC-1128 drank in water, inhaled it like breath. It filled her stomach, her trachea, her lungs. And then she was full—so full of it that the boundary between her and the river seemed to no longer exist.

At first, she had struggled in terror, but as she merged with the water, a deep peace pervaded her. She floated in serenity for what could have been a moment or a millennium. She could no longer tell the difference. All time was an infinite now. She drifted through multicolored clouds, intoxicated by luminous hues she had never before seen. Their beauty birthed an urge to move in joy, celebrate the magnificence of existence, and she spun herself end over end. She felt as if she had become a curl, a smile on the face of the sky, twirling through the iridescent fabric of creation.

Suddenly, she found herself speeding toward the bright eye of the tunnel's opening. What had happened? Hadn't she jumped? Had the stress of the escape played havoc with her brain? Before she could contemplate those questions, a voice came. "You have to go back. It's not your time yet, and there is something you wanted to accomplish." Although an imperative statement, she understood that it was not a command. She had a choice. She could stay in this place of bliss forever.

Now a wave of long-forgotten memories flooded her mind. Recollections of eons of existence entered her awareness all at once, and in that tide of knowings was the inevitable resolution to the choice she now faced. She would go back. She would return and accomplish her purpose.

She was instantly sucked backwards. Faster and faster she traveled. She felt herself shifting through layers, density accumulating. It was as if what she had just experienced was made of some ultra-fine substance that could not transfer back to the material world. And as she fully re-emerged into her physical body, the memory of what had happened dissolved back into its own essence.

She felt the ache of her stomach's convulsions and vomited a stream of water. Each cough brought agony to her lungs, but her desperation for air overcame her pain, and she gasped in oxygen in long, heaving breaths.

When her eyes opened, the wonder of what she saw magnetized her attention. White hair. A thick mane of it so pure and perfect that it stunned her. She struggled to regain her mental bearings, to piece together what had led to this moment. She remembered the transport, the tunnel, the jump, the overwhelming power of water. Then it struck her. The face in front of her was not her transitioner. It was a man, surely, but one far beyond fifty. She had never seen such a crown of glory on someone's head. And as she looked into his eyes, she saw something else that she had never before beheld. She was witnessing the quiet grace of the aged.

"Calm now. You're going to be all right. We'll see to that. We caught you in our net." He tilted his head toward a pile of rope on the rocks—a seine net that, from the smell of it, had also caught its ration of fish.

We? There are more than one? There are people on the outside! The realization screamed inside her. Had a transporter team once jumped at the bridge? If so, how had they survived nature's fury long enough to grow old? As the questions swirled inside her head, a second face came into view. *A boy!* Not more than ten, he peered at her with a face of consternation.

"Let's get her home, Grandpa. She's really cold."

Home. Of course they would have a home. But if he's only ten years old or so... A family. There's a whole family out here! She closed her eyes and let it sink in.

"Can you stand?" the old man asked.

She didn't know. Her legs felt numb and her lungs and head were bursting with pain, but she nodded yes, because she knew she needed warmth and care, needed to see this home.

As they helped her to her feet, she was able to rasp her question out. "The man with me...?"

"If there was someone with you, he's downriver by now," the old man said.

He turned to the boy. "Trask, can you get her home?" The boy nodded. "Send Josif and Talor to help me," he instructed.

The boy steadied DC-1128 as she took her first stumbling steps over the river rock. The old man headed downriver, not knowing that Darby Tate had not suffered DC-1128's fate. He had made it to shore long before the seine net snatched DC from death's grip. And now, Darby sat on the cold stones upriver, wet and shivering as the first fingers of dusk cast their shadows.

Chapter 13

The fire warmed DC down to her bones. She imagined the stones of the hearth held stories as old as the Earth itself—stories of cold and warmth, of death and survival, of serenity and struggle. She snuggled more deeply into the blanket they had wrapped around her, its earth-tone patterns of zigzags and circles surrounding her with more stories—tales of the people who had called this place home over the centuries. Everything here seemed to hold an old story, and as she relaxed her gaze into the red embers, her imagination created generations of lives that had walked on these floors, sat in this chair, gathered warmth at this hearth.

She had never before felt the penetrating heat of an open flame. Under the dodec, no fires were allowed, no unnecessary combustion to create airborne wastes. What else had she sacrificed in that self-contained world? How had it contracted her into a person smaller somehow than those who shared this house?

It's all right. I'm out now, she thought. And as she gazed at the dancing fingers of light, she could feel herself already expanding.

A cup of steaming broth appeared before her. "Thank you," she said, and took the offering.

The woman who gave it was short and plump, a bun at the back of her head and a no-nonsense countenance in front. She had taken on the task of DC's protector, shielding her from the flood of questions that the rest of the family was aching to ask. Such was her power in that house that she held every member of it at bay with a mere glance, allowing DC to rest and regain her inner balance.

DC was curious, too. Like a creature of the sea suddenly walking on land, she wanted to know its inhabitants. But for now, she knew the important thing. She was safe. And she would have plenty of time to immerse herself in this new group. And so she was content to heat her skin at the fire and warm her innards with the soothing liquid—content to let her mind rest.

It felt as if she needed this time for healing—from what, she knew not. Her ordeal in the water had been frightful, but not catastrophic. No, it was not that. There was some deeper trauma. A much more menacing destroyer had inflicted its damage slowly, and she could feel it poking its head below the surface, scanning her inner world for what it could lay claim to.

She heard a door open behind her and the old man's voice in a low tone. "We couldn't find him. It's too dark now. We'll look again tomorrow. How is she?"

"Warm by now, I imagine. But she's got an anguish to attend to," came the woman's reply.

The thought of her transitioner brought DC back to the day's events. She had selfishly revived him to aid her escape. She had told him to trust her and jump, even though she wasn't sure that a river ran below the bridge. She had saved him from the Consolidate's death potion but could not save him from the rage of nature. As DC-1128 berated herself for her failings, the anguish that Grandmother Sylvan had mentioned remained unattended.

Chapter 14

Darby Tate had never been so cold. Even death hadn't chilled him to the core like this. He had found a broad tree trunk to shield his body from the breeze, but he had no blanket to cover his wet clothes. How could he know to remove them until they dried? His world had been devoid of the need to survive. Like everyone else in the Consolidate's care, he had walls and a roof to keep in warmth and enough food to keep hunger at bay. Shelter and sustenance for all. That was the Consolidate's promise, and it had endeared many people to the ruling class. Never mind if the food was rice and the roof was tin. Even those who preferred to do nothing could live to fifty with some degree of comfort. There was no need to learn which plants you could eat or how to endure a freezing night.

His chattering teeth sounded like castanets. Drowsiness descended on him, and he longed for the comfort that sleep would bring. His mind drifted into the void between, where images rise like momentary ghosts before dissolving back into blackness.

A flash. A tunnel. His mother. A path through a park. Flowers that glowed from within. Himself as a child. The time he called his father a loser. The time he saved an injured cat. Revelations and insights, feelings and flashbacks. Moments of joy, of anger, of kindness, of shame. The disjointed movie immersed him in its script. And then came the realization that this was not just a collection of meaningless images. It was a rerun—a selection of experiences that molded the personality to which he clung in order to see himself as separate from all other selves.

He pulled himself toward wakefulness. His brain felt as heavy as a paralyzed limb, but he dragged it back into the cold night. He had to think, to remember. From the time that she revived him in the morgue until this moment, he had not had time to reflect. Everything had moved so fast. But something had happened before their escape. Something momentous. If he could only recall it. He closed his eyes and tried to coax the images in, but they were as stubborn as glue dried in its tube.

Use manufacturing mind. Focus inward, he said to himself. All those years of working at the thought facsimilator now had a greater purpose, and he gathered his intent and concentration. He emptied his mind and felt for what he was trying to extract back out. And then the memories came, at first just a trickle.

I did die. I remember. I floated and saw my body below me.

The trickle grew into a stream, and he recalled the tunnel, the light that was living, the multi-holograph review of his life. The stream became a torrent, and Darby Tate remembered it all—the feeling of love as a substance, the reunions, the questions and answers, the knowledge and knowings, the journey back toward his source, and the fantastic force as he slammed back into his body.

She brought me back. Oh, why did she bring me back?

In that instant, the answer infused him, and he knew that he would survive this frigid night. He knew that one day, he would stand before the sacred ones, and she would be his witness.

Chapter 15

DC awoke to the smell of fried eggs and the sound of hushed voices. They hadn't waited breakfast. They knew she needed rest, and they needed fuel for their chores. She heard a door open and feet leaving. Then the house was quiet.

The thick robe laid out on the chair by the bed offered its invitation, and DC slipped it on. A glance around the room showed that the rest of the items in it belonged to a child—a doll and stuffed rabbit, small shirts spilling out of a drawer in the dresser, a flower-adorned box on top of it, and a rocking chair small enough for an elf. DC opened the door and followed the scent down the hallway.

The woman with the bun was in the kitchen. She had introduced herself the night before as Grandma Sylvan. Now, the no-nonsense countenance needed for the large brood of that house melted to softness. She handed DC a cup of mint tea and sat her at the table.

"I want to thank you," DC began. "You have been very kind."

"Well, my dear, we are the same person. And you're very welcome."

DC thought it an odd reply, but she knew that no matter how close this place was to the dodec, it was still a foreign land.

Grandma Sylvan returned the teakettle to the stove and began asking questions without asking them. "We rarely get a guest from the city," she said. "Your family will miss you."

"Oh no, I don't have a family," DC answered.

In this way of making presumptions, she drew out DC's story. Over eggs and biscuits, DC told of the escape through the transport tunnel. She explained that everyone in the dodecahedron believed that no one lived on the outside, that it could not be survived. Over a second cup of tea, she described what life was like for the people of the dodec, and what life was like for her.

The soft empathy in Grandma Sylvan's eyes kept DC talking, and soon she was back in time to her childhood, her alcoholic father and fearful mother, having no brothers or sisters to play or even fight with, her shyness in school, how she met her best friend at age fourteen and finally had a confidante. Then forward in time to her young adult life, how she discovered that people were manipulated like puppets, her decision to work for the Consolidate to find out enough to defeat it or leave it, her job at the Transitionary.

"My title is transition witness. I witness people die— get killed, actually—and I verify their deaths. Dozens every day."

She paused and watched the woman's eyes, but she could read no judgment there. She needed a response and remained silent to wait it out.

"Of course you did," Grandma Sylvan finally said. "Bless you for being the one to have that experience for us all."

It was such a strange statement that DC couldn't go on. There was no forgiveness in it, but rather a lack of the need to forgive.

She heard boots stomping on the porch, and a tall boy clamored through the door all out of breath, kicking off his boots and pulling off his over-sweater all at once. When he saw the visitor sitting there, he froze for a moment, but the sound of other feet thumping to get the mud off prompted him away from the entryway, and he walked into the kitchen all gangly-legged and offered his hand.

"I'm Finn. Nice to meet you," he said.

As the others piled in, Grandma's no-nonsense countenance returned, and they approached DC one by one and gave their introductions. Lucas, Micah, Trask, Annabel. They smelled of fresh air and brown earth. Their energy was such that they would have talked all at once, peppering her with questions, but ever mindful of Grandma's gaze, they sat politely around the table and waited.

"DC is from the city," Grandma began. "She decided to leave it, and the only way out was to jump from the bridge."

"Did you break anything?" little Annabel asked. She lifted her pant leg. "I once broke my leg and the bone came clean out," she said, showing the scar.

"How do you breathe in the city?" Micah chimed in. "It's all enclosed. Are there air holes?"

Before she could think of an answer, Trask asked, "Do you drive a flycar? What's it like?"

And so it went on for an hour as DC satisfied their curiosities. And she learned about them as well—their ages and chores, their talents and favorite foods, how their parents had died in the fire, how Finn had known that a visitor would be coming.

With their curiosities satisfied and their stories told, they pulled DC from her chair to show her their favorite room. Over the generations, when members of the family traveled, they would rummage through abandoned buildings where they found treasures of information bound between cardboard covers. Books on dozens of topics now filled the shelves and boxes in their library room, and not one had been left unread.

The children thought it must have been a strange world their ancestors had inhabited, where every bit of information, whether how to build a home or a bomb, was written down on pieces of paper. Grandma had taught them how to tap directly into knowledge, so most of the nonfiction books had little utilitarian value. But there were some topics that they would have never thought to inquire about, with titles such as, *Hawaii on Ten Dollars a Day* and *Get Rich Cheating*. And the novels were sheer delight. The children were amazed at how the storytellers of those days wove tales of violence and uncontrolled passions, of unimaginable cruelties and unnecessary sufferings. *The Wonderful Wizard of Oz* was Annabel's favorite book of such ilk.

Finn wanted to show DC his best-loved book, *Memoirs of a Psychic Spy*. In those days, they called them remote viewers, Finn told her, and the one who wrote this book worked for the government. Finn was surprised to learn that DC knew nothing about such things, so he explained that nowadays, many people had the gift of seeing, and that those who took up the training could read any target, past or present, and could even watch as probabilities within the great field of possibilities coalesced into future reality.

"I can do it too sometimes," he said. "This morning, I could see where your friend was. Grandpa has probably got him by now."

Her transitioner. She had been so immersed in this new experience that she hadn't been thinking about his death.

"You mean he's alive?" She felt her breath catch.

"If I saw right, he is," Finn said.

As if on cue, the door opened, and Talor and Josif entered carrying a stretcher made of branches and canvas, with Grandpa behind them.

"Hurry," Josif said. "Add wood to the fire."

They laid him down at the hearth, and DC rushed into the room and knelt beside him. Without thinking, she grabbed his wrist, but there was no pulse monitor to answer her question. His lips were blue and his hand like ice. And yet there was breath! She watched his chest rise and collapse back, rise and collapse back.

The wave of relief she felt surprised her, as it meant that his life somehow mattered to her. For what reason, she did not know. Wasn't he a stranger—no more than a transitioner to aid her escape? A second person in brown coveralls to complete the disguise of transporter team? A second body to drive the transport while she fended off any pursuers? A second set of eyes to watch for danger on the outside? A mere accoutrement of survival? Why did she care now that she needed none of these things?

DC-1128 had no way of sensing the transformation that had begun, no way of knowing that the woman who went by her Directory of the Consolidate employee identification number was a product of the dodec, and what it had molded could not exist outside of it.

Chapter 16

Darby Tate's first awake breath felt like his last. From the moment he awoke, it seemed as if he was no longer breathing but that the world was breathing him. Its exhale filled his lungs with air, its inhale took it back.

And that was not the only difference. A passion had awakened in his breast, and it burned there like the sun. He opened his eyes and remembered it all, every bit of it. In the morgue, on the other side of death, he had found his true self, had almost merged into it. Now, back on this side of the transition, he seemed no more than its image, a reflection in still water, a figure in its dream. It would not be enough to be that. He had to get back—back to the source of himself. But not through death. From the moment he awoke, he knew he could find his true essence here, while inside this thing called life.

When he had awakened in the morgue, the physical world had felt like a movie set. The worried face that had greeted him seemed like an actress who had become her character, performing in a comedy she perceived as a drama. His mind still intoxicated with the euphoria of death, he could not help but laugh at the absurdity of it.

The same face greeted his second resurrection, this time with a softness that welcomed his rebirth into the world.

"Hello again," he managed to get out before a shiver overtook his body.

"Let's get him out of those wet clothes," Grandpa Sylvan said.

DC-1128 retreated to the kitchen with Grandma Sylvan for propriety. The men could dress him this time.

Grandma placed a bowl of blueberries on the table between them and grabbed a handful of the purple globules. "The river gave him back to you."

The statement caught DC off guard. "To me?"

Grandma nodded and shoved the bowl of berries in DC's direction. "In the city, did you learn much about the natural world?"

"Well, yes, I studied nature. I learned everything I could in hopes of surviving it."

The berry juice had flooded Grandma Sylvan's mouth, and she spoke with an indigo tongue. "Where two streams meet is called a confluence, and there, a river is born. From that moment on, it has no choice but to empty itself into the ocean."

DC waited. How could she reply to such a statement when she didn't know what Grandma Sylvan was getting at? She tossed a few berries into her mouth and felt the skins pop between her teeth. This would not be the last of Grandma Sylvan's riddles that DC would store away until the day it revealed its meaning.

Chapter 17

As the days passed, Grandma continued to release snippets of wisdom like mice dropped into a barn for the cat to catch. DC gathered them like golden nuggets, memorized every phrase and inflection. She was now a part of this new world, and she needed to know its tenets and logic. And so she absorbed every word and sensation. She let a few weeks pass without worrying about the future or the past, without thinking about her next step. She breathed Grandma's sagacity into her deepest self, and she would have stayed in that warm-hearthed home forever—knew that the invitation to do so was open and genuine. But she had made a promise to herself, and it would drive her toward a more perilous fate.

Desire is a fuel. It inflames whatever's burning. It propels whatever moves. If consistent and true, it has the power to define a life, lay out its path and determine its journey. And DC-1128 had that kind of yearning. She had vowed that if the outside world could be survived, she would return to the dodec to rescue her friends, grant them their emancipation, make them her family. Vostro and Orion and Gemini and Ari. She had never really cared whether the Consolidate stood or fell. She had only wanted freedom. But what use was it without the ones she loved? What use was any of it without Ari?

Little did she know that her transitioner, too, had a passion kindled. In his dying vision, he had seen the sacred ones, and now he felt that he needed to seek them as much as he needed to breathe. His mother's stories had not been mere fairy tales. He had seen that they really existed, and he knew they would have the answers he craved. They would tell him how to reclaim the source of himself, how to get back to his essence.

One other person in the Sylvan home had an unfulfilled yearning. The boy, Finn, knew he had a gift. Information came to him in images. The distance might be time or miles, all the same, he could see what lay ahead. But it wasn't consistent, and it wasn't at will. If he was to use it for good, he must be able to control it, to choose what he saw and for what purpose. He must find a mentor who could coax his gift into its full fruition.

"I'm going to go to The Village," he told DC and Darby one day as they were cutting and stacking wood for the winter. "There they have masters in all of the mental arts."

DC and Darby had learned about The Village during their first days at the Sylvan home. A week away by foot, it was the closest of the many towns spread throughout the countryside. DC had been shocked that she could live her entire life knowing only about the five great dodecahedrons of the Consolidate, while an entire society was thriving on the outside. How could no one have known about these people living in freedom?

"That was part of the treaty that ended the World Civil War," Finn explained as he grabbed another armful of split wood. "We have to maintain our distance and not interfere."

"Why does your family live here instead of The Village?" DC picked up two more pieces of wood that Darby had split and tossed them to where Finn was stacking. "It sounds like life is easier there."

"Grandma says our home holds our history. Her great-great-grandparents moved here after the war. So many houses were empty that the survivors had a lot of places to choose from. Grandma says this home was a wise choice, because it's out of harm's way—high enough above the river during floods and far enough from the mountains to avoid landslides. The metal roof protects us when the balls of ice get as big as fists, and the trees are close enough to shield us from the worst winds."

At least that was one thing the Consolidate had not lied about, DC thought. The weather outside the dodecs was fierce, with tornadoes and flash freezes and lightning sometimes striking as frequently as a typist's keyboard strokes. Yet the people on the outside had survived it for seven generations, and so had those in the Sylvan home.

"Grandma says it has good bones, and everything else can be rebuilt," Finn said.

Darby lifted another log to the stump. He, too, still had many unanswered questions. He asked if Finn knew about the sacred ones.

"I've heard of some special people in The Village who keep everything in balance, but I don't know what they're called," he said.

That must be them, Darby thought as he struggled to pull the ax out of a knot. He tried to hide his excitement, but DC noticed every nuance.

The thing she wanted to ignore was his fight with the log, but she quickly became impatient.

"Let me give it a try," she said, and he reluctantly handed over the entire contraption, log with ax attached. She dropped the log against the splitting stump in the opposite direction of the split, and the log released itself. She lifted her shoulders in an I-don't-know-how-I-know-these-things shrug and handed the ax back to Darby, glancing at his face to see if she could read a reaction to her playful show of superiority. There it was, a slight upward glance and rise of eyebrows. She pretended not to notice.

"Tell me more about these mental arts you talk about. What skills do people have?" she asked Finn.

"Well, it's everything that needs to be done. Some people specialize in moving objects, others are manifesters. Some people can see into the body and heal it. And then there are the weather wooers. They bring the rain when needed and move the worst storms away from The Village. And of course, there are people like me, who can see things at a distance, and people like Grandma, who can talk to the ancestors. I'm sure there are more, but that's what I know of."

The idea that now took hold in DC's brain rapidly sprouted. "Do you think some of the villagers might be willing to help me get my friends out of the dodec?"

"Probably," Finn said. "We all serve each other."

In that moment, DC knew why these three lives had converged at this place and time. She knew that the next step on each of their paths was the same step, and that they would take it together.

"I'm going to The Village with you," she announced. "And Darby's going, too."

Darby lifted his eyebrows in an I-don't-know-how-you-think-you-can-decide-for-me expression and loosed his ax on an innocent log. But he offered no objection. He was beginning to learn that once DC had made up her mind, there was no turning back.

So focused was her intent, that the moment the winter's wood was stacked, she began her preparation for the journey. Back at the Sylvan house, she went straight to the small pile of belongings she had brought with her when she escaped the dodec, re-evaluating each item in light of what would be needed for the trip to The Village. And over the ensuing days, Finn and Darby joined her in preparing for the journey, drying strips of fish, sharpening the hatchet, and waterproofing their boots with bear fat. Each day, they watched the sky for clues of coming weather. For the seven days of the trip, they would have no safe haven. Only their wits, and perhaps Finn's foresight, could help them make it to The Village, where Finn would find a mentor, DC would ask for allies, and Darby would seek the sacred ones.

Chapter 18

Their journey began at the place where the transport had surfaced from underground, and DC and Darby could see the tunnel that had birthed them into this new world. Where it ended, the tracks emerged into open air, arching up and over the river like some great steel tongue.

As Darby hoisted his pack over his shoulders, DC moved close to him. "When I go back to get my friends, you'll go with me, right?"

Darby could think of only one thing he wanted inside the dodec. It was hidden under a floorboard. But to risk his life for those two blue stones? Wasn't his mother's memory enough?

"That's a lot to ask," he said, "I'll have to think about it." His selfishness embarrassed him, and he looked away from her and stared at the roiling waters in front of him.

The river ran so wide and wild that it had swept all the old bridges away in the years since the dodecahedrons were built. The Consolidate needed only one new bridge, and now its tall trestles would provide passage for the three travelers on the first leg of their trip.

They donned their harnesses and cinched themselves together to prepare to traverse the girders. DC held the small backpack she had taken from her desk at the Transitionary, and in spite of its time in the river, all of its contents remained intact. A bedroll now hung from its bottom straps. Darby and Finn carried the extra weight of dried fish and camping implements, dividing the burden by what could be borne.

Finn had traversed the bridge's girders twice in his life. He had first crossed at age ten, when the days of dryness had diminished not only what lived in the garden, but even the wild plants in the woods available for harvest. He had seen in his mind's eye that the land to the south had been spared the drought, so he had gone with his father and three of his brothers to gather greens and roots for the winter. His gift of sight had helped keep away hunger that year, and he was grateful for it.

The next time he crossed the great river, all of his siblings were with him. Days upon days of dry lightning strikes had set the forest ablaze, and as the wind propelled it down the mountain toward their home, the children went with Grandma and Grandpa to the safety of the river's far shore. The river's girth was so wide that even the embers carried on the wind would not reach across it. Their mother and father had stayed behind to drench their home with water from the well, promising to join the rest of the family if the fire got too close.

When the fire had died, the children found their parents' charred bodies near a smoldering log half way up the path back to the house. Whether they had been overcome by smoke or hit by a falling tree, the family never knew. Finn could not see it. Neither could his mind's eye see why the house had been spared, whether it was due to his parents' efforts, a shift in the wind, or Josif's gift of focused intent. But the thing that had jabbed daggers of sorrow into his heart was that he had not seen in advance that his parents would die if they stayed behind.

On the day of their death, he had made a pledge to himself. He would not let his gift come and go at its own whim. He would learn to use it at will, to direct it for the benefit of his family and all those with whom he came in contact. The gift had been bestowed upon him freely, and he would give freely of it.

Now, he was old enough to seek a master seer, so this journey across the bridge had its own purpose. And it was different than his first two river crossings for another reason. For the first time, he would be leading it. Though only eighteen, he had the most to offer this traveling trio, with his knowledge of the land and the weather. He knew how to read the night sky for direction and the day sky for weather warnings. He knew which plants could be eaten and which were used for healing. And when he had heard of his traveling companions' reasons for going to The Village— their fervent desires—he had wrapped his heart around them and vowed to get them safely there. But first, he must get them over the river.

"Leave plenty of slack in the rope," he instructed them. "When I get to a girder, I'll stop and wait for DC, then you, Darby. The moss that's grown is dark and you can't always see it, but assume it's there, and it's slippery, so test every step."

DC and Darby had never seen moss in the humidity-controlled environment of the dodec, but they trusted Finn's assessment of it. And as they climbed onto the colossal steel structure, they felt for secure footing with each step. They found very little. So slick was the surface that they had to use their arms to hold much of their weight. They were thankful for the loops of rope around their thighs and waists acting as harnesses. As Finn reached each new section of girder, he cinched the rope that tethered them together at a crossbeam and then motioned them to follow. And so they made their way, inch by inch, over the writhing waters.

DC was mesmerized by the power of the river below her, elated by its ferocious freedom. It was so much greater than her tiny life, that it deserved to take her if that was its wish. It nearly had once, but it spit her back out into Grandpa Sylvan's net. Now she wondered, was she that unpalatable?

Darby was not at all awed by the roaring torrent. He saw it as a menace, not some sublime thing. From his perspective high up on the trestle, he could see that when he had jumped from the transport, he must have fallen close to shore, because no one could possibly swim half of the river's width.

He didn't know whether the fear he now felt came from the memory of his struggle in the river, or the knowledge that if he fell into it now, he would not make it back out. Although he took each step with the caution of a tightrope walker, his arms began to shake. He looked at the churning rapids, and his perspective suddenly shifted. It seemed like the water was standing still, and it was he who was moving so fast. He tightened his grip, and there it froze, ten white fingers clinging to the crossbeam like some stubborn root. From far away, he must have looked like a spider's prey, caught in a great iron web.

"Don't look down!" DC yelled, but the roar of the water half drowned out her voice, and the shrinking of his world blocked out the rest. It shrunk down to a pinpoint and disappeared, and Darby Tate's foot slipped.

Chapter 19

Finn was helpless as he watched the weight of Darby's falling body jerk DC from her perch, and it pulled him off the girder, too. Darby's body slammed into a support beam, and the three of them dangled there like some fisherman's catch.

Finn looked up to his knot and hoped it would hold. It had kept them from falling into the river, but what would he do now with three-hundred pounds of dead weight holding him down? Before he could even clear his mind to form a plan, DC was hollering up at him. "Throw me the extra rope."

She had righted herself by wrapping one arm around the rope above her and one leg around the rope below. Now she held out her free arm to show Finn his target. Although she was no more than ten feet below him, the wind gusts could carry the extra rope beyond her reach, so Finn waited for nature to hold her breath before dropping the spare cordage. DC caught one tip of it and gathered the rest up. The center of the X where the crossbeams met was above her, and she flung the rope around it, then she looped it through the harness around her waist.

"Bring it back up through the middle before you cinch it," Finn yelled down, instructing her in securing a good knot.

She tightened and tested the knot, then yelled back up at him, "I'm going to cut you loose."

Finn now understood what she was doing. The rope she had just tied now held Darby's weight and her own. Cutting the tether to him would free him to move.

DC reached back into her pack. She pulled out the particle-beam pistol and aimed at the tether leading up to Finn. The beam sliced right through, and she felt the jerk of her rope taking up the slack.

Finn, now freed from the extra weight, untied his rope and stuffed it into his pack. He would have to free climb to reach them.

DC watched with apprehension. Life in the dodec might be too dull, but she wasn't sure she had the stomach for this kind of adventure. She had witnessed thousands of deaths, but never of someone she cared about, and she prayed that Finn would not be her first.

He shimmied his way down to the beam just above where DC and Darby dangled and secured himself to it. He threw a rope over the beam above him, tied one end to his harness, and threw the other end down to DC. He would use this as a lift line, with his own weight as a counterbalance.

"Tie this around your harness," he instructed. "I can't pull you both. You're going to have to get to the beam. I'm going to swing you."

DC cut herself loose from the beam so that she would be able to swing freely, and Finn pulled on the tether to begin the momentum. The dangling duo looked like a pendulum in a grandfather clock, gathering momentum and distance until DC could reach the crossbeam. The moment she grabbed it, Finn dropped all of his weight onto the lift line, and the counterweight enabled DC to keep her grip. Inch by inch she climbed up the crossbeam, the strength of

Finn's pull helping her lift Darby's weight, until she reached the horizontal beam and pulled herself onto it.

After securing herself, she joined Finn in retrieving the still unconscious Darby Tate. The way he hung there, stomach up, arms and legs dangling behind him, it looked as if he'd given up in the middle of a backflip.

As they pulled him toward their precarious perch, they noticed the blood that was matting his hair.

DC didn't care about that. Perhaps it was the sustained rush of adrenaline. Or perhaps she simply had no patience left. For whatever reason, she felt anger rising inside her. And when Darby's face was in reach, she leaned down and slapped it.

"Wake up, you idiot! Now's not the time to sleep," she screamed.

But still, he dangled limp. She reached into her pack for her flask of water and poured it onto his face. He sputtered awake and upon instinct grabbed the beam.

"I should have let you die this time," she scolded. "Now get ahold of yourself, or you're going to kill us all."

Unlike the last time he was revived by this woman, Darby did not smile or laugh. This time, the drama of it felt completely real, and he was fully immersed in the emotions of the moment. They helped him onto the beam, and he tied himself off so they could all rest and regain their strength, while below them, the river ran her carefree race toward the sea.

Chapter 20

From its source fourteen-thousand feet up in the mountains to its mouth at the ocean, this river had danced the ancient dance of land and water. Ten million years ago, outpourings of lava had forced her into her course. Eight million years later, a new mountain range began to uplift, but the river would not be moved this time, and she cut right through it. Her massive flow carved deep canyons and gorges. She gouged out basalt rock, creating channeled scablands, and deposited rich sediments in the valleys.

Fifteen million salmon fought her currents each year to earn their deaths, and their offspring rode her rapids back to the sea. A bounty for the life along her banks, she fed the bears and eagles and quenched the thirst of all the other living things within her reach.

Men had lived at her shores for millennia, and she had freely offered them her gifts. In return, they had given her honor, creating songs and stories of her greatness. But four-hundred years ago, a new kind of man had come and demanded more than she could offer. These men gave her a name—Columbia—and tried to tame her. They cut large swaths of trees near her banks and let the sediment fill her. They dammed her flow to make power. They used her to dilute their radioactive wastes. They sucked out her water to moisten their crops and replaced it with runoff laden with deadly chemicals. And so the life in her began to die.

Oh, she had taken a few of them, too. The shifting sandbar at her mouth had claimed so many ships that they called it a graveyard. But it was a small trade for the life of a mighty one.

It was only during the last two centuries—a mere moment from her perspective—that the humans had returned to treating her with kindness. And as all life does when freed from ongoing assault, the river had healed. Millions of salmon and steelhead now rested in her eddies, and her water again ran clear and free.

On this particular day, she would claim no more lives, for her relationship with the species that walked upright had returned to balance, and she knew with the wisdom that requires no thinking that each thing has its appointed time to die. And so the trio of travelers reached her south bank safely. And this night, they would eat the kokanee she offered and revive their strength listening to the melody of her currents.

Chapter 21

"If you'll gather wood for the fire, I'll go find some plantain for a poultice," Finn said to DC, dropping his pack to the ground.

Wood burns. Roots nourish. Branches shelter. Leaves heal. Our lives really do depend on the trees… and rivers and skies. Just as DC was letting her thoughts drift, erasing the tension of their ordeal on the bridge, she noticed Darby starting to set up the tarp.

"What are you doing?" she snapped. "You've got a wound that's been left untended. Sit down and put pressure on it until Finn gets back. I've saved your life twice. I don't want to have to do it again." She didn't know where the sharpness came from, so she chalked it up to the strain of the day.

"What's irritating you?" Darby asked

She opened her mouth to answer but thought better of it. A spat would signify some kind of intimacy, wouldn't it? She stomped off into the woods to find fuel for the night's fire.

How could this man infuriate her so? She barely knew him, and yet it felt as if their lives had been connected for decades. Somehow, she sensed his foibles and faults, his strengths and inclinations. Or did she just imagine it? What did she really know about him, after all? His name, and that he had borne half a century of drudgery under the dodec. She knew that he felt he never fit in, that he became a manufacturer because he preferred working from home, away from other people.

Not much to crow about, DC thought. *But who am I to talk? At least he didn't kill to make a living.*

She respected the members of the manufacturing class for their mental capacities. Manufacturing had once been done by physical exertion. But a Consolidate company had created the thought facsimilator, and now no physical energy had to be used to make material things. Now, you could browse one of the Consolidate's electronic catalogues, and when you saw something you wanted and placed your order, a picture of it, along with your description of any personalized changes, was sent to the optiscreen of a manufacturer like Darby, who would enter the product number, imagine your changes, and focus on the image in its three-dimensional fullness. His electrode-studded headband transferred the image into the thought facsimilator, which then sent it to a 3-D printer. It was on-demand, fast and personalized—perfect for a society in which consumption of goods was the considered the highest good.

As a manufacturer, Darby would possess an admirable capacity for sustained, focused concentration, and DC esteemed that, but she seemed to find reason to criticize almost everything else—his crazy reaction upon awakening at the morgue, his fall at the bridge, even the mission he was now undertaking. *Sacred ones, schmacred ones,* she said to herself. *Some hallucination he's following.*

Her thoughts were still tussling when she returned to the campsite with an armful of branches. Finn was already back, placing leaves on Darby's head wound.

"This will help prevent infection," he explained. "When we get some water boiling, we'll make a poultice, and that'll help it heal faster."

With the cut now mending, they set about putting up camp. Finn caught a fish and showed Darby how to clean and skewer it for cooking.

The sound of fish skin sizzling over the flame reminded Finn that he was the one who had to pay attention to their meal. His friends were not yet experienced in living from nature's gifts. He lifted one flap of flesh and showed them how to check the fish for its readiness. Steam rose from the pink meat like a soul from its cadaver, and the smell of it made their stomachs rumble.

They shared their catch on one plate, each plucking a few flakes of meat and then passing it on. The tender fillets filled their bellies while the hot juices flooded their tongues, and although the two dodecians had eaten meals all of their lives, this was a new sensation, as if nature herself was sharing some intimacy.

Sated and serene, they sat around the campfire, the yellow flames bathing their faces in dancing light. DC avoided Darby's eyes. She focused on Finn instead. She wanted to know more about his ancestors and the villagers of today. She still had so many questions. How had the villagers come to be separate from the people of the dodec? How had they learned the mental skills that were still foreign to dodecians? Did the rulers of the dodecs know they existed? And if so, what was their relationship? What version of history did his people tell?

Chapter 22

"Before the World Civil War, not only this river, but all life started to die," Finn began. "The fish were so poisoned that people could no longer eat them. The trees were so weakened that they succumbed to diseases. Patches of garbage littered the oceans. Almost all the water had been blighted—the rivers, the aquifers. They filtered the dirty water and sold it back to the people. In fact, all the free gifts of nature were made into commodities—seeds, land, trees. People worked all day so they could buy things they needed just to remain alive. Even staying warm had a price. The fuels they sold put chemicals in the air that changed the weather. Storms became severe, and droughts became frequent. Even when rain was plentiful, the fruits and nuts and kernels were getting smaller and smaller. It was as if life was withdrawing itself from the planet."

Finn paused, his heart made heavy by imagining what his ancestors had endured. "Then came the Great Shift." His last two words carried a tone of reverence. "That's what the ancestors called it."

"What was it?" DC asked, already so enthralled by the history lesson that she could barely wait for Finn to take breaths between sentences.

"Well, it was only a small portion of the people, but they had a change of heart. Grandma says they chose to believe in unity, and the love that they already had could then flow freely."

As DC listened, she watched the campfire's flames sway, merge and separate, moving to some unknown force contained in their very essence.

"How did they actually solve all those problems—the bad water and what they had done to the air and land? How did they stop everything from dying?" The fire spit an ember at her with a loud cracking sound, and she quickly leaned sideways to avoid its path.

"It became clear that every problem they faced boiled down to fear. And the antidote to that was the understanding of unity."

Finn saw the puzzled look on her face and realized he'd have to explain further. "You see, we used to think we were separate. That you were encased in your skin and a different person than me inside my skin. That's the illusion that creates fear."

What illusion? I still think that. DC was too self-conscious to say it out loud.

"If that's what you believe, you have to protect yourself from everyone else, so you do everything only for yourself, no matter what the harm to someone else or the rest of life. It wasn't just a problem with the people in power, because it was what everyone believed and how everyone behaved."

DC thought about how she had often complained that the Consolidate subtly enslaved the people for its own benefit, yet hadn't she done similar things? Hadn't she hijacked Darby's death to help her escape, told him to jump not knowing what injury or pain he might have to endure as a result? Yes, she had done all of that for her own benefit without thought of the consequences he might face.

Finn interrupted her thoughts. "Their religions got some people to act kindly toward others, but even that was in their own self-interest, because they thought they would get a reward later. It wasn't from the knowledge of our oneness."

He explained that the transformation that led to the Great Shift began after experiments into the smallest pieces of matter had shown that everything was part of one great field of energy—an unbroken wholeness.

"Some people began to realize that even though everyone seemed to be separate, they really weren't. If their best science was true, everyone was really just a different aspect of one thing, and anything done to anyone was done to all, to the whole."

He paused for a moment. He could sense that this knowledge, though centuries old, was still a new concept to his companions, and he gave them a moment to begin absorbing it. "That shifted their focus from 'me first' to 'we first,' to a true concern for the welfare of others."

DC didn't let the new knowledge sink in too far before blurting out the contradiction she saw. "And that led up to the World Civil War? Sounds more like a great rift than a great shift."

"Well, it did cause a rift with the ones who had held power. You see, the new unity and lovingness of my ancestors helped them remember their gifts, reintroduced them to an inner technology that must have seemed very threatening to those in power."

"Inner technology?" Darby asked, finally joining the question-asking.

"Our gifts, like seeing and healing and manifesting."

93

"Oh," Darby said.

Finn explained that his ancestors' first experiments with this inner technology entailed combining their intent to try to influence numbers randomly generated by a machine. When they saw they could do that, they took on larger tasks, like reducing the size of a hurricane before it hit land, or trying to prevent a skirmish between neighboring countries.

"The people in power saw what was going on, and they considered it a great threat, because they realized that the combined intent of the people could become stronger than all the power they had amassed."

DC wondered how this information could have been kept from the people of the dodec for so many generations. *Have we had the ability to free ourselves all along and just didn't know it?*

Although Finn did not hear her question, his next sentence answered it. "Remember, it was only a small portion of the people who gained this new awareness at first. There has to be a critical mass before any real change can be made."

He explained that the masses remained lulled and dulled, fearful and self-focused, but the people in power worried that the new awareness of the few would eventually spread like a virus.

"When their old tricks of manipulation failed to stop the spread of unity consciousness, they used violence. They labeled our ancestors anarchists and claimed that everyone else was under attack. That gave them an excuse to release weapons that had remained secret—weapons that made earthquakes and weapons that spread pain through waveforms, weapons that stunned the brain and weapons that dissolved tissue. They even weaponized weather. That's why it's still so bad now."

Finn explained that the destruction was blamed on his ancestors, and most of the survivors were lured into the cities, to the great dodecahedrons being built for their safety. Those in power called the dodecians "patriots" to hook them with pride and convince them that the war had been necessary. They knew the potency of fear, so they continued to present an onslaught of enemies—anarchists, weather, germs, earthquakes. Even the rays of the sun were cast as an adversary. And most people, in their innocence, in their harried brains and shielded hearts, believed them.

Only the ancestors—the ones who understood the truth of unity—saw the subtle enslavement and stayed outside of the dodecs. Their new skills grew rapidly—talents greater than any weapon. The dodecs had a waveform cannon that could fire a devastating blast of energy at the new villages where the ancestors gathered, but the villagers could shield against it using only combined intent. The dodecs could send silent unmanned planes to view a village, but the villagers could send their vision right into a person's mind to learn in advance of his plans.

When it became clear that all of the outer technologies were no match for the power of the human heart and mind, an agreement was made, Finn explained. The people in power would consolidate all of their holdings into the dodecs, and they would leave the ancestors alone. They would stop taking from the Earth and returning nothing but poisons. Their world would be the five great dodecahedrons of the Consolidate and nothing more.

And in the decades hence, the ancient river had recovered her flow, healed and rejoiced in the returning fish and the life burgeoning along her banks. The descendants of the ancestors now lived in freedom, and the people under the dodecs still didn't notice their yokes.

But some do, DC thought. *And I will move heaven and earth to get them out.*

III

Chapter 23

It took a body as big as Vostro's to lift his cows, legless as they were. He moved his best producer to her stall, its walls just wide enough to hold her torso. He reached through the hole in her side and pulled a wad of cud from her stomach. *Perfect texture*, he thought. He had to admit this was a more profitable way to make milk than how his grandfather had done it. All the unnecessary parts had been bred out, even the voice box, and the udder made almost as large as the rest of her.

Profitable, yes, but he thought it grotesque. Something was not right about it, and it made his entire world amiss. But this was business, and he had to compete with synthetic milk.

"How can I make it as cheaply as your chemical concoctions?" he had once asked Ari. "You can't," Ari had replied. "Soon there will be nothing left not made by men like me." He had puffed out his chest to show he was joking, but they both knew the truth behind the humor.

As a boy, Vostro had loved the Jerseys, the warmth of their bodies when he leaned against them, how their breath misted in the mornings when he went to check the milking machines. He especially loved their eyes. As gentle as daisies, they gave him something his mother never had. But now, the Jerseys' eyes were empty sockets—just another unnecessary part. And his mother was dead, her bitterness having eaten through her brain like acid, so that several years before her Listing, she just sat in her chair staring into the distance.

At least a cow gives milk, he would say to himself during the years of her dementia. He wanted to apply to the Consolidate to list her early, but his wife would have nothing of it. "She's your mother, not one of your heifers," Mari had scolded. "I don't care if she never loved you. Maybe she had to become as hard as her world to live in it."

Vostro dropped the fistful of cud back into the heifer's stomach and crouched down for his next task. The stainless steel milking bucket bent his reflection. *This world has distorted us all,* he thought. He reattached a vacuum tube to the pump before hooking it up to his top producer. Teat cups, pulsators, transfer pipes. His milking stalls had hundreds of them. Soon all would be used for another purpose, not for pulling out mother's milk, but for the bombs that would bring the Consolidate down.

Chapter 24

Orion's optiscreen was forever blinking. He had programmed it to keep him in the loop on anything of consequence, and it flashed its messages in front of his eyeballs every few seconds.

"Emergency Security Management Team meeting, 10 a.m. in the VP's Office." That was the message he was meant to get. But he had also hacked the message sent by the security vice president to the directors of the Consolidate. That's how he knew what the meeting would be about. When he got there, he'd have to act aghast when the vice president of security announced that a transition witness and a transitioner had hijacked a transport right under their noses. He'd have to join in pointing fingers at everyone but his own subordinates. His staff had nothing to do with it, of course, as artificial intelligence technology had not been used to aid the escape. But it would be assumed that the escapees had inside information, and all at the meeting would be trying to reroute the blame away from themselves.

At age nineteen, Orion was the youngest department head in the Security Division. At eighteen, he had hacked the Consolidate, and it immediately co-opted his skills. Anyone who could break through twenty-two layers of firewalls and artificial intelligence blockades had no choice but to use his talents for the power elite.

At first, he was all ego about it. Those at the top deemed him the best of the best, and it filled his young mind with pride. They heaped pay and prestige on him to buy his allegiance, and he was easily for sale at that price. His eagerness spilled out of him like spaghetti in a too-small dish, and he served his masters dutifully.

But that all changed on the day he went to Ari's office.

He had gone to the Division of Chemical Sciences building to look for a tifiog—an artificial intelligence machine gone rogue—one that not only learned on its own but had started making choices. Such a thing was a potential liability, much like a human who thought too deeply. It was Too Intelligent For Its Own Good—tifiog for short—and it must be unplugged, deconstructed, destroyed. The chemical sciences building seemed to have more than its fair share of these misbehaving machines, and Orion had been determined to find out why.

When he had walked into the office of the brain chemistry lab leader, what he saw set his synapses to firing in such haphazard chaos that they would never again return to order. She was petite and pale, with hair as gold as honeycomb and lips as pink as flamingos. She moved as if made of air, and as she walked past him and out the door, he sensed a breeze that would forever pull him in its wake.

The man behind the desk had shattered his trance. "Ari Stockton," he said, and he held out his hand. "And that was my daughter who made your jaw drop." Embarrassment had flashed across Orion's face that day as he tried to realign his synapses. "She's only seventeen, and it looks like my left arm is bigger than you are, so you better rethink it," Ari had said in his best deep voice, while he silently thought, *What an asset. An artificial intelligence expert with a young enough mind to mold.*

That was the beginning of their friendship and the end of Orion's loyalty to the Consolidate. He had once been for sale, but within months, his allegiance was completely out of stock. Little by little, Ari had reeled him in, even revealing what chemicals the Consolidate put in the water to keep the populace docile. And one day, it was no longer just his desire to catch a glimpse of Gemini that brought Orion to the Stockton home, but his belief in what The Group was doing.

His synapses were now firing as a rebel mind, a tifiog of sorts. But it wasn't until today that the Consolidate would treat him as such.

On his way upstairs to the Security Management Team meeting, a new message flashed in front of Orion's eyes, although it was not meant for him. "Threat confirmed. Ear 7316." He typed the number into his wristgear and read the results. "270 Park Street. Occupied (2). Ari Stockton, 49, DC brain chemistry lab manager. Daughter, Gemini Stockton, 17."

His heart nearly stopped. If it had synapses, they would be firing like a pinball machine on methamphetamine. The Security Division had an ear in Ari's home. Gemini's home. The greater implication hit him. The ear would have picked up his voice, too, his name, and his plans to help with the overthrow. They would know he was a tifiog, and even now, they would be making plans to unplug him.

He sat quietly through most of the Emergency Security Team meeting, carefully watching the security vice president's eyes. Did they narrow when they glanced in his direction? Did the pupils dilate?

"I'm surprised your AI-bots didn't pick up any hint of the planned escape," the vice president was saying to Orion.

He rerouted some of his synapses to answer the question. "We don't have eyes in the morgue," he replied. "If there had been any electronic activity in advance of the escape, the bots would have known it. I suggest we add a few eyes down there, and take a look at why Transport Control didn't spot the unauthorized entry." Blame rerouted. Finger-pointing accomplished. But Orion had a bigger accusation to evade, and as soon as the meeting ended and the room emptied, he approached the security vice president.

"The transition witness who escaped belonged to a rebel group that I infiltrated. It poses a category-three threat. When would you be available to discuss it?"

Chapter 25

The windows of Trinket Village seemed particularly bright this night, the baubles inside sparkling their false promises. Gemini never bothered to go inside. It was enough to know she could buy any of them. And she was pulled by a different longing.

As she made her way to the chemical sciences building, the night sky suddenly turned to light. Every inch of the dodec's polygons was lit with the same image. Dark hair fringed the man's scalp and his jaw was slightly slack. Gemini looked up into the kind eyes and thought she saw a twinkle there. His voice emerged melodious and comforting.

"My dear friends, I bring you good news. Many of you are talking about the dancing lights in the sky last night. Our precious dodec has shielded us once again. We suffered no damage from the solar storms. Several strong flares on the earth side of the sun bombarded the atmosphere with deadly radiation, but none was measured inside our city. You are safe. You are protected. That is my promise."

The Benefactor sat as still as a chameleon merging into its surroundings. But his eyes were animated, beaming confidence and compassion.

"We had faced a much more serious threat inside our precious dodec. But as of today, that, too, has been resolved. A rogue group of dodecians had devised a devious plot to cause much damage. I'm afraid that many of you would have been in harm's way had they not been stopped. Our Security Division, working from a tip from a citizen, was

105

able to identify and dismantle this terrorist cell. You are safe. You are protected. That is my promise."

He paused and took a deep breath, as if it was time to depart from the script.

"On a personal note, I want to thank all the citizens of the dodec for contributing to our collective well-being. Your patriotism and vigilance are a blessing to us all. It is an honor to be your Benefactor."

A sweet smile touched his lips, and the dodec's glass panels went blank for a moment before again revealing the world outside, the dark sky and twinkling stars—another projection that hid the truth from the innocents inside.

Gemini continued down the street, buoyed as always by the Benefactor's public address and wanting to share her happiness with her father. He had looked so concerned about her since DC-1128's disappearance, but how could she tell him that the Consolidate itself had filled the gap in her heart? As she walked through the glass double doors into the chemical sciences building, she mused that the actual DC—the Directory of the Consolidate—had become her second parent, and that she could truly blossom in the larger light of that overarching entity.

She usually knocked at her father's office door before entering, but this time it was ajar. Through the one-inch gap she could see that something was amiss. Papers sat haphazardly on a chair and overflowed onto the floor. Her father with his obsessive neatness would never leave it like that. A chemist had to be tidy. Even one errant drop of the wrong substance could cause an explosion. As she opened the door, her heart dropped into her stomach. The desk drawers were open, the furniture askew and the cushions slashed. Gone were his wall monitor and the framed print behind his desk.

"Gemini Stockton?" The voice came from behind her, but her mind was still whited out, so all she could do was nod and close her open mouth. A hand grabbed her arm hard. "Come with me, please."

"Where is my father? Is he all right?" The words tumbled out half-choked, and tears blurred her vision so that all she could see was that the man wore a black suit. "Tell me if he's all right!" she shouted as he pulled her down the hallway. "Is he all right?"

Her mind flashed back to the day of the accident. As Gemini had walked toward her elementary school's gates, looking for her father's car, her mother's best friend had intercepted her. Whether she read it from DC-1128's face or had some invisible connection to her mother that relayed such information, she immediately sensed that her world had changed forever. "Your mother and father had an accident." DC's mouth kept moving, but Gemini's young ears had heard only vague syllables, for fear, as black as a hook, had pierced clear through her, and she could not resist as it pulled her into its depths.

"Calm down. He's fine," said the man who now held her in his grip, his voice jerking her back to her present predicament. Several chemists peeked around corners as Gemini was led down the hall, out the big glass doors of the chemical sciences building and into the back seat of a Security Division flycar.

As she rode in the flycar, her mind was all a scramble. She could get nothing more from the men in the front seat, so her brain was talking to itself in three directions. *Why did they search his office? Are they taking me to see him? The quiche is in the oven. Three-hundred and fifty degrees. It will burn in half an hour. Are they at the house now? Maybe they'll notice it. Is this why DC-1128 has been gone all these weeks?*

Between thoughts, in the way that fear connects similar incidents, came flashes of the days after the accident—her father in the hospital, his face and chest wrapped in gauze and tubes protruding from both nostrils. The feeling in her chest as empty as a canyon. DC-1128 rubbing her back for comfort as she pressed her face into her pillow and soaked it with her heart's saltwater river. The loss of her mother had cut a wound so deep that no other love would heal it. But then she saw her father's grief and dammed her own flow of sorrow in order to become his comfort. She now believed that being strong for him back then had made her strong forever. She could not see that she had simply partitioned her heart and learned to live in the fortified portion.

Back then, they had told her so little, only that there had been an explosion at the lab where her parents worked side by side. Years later, she had drawn every detail out of her father—the precise chemical mixture they were working on, why it burned skin and how large had been the shard of glass that cut her mother's throat. Most of all, she wanted to know why that particular chemical compound had import. How was its intended function significant enough to take away her mother? She had not been satisfied with the answer, and in the unguarded part of her heart, she would always search for another.

The flycar landed near the top of Consolidate Headquarters, and Gemini refocused on the present moment. The room they put her in was big enough for a table and two chairs and little else. Its blank walls helped her empty the tumult in her head. Someone would come in eventually, and she would not cooperate unless they took her to her father. And if they refused to do that, she would demand to see the Benefactor.

She had no way to know that her father was so close, just two doors down, watched by, attached to, and evaluated through machines from which no one could keep a secret.

Chapter 26

Sometimes Orion could feel a seizure coming on. It was as if everything was a bit more distant, had somehow receded. That's how it felt now, sitting in his office. But he was still conscious, upright and thinking. Years ago, the doctors had diagnosed him with cryptogenic epilepsy. They could offer nothing more than a prescription to treat the symptoms, but the drugs made him dizzy and fatigued, so he didn't take them. Thanks to his affiliation with The Group, he had learned that the Consolidate would not allow its medical schools to teach the real cause of any illness if something inside the dodec was the culprit. Orion sometimes thought that they wanted people sick. Why else would it be illegal to use the word "cure" for anything other than a profitable chemical compound that they controlled? His best hope was Ari, who had mentioned that his new project, although addressing issues much broader than disease, might stop the seizures once and for all.

For half an hour now, he had been feeling the gap between himself and what he saw and heard in the world outside his skin. Yet he hadn't blacked out. He had to stay conscious now. He needed every minute to think his way through this crisis.

They would have arrested me by now if the security vice president didn't believe my story. Or are they just going to watch for a while? Oh, my Gemi, what are they going to do to you? What have I done to you? It's not my fault. They had an ear in the house. For how long? I can't help them if I'm imprisoned. His synapses were nearly humming. *What did they hear me say? I've got to try to remember every word. Are they already collecting data from the others? Maybe I can hack the micro-expression cam. I've got to be ready for my turn or I won't be hacking anything. Ari's muscle-relaxer patch. Where did I put it?*

And so his frantic thoughts continued, taking him farther and farther from the world outside his skin, until the knock at his door snapped him out of it.

"Director Wolfe wants to see you in fifteen minutes, her office," Orion's executive secretary said, unaware that her boss might now be on the Consolidate's most-wanted list.

Director Wolfe was responsible for five divisions within the Consolidate, including security. The only person higher than the three directors was the Benefactor himself. *Or is the Benefactor just their puppet,* Orion often wondered. No one had seen him in public for years, and his appearances for his weekly addresses seemed funny. His face was animated, but his body seemed rigid and a bit out of proportion.

Director Wolfe seemed a bit rigid too, Orion thought as he lowered himself into a chair in front of her mahogany desk. The desk seemed larger than his entire office and made him feel smaller than his usual self, which already was diminutive. He wondered if there were sensors in the cushion upon which he sat. Eyes in the ceiling trim?

"I wanted to personally thank you for your work in uncovering the plans for the coup d'etat," the director said.

Though she simply sat there in her high-backed chair, Orion could feel her circling, patiently waiting. He imagined saliva dripping from her jowls like the predator she really

112

was. His heart beat in his ears. He was definitely back in his skin now, every sight and sound more acute than ever before.

"Thank you, ma'am. Just part of my job."

"No, not really." The wolf let it hang there in the air, bait for a small prey.

"I could say that anything related to security is my responsibility, but truthfully, I've just always been attracted to intrigue, and this was a sort of sport for me." *Choose your words carefully. Each one must hold some truth if it's to hide what's true.*

"Then you've hit a home run. Are you a baseball fan?"

"Hockey, ma'am. Requires more strategy."

"Of course. In that case, you made it past the goalie."

It held multiple meanings, and Orion wondered if that's how Director Wolfe saw herself—as the person that nothing gets past. Was she insulted? Would she close in for the kill without the rest of the pack? Orion acknowledged the statement with a small nod and waited for the pounce.

"The vice president of security will take the case from here. But on behalf of the Benefactor and all the directors of the Consolidate, we appreciate your skills as a self-appointed field operative."

Double meanings again, but he was still intact, and it was an obvious dismissal. As he walked toward the office door, he felt like a mouse that had jumped away from the jaws of a sprung trap.

"Do you have family, Mr. Solomon?"

Very few people called him by his last name, and he turned to see if the hammer was still cocked. "Just a mother and brother."

"They'd be very proud of you if they knew what you had just accomplished. And your future wife will be lucky to have someone with such a promising career."

"Thank you, ma'am," he said, and then stepped off the trap's platform and out the door.

For the rest of the day, the director's last comment haunted him. *There's no chance now*, he thought. *She has no future at all now, let alone as my wife.*

Director Wolfe's post-meeting thoughts were the opposite of Orion's in that they exuded calm confidence. *There is more than one way to kill a mouse. Poison is more convenient. The animal disappears to die, so there is no mess to clean up.*

Chapter 27

When they took her down the hallway to another room and sat her in the chair, she could smell it. Her father had been there. Two people who are close enough will know the scent of each other's skin still lingering in the air. In front of a camera and hooked up to a myriad of sensors, she felt like an intensive-care patient. But these devices had a purpose other than saving her life.

"Your name and age."

The technician is so deadpan that he could probably fool these machines, Gemini thought. "Listen, I'm going to cooperate. I believe in what you're doing. I just want to see my father first. There's been a mistake. He's not the biggest patriot, but he would never break the law."

The camera was scanning below the surface of her skin to the minute movements of every muscle—the split-second indicators of emotion.

"Your name and age, please."

"If I answer your questions, will you let me see him? You have to answer my one question first."

The technician's deadpan became a slight scowl, and Gemini didn't need a slow-motion replay to see it. "If you don't answer *my* questions, you may *never* see him."

"I'll do everything I can to help the Consolidate, but please, at least let me know if he's all right."

The metrics showed she meant what she had just said. She was, indeed, a patriot, and those infallible results from the first few moments of her interrogation rerouted her fate.

Or perhaps circumstances are created to route us to a predetermined destination. Either way, Gemini Stockton's career as a politician had just been launched. She had labeled herself as perfect bait. She would be placed as an aide in Senator Smallman's office. For a home, she would be sent to Orion Solomon's house.

Chapter 28

From his small cell, Ari had created a new formula all in his head, connecting and labeling the hexagons, then stamping the image into his brain like a brandishing iron. But it had no importance. Rather, it was a distraction, reducing his worry to a quiet rumble beneath the surface.

Since his arrest a week ago, he had been alone with his fear, and it was an irritating cellmate. It invited his imagination to a game of poker and refused to reveal its cards. But Ari still played the game. If Gemini was in custody, he may as well fold his hand. If she was safe, he had a royal flush.

He heard the clank of the latch on the strike plate, and the steel door slid open. The guard motioned him up and led him down a hallway to a room containing nothing but two chairs. When he saw her, from his toes to his temples, his entire body sighed in relief. She was safe. And not only that, she was free, not locked up or shackled. Their hands met and their eyes locked, and in the way that a father transfers love to his daughter, he filled her with his affection.

"Oh, Dad, what have you done?"

The Consolidate had done away with trials and juries years ago, but his own daughter? *Has she convicted me without even asking a question?*

"Are you all right?" He didn't really need to ask. Other than the worry lines at her eyes, she seemed to beam.

"Yes, I'm fine. But how about you? What's going to happen?"

He had no idea what fate awaited him. Had the Consolidate ever had to deal with insurgents? At least his insistence that Gemini know nothing about The Group had saved her. He didn't care what happened to him. In six months he'd be fifty anyway.

"I don't know, Gemi. How'd you find out I'd been arrested?"

"I went to your office and," she paused, "you weren't there, but a man was. He brought me here. They asked me some questions, and then they sent me to stay with Orion."

"Orion?" If eyebrows were vent pipes, Ari's would have gone through the roof.

"Well, his family. He has a mother and brother. You know that. I have to stay until I'm eighteen, but I don't mind. I have my own room."

Ari's scientific brain couldn't fit the pieces of this puzzle. Although he had not given Orion up during his interrogation, he didn't need to. With one machine reading his brainwaves, another his pulse and another the fleeting expressions of his face, they extracted the answers without him saying a thing. They only needed to ask the questions, and his autonomic nervous system would answer truly. They had asked about Orion, so they had to know his complicity. So why was he free? Had his allegiance to the Consolidate never wavered in the first place? Had Ari recruited a double agent?

"Gemi, listen to me. I don't want you to trust anybody. Do you hear me?"

"What are you talking about? No one's trying to hurt me. But you," she glanced away for a moment, and when her eyes returned to his, they showed her distress. "How could you do this? What's so bad about the Consolidate that you would risk everything?"

He knew the precise accusation even if she didn't say it. How could he risk getting taken away from her, when she had already lost one parent?

"Gemi, you know my age. How much does it matter?" He didn't care what they had told her, and he would not defend himself to her. The overthrow was for her, not him. He half expected to die in the attempt. It was Gemini who would have seen a brighter day, would have lived to see her grandchildren and maybe even her great-grandchildren grow up in a better world. But now he had failed her. Or perhaps he hadn't. It depended on what Orion's freedom meant. He stared in silence at her, wanting to say a lifetime of I-love-you's in one frozen moment.

"Do my friends know I'm here?" he asked.

"Well, Orion of course. DC-1128 is still missing. I'm going to ask Senator Smallman if he can find out what happened to her. Oh, I almost forgot, I'm going to start working in his office after school."

It wasn't the announcement but the spark in her eyes as she made it that startled Ari. What had he failed to notice about his own daughter? While he had been immersed in his project, had she been walking toward the jaws of the monster? She had questioned his motives while defending the Consolidate. She was thrilled to get a job in a senator's office. What direction was fate taking her? As his mind raced forward in time to one possible future, his sense of urgency returned. Even while imprisoned, he must look for a way to help accomplish The Group's mission. Forget the greater good. There was only one dodecian who had to be saved from the Consolidate now.

"Gemi, you must take care of yourself. Be smart. Don't let anyone do your thinking for you. Question everything. The truth is always there, but sometimes you have to dig for it. Go to the house and get my books. Read them. All of them. You have to know more about your world than what they tell you. If the only thing you ever do is..."

"Is that what happened to you?" she interrupted. "Something in those books?"

This time, the accusation pierced him, but before the sorrow could bleed him, a guard came in and announced, "Time's up," and led Gemini toward the door. When she glanced back, he could see in her eyes her love for him, mingled with disappointment.

Chapter 29

Vostro had told his delivery driver to take the day off. "Spend a day with your wife and children. It'll stay on the clock. You deserve it for doing a good job," he had said. Now, as he drove the two-thousand pounds of milk along its route, he thought about his own children. He knew his wife would not forgive him if he left them fatherless, and his arrest now seemed imminent.

Ari was in custody. Orion was avoiding contact. Only Gemini had stopped by with news of her father. "He seems to be holding up fine. He told me to tell you that when he gets out, he'll drink blue vodka with you out of a test tube." It must have held a message, but Vostro couldn't decipher it. He also didn't know why the Consolidate hadn't arrested him yet, but he suspected they wanted to watch and see what he did.

So they don't know everything. Ari wouldn't tell them. They want me to lead them to the others. He was worried he might be doing that at this very moment. His group of conspirators, also known as The Uptown Group, had two counterparts, one in the manufacturing district and another in Old Town. And he was now headed for a rendezvous with a member of The Manufacturing District Group. He had no idea where the Consolidate had ears and eyes, so he would have to be careful not to give anything away.

Orion had told him that they could mount a camera and microphone onto a mechanical insect and remote control it right onto your windowsill. But what was he to do about it—be afraid of every mosquito in his milking barn? Had some little arthropod watched him loading the milk machine parts into the delivery crates? It didn't matter. It had to be risked. He expected that he, too, would be in custody soon, so this might be his only chance.

A member of The Manufacturing District Group would be meeting the delivery truck at one of the supermarkets. The crates marked with small black stars held the milking machine parts. They would be unloaded along with the crates containing milk into a supermarket cooler and later retrieved to be assembled, not by a thought facsimilator but the old-fashioned way, by hand, into deadly devices.

Vostro still had hope for the plan because of the size of the two other groups. Each had three times the membership of his, so they still had the manpower to carry out the plan. But could they accomplish it without Orion's help? If Orion had been compromised, they would no longer have someone who could redirect the Consolidate's detection devices while they placed the bombs. They would need time to re-strategize or find a new recruit in the Security Division.

Two buildings were on The Group's target list: Consolidate Headquarters and the Transitionary. Both would crumble at the same moment, at a time when the Benefactor and all three directors of the Consolidate were at their desks. Every critical part of the system must be targeted so that the body of the Consolidate could not be reassembled.

Vostro knew all about missing body parts—which ones could be bred out, and which an animal needed to continue fulfilling its purpose. He was certain that without its brain and nervous system, the Consolidate could not operate. Its arms and legs and torso would wither and die. But just to be certain, they had devised a way to rally the people to their cause. If Consolidate Headquarters was the brain and nervous system, the Transitionary was the bowels of the beast—not necessary for its existence, but symbolic. Its downfall would stir the populace. When they realized that their mothers and fathers and sisters and brothers and husbands and wives and friends and colleagues did not have to be taken away for premature deaths, they would be shaken from their complacency to help complete the transition to freedom. Of this, Vostro was certain. For who would not fight for the life of a loved one? If they had not fought before, it was only because there was no way of winning.

We still have a chance, he thought as he drove his truck away from his dairy. *His* truck. *His* dairy. He still felt a sense of ownership, even though it hadn't been true for two generations. The Consolidate had steadily gobbled everything up. It allowed past owners to stay on as managers. It showered them with extra purchasing credits. But they then became no more than Consolidate slaves, Vostro thought.

Not for much longer, he said to himself as he headed into the manufacturing district.

At each supermarket on the route, Vostro was amiable with the workers at the receiving dock. To one he said, "This is the best milk on the market." To another, "It will last more than a month if kept below forty." Anything to misdirect his enemies. If they were listening, they would expect a coded message, and they would focus their suspicions on the innocent loading dock workers, not his co-conspirators.

123

He did not know which supermarket The Group had chosen to receive his special delivery until he saw the bright orange hair in his rearview mirror. The overhead door opened to reveal two men on the loading dock, including one with the carrot-top of Simeon Sing. Surely that flaming mane had no purpose for survival, so Vostro wondered why nature had chosen to express such a gene. *Maybe she just likes variety,* he thought.

It was Simeon, not Orion, who was the brains of The Group, and Vostro sometimes joked that Simeon's hair was that color because his mind was on fire.

"Sign here." Those were the only two words Vostro said to him, and as he did, he pointed to a little black star that marked the signature line. He was sure Simeon would make the connection to the stars marking the crates, and as he watched them unload crate after crate onto the waiting pallets, he knew the value of Simeon's razor-sharp mind.

The last two stops held no significance, giving Vostro a chance to let his tension drain. And at the end of the day, as he pulled his empty truck into the barn, he felt confident that if the Consolidate had been watching, he had thrown them off.

He parked the truck and entered the milking barn to check on a Jersey that had shown signs of mastitis. He leaned his head and shoulder against the Jersey's side and stirred the warm milk in the bucket, looking for flakes and clots. He took his time, enjoying the feeling of the thick liquid caressing his fingers. Then he reached for the udder to find out if it was hot to the touch, and as he bent further to feel the other side of the udder, he saw two sets of highly polished shoes next to the stall. He looked up to a man and a woman with no expressions on their faces. He pulled his towering frame upright to address them.

"Will you let me say goodbye to my wife?"

IV

Chapter 30

For four days now, the trio of travelers had trekked through the fertile forest. The cracked remains of a hard black surface was below their feet—an old road now pierced by tender roots of moss. Nature takes back what men have built, as if to show what is and is not permanent. The old trees still stood. With two hundred years of freedom from assault, they had spread their needle-laden arms into great green canopies.

DC was pleased that she could see all levels of these wooden giants as she walked the once-paved path. On the mountain that rose sharply to their left, she could see gnarled roots clinging to the rocks on the incline—strong fingers that anchored these great beings to the earth. The land to the right dropped off into a ravine so steep that at clearings, she could see the treetops' pointed crowns reaching skyward. The scent of needles and pine sap assaulted her nostrils with sweetness.

She remembered Ari's explanation of the exchange between humans and trees, one absorbing the carbon dioxide the other exhaled and providing oxygen in return. *Even here, all is breath.* The thought led her back to her old world. She did not want her mind to go there, as it disturbed the new peace she felt. But she would never forget about her friends, nor what she had done in the transpods. The latter would forever be a deep cut in her heart. But here, it might heal, she thought, perhaps leaving ropes of stiff tissue like Ari's cheek, but no longer an open wound.

Ari, her strength when she felt weak, her confidante when she needed to talk. Who had comforted whom more when her best friend—his wife—had died? She felt the guilt he bore for the accident as if it was her own. He had worn it on his countenance for months. Then one day, it secreted itself somewhere in his chest, its roots cracking through his heart like the moss on this old road. Yet soft! DC knew the softness of Ari's heart, and she cherished it. But it had seemed a forbidden thing to claim the love that belonged to her dead friend. And so she had focused her affection on little Gemi, so vulnerable at only seven, so lost without an understanding of death. And through this attention she had found a deeper love, the kind that only a mother knows, and it satisfied her longing.

As she listened to the crunch of brown needles beneath their feet—brittle things breaking on the tender moss—she wondered if she would make it back to the dodec before the overthrow. She knew now that there was no need for The Group to risk their lives. They could simply leave the dodec. It was safe on the outside. They could leave the rest of the dodecians to their sorry existence, and join her in freedom.

Drops of rain hit the canopy of needles, giving cadence to her thoughts. She donned her UV cloak to keep her head and shoulders dry. Perhaps it had been needed many years past for protection from the sun's ultraviolet emissions. But living things heal themselves when free from fresh offensives, and the atmosphere's ozone holes had closed. The Consolidate kept the threat alive because fear requires no prison guards. People step willingly into their little cells for the sake of safety and do not want to break out.

The UV cloak was now solely for comfort, and DC was glad she had it as the patter of rain picked up its pace and found its way through the branches. Great drops of liquid hit the hood of her cloak and splattered on its plastic surface. Faster and faster they came, until finally a fury of rain was pouring down from the darkened sky. The rivulets in the cracks of the old road became streams overflowing their asphalt banks. The atmosphere began to exhale, tickling the fingers of the trees, and then steadily increasing until entire branches were waving their warnings.

"Let's get out of this!" Finn had to shout to be heard over the pummeling of wind and water. He gestured to their left, where a rock outcropping rose sharply, providing a partial shield from the growing tempest.

Although traveling companions for less than a week, they did not need to communicate as they scrambled to put up their shelter. Darby unstrapped the canvas from where it was fastened to the bottom of his backpack and began assembling the framework while DC pounded the stakes into the muddy ground and Finn made sure the ropes were tight. Together, they unfolded the canvas. The wind tried to take it, and it required all their strength to stretch it over the skeleton of poles and secure it. Even after it was in place, they had to help the ropes hold it down, so fierce and insistent was the wind. Without free hands to lay a ground tarp, they simply squatted above the mud, each holding a corner of their protective cover.

They were wondering how long they might have to maintain this position when they heard a rumble like thunder from the hill that rose behind them. And with no other warning, a river of mud engulfed them.

Muck. Ooze. Sludge. Viscous earth. The landslide had picked up the speed of a diving eagle on its flight down the mountain. But this one had weapons much larger than talons and just as sharp. Small trees and large rocks were carried in its wake, and it hit them with the force of a thousand hammers.

And then they merged with the onslaught. They rode the thick liquid on their backs and stomachs like unwilling surfers as it bore them over the land's flat surface before plunging them down the ravine.

As she felt herself falling, one word left DC's lips. "Ari."

Chapter 31

Just as aqueous rivers empty themselves into a larger body of water, the torrent of fluid earth deposited itself into a large pool of mud at the bottom of the ravine. Lodged against a tree trunk, DC could tell she was bruised and battered, but under her covering of muck, she could not see the damage. It hurt to move her hip, and her arm stung in dozens of spots as if it had been a block of parmesan slid against a grater, but she was able to pull herself up from the thick goo to look for the others. She was barely able to see through the downpour, and yet she was thankful for it, as it was cleaning the gray sludge off her skin and clothes.

After just a few steps, she spotted Finn. He was on his feet and looked winded but uninjured. A few yards away, she could see an arm sticking up like a flag of surrender. She slogged her way toward it. It felt like her feet were suction cups. Attached to the arm, she could see Darby, his face half-buried, dazed but awake. She pulled his head up and stuck two fingers in his mouth to make sure that no mud blocked his breath.

"I'm getting tired of saving your ass," she said. This time, there was sympathy in her voice and even a hint of playfulness.

For a moment, Darby forgot his predicament and wondered how this woman could go from nail-tough to tender from one moment to the next. *The female of the species,* he said to himself. Little did he know the conflicting emotions that pulled DC like a tug-of-war rope.

But neither did she understand his temperament. He assumed that she saw him as emotionless and boring at best, infuriating at worst. *Too bad she didn't know me before. I'd have given her a run for her money.*

His entire life, he had been different than other people, unappreciated by the average dodecian. But this woman would have liked his uniqueness, he thought, would have enjoyed his quick wit and fast-forward thinking. She might even find him fascinating. But he wasn't like that anymore. It seemed as if a large part of him had died in the transpod, or at least gone underground. He used to be action-oriented, clever and somewhat rebellious, the one person not glued to the fun tunnel—as a child, the only one running down a hill, arms outstretched and screaming like an eagle.

As an adult, he still hadn't fit in. Instead, he had developed the confidence to stay true to himself. *She would have liked that. She would have at least thought I was interesting,* he thought.

But ever since his first death, things like that didn't matter as much. His personality no longer mattered. In fact, sometimes it felt as if he no longer had a personality—that he was no longer the actor in his own drama, but rather the observer of it. If not for the occasional twinge of fear this brought, he felt quite good, even happy. In fact, most things now seemed funny to him, slightly absurd or at least amusing. He must seem goofy to her, laughing at things she thought were serious. And boring, only talking when necessary.

"Can you get up?" she asked after scraping a few inches of mud off his chest.

There used to be a part of him that would want to make an impression, and he willed it to the surface. "I'm your golem. Whatever you command."

He hoped she'd appreciate the humor, and he searched her face for the hint of a smile or even a smirk. The corners of her lips turned up a smidgen, and that was enough. He moved one leg to test it, and then the other. Each body part felt intact, and he eased himself out of the blanket of wet earth.

Finn had made his way to them and was now on his knees searching through the muck where Darby's back had been. Through the clatter of rain he hollered up to them, "We have to find the packs."

Only DC's pack remained on her back. The other two could be anywhere in the thick river of liquid earth.

"We need to make shelter first and take care of any injuries," DC hollered back. "Are you hurt?"

"A few scratches I think."

Finn pointed to the largest tree within seeing distance that was outside the pool of mud. It looked like it was on flat, solid ground. His two companions understood, and the three of them made their way to the spot. They searched their surroundings for the longest sticks they could find. They leaned one end of each stick up against the massive trunk, fitting them into indentations in the bark and fanning them out into a semi-circle along the ground. The men pressed the bottom ends of the sticks into the drenched dirt to secure them as much as possible. Meanwhile, DC had taken the particle-beam pistol from her pack and was slicing live branches from nearby trees. Laden with needles, they would make a fine roof for the lean-to. With laces from their boots, they secured the branches to the framing at strategic spots, and although cobbled together, it held.

Together, they huddled and shivered inside their makeshift shelter until the sky had cried itself out.

When they emerged from underneath it, they assessed the damage to their bodies. Other than DC's sprained hip, they had suffered only cuts and bruises. Finn set out to find the first-aid they needed—spicebush for their bruises and comfrey for their cuts. He had also seen some sword fern, the roots of which would make a hearty stew for supper if they could start a fire in this wet mess.

Wood burns. Branches shelter. Roots nourish. Leaves heal. The mantra now repeated itself in DC's mind like a lullaby, and she was comforted by the truth of it. She had seen both sides of nature, what it could give and what it could take, and she both loved and feared it, much like she had felt about her father.

Her fresh cuts made her think of her father, and as she walked through the wet forest to look for any piece of wood that might burn, the past took root in her mind. As a child, she could not help but love her father, even after he started drinking, even after her mother fell victim to his rages, and even after she, too, bore the bruises of his anger. She learned to hate him when he was cruel, love him when he was gentle, and not trust him in between. It had caused a split in herself that still had not mended. Now, in the solitude of her search for dry branches, as the sting of the fresh wounds on her skin began to fade, she wondered if nature had any tonic for the invisible cuts of childhood.

As they sat at the fire that night, brewing their stew, herb poultices fastened over their worst gashes, DC couldn't stop translating every word her friends spoke into her own private, internal discussion about her father. Even Finn's talk about the weather could be related to her childhood wounding.

When he said, "The weather is bad now, but it wasn't always like this," DC's thoughts jumped to, *That's what my mother used to say, too. 'He wasn't like this until he started drinking.' A lot of good knowing that did.*

"There was a time when storms like this came only once in a while," Finn was saying. "You could live your whole life and never see a really big one—the type that takes peoples' lives. But then they weaponized weather. And they were using fuels that burned dirty. They knew it could change the weather, but they were addicted to their fuels, so they were in denial about it."

DC understood denial. When her mother would notice the bruises on her child's arms, she would say, "Honey, you have to be more careful." *What had she meant by that?* DC wondered. Did she think her daughter was simply clumsy, had bumped into the sharp edges of furniture or tripped on a carpet? Or was it a subtle warning to avoid invoking the drunkard's ire? Either way, it was a form of denial, and from it, DC had learned to not look the hard truths too closely in the eye.

"We think that someday, the weather might heal itself." Finn was saying when DC brought her attention back to the present.

The group was silent as Finn stared into the fire for several moments. Without looking up, he said, "I'm sorry I didn't see it coming—the storm and landslide." Just as DC's thoughts had been trapped in the past, searching for

137

answers, so did Finn seem to be apologizing for something else—for not foreseeing some past disaster—the one that had taken his parents' lives and set the course of his own.

DC sensed the connection, and the motherly instincts that the Consolidate's trait test had once identified now surfaced. She felt a flood of affection for this young man who had bravely taken on the task of guiding them to The Village. She wanted nothing more than to comfort his self-doubt.

"There's more than one way to save a life," she said. "If not for your knowledge of plants—if you didn't know which ones are good for food and for medicine—we might not make it to The Village."

"Well, we're not there yet," Finn replied. But she could see his frown had softened.

Chapter 32

The next morning began with a hunt for the packs. They scanned the surface of the congealing river of mud, but it would take weeks to dig down and search every foot of it, and after an hour, they gave up. The rest of the journey would have to be accomplished with the items in DC's pack, with nature providing whatever else they needed.

Her pack contained everything that she had escaped the dodec with, except the brown coveralls, which she left behind in favor of more practical travel clothes provided by the family. She had shared some of the protein powder with the family, just because it was a novelty to them, but the rest of the powder was still in its container, next to the fire orb, pistol and thinsulate blanket.

After her rescue from the river, when she had emptied the pack to dry its contents, she had found something she hadn't put there wedged into the bottom of a zippered side pocket. The two tiny vials of clear liquid were surrounded by a piece of folded paper held in place by a rubber band. The river had watered down the ink, making most of the note illegible, but she could tell it was Ari's writing and had been able to decipher a few words: "shamans used" and "dimethyltri..." and "beyond the veil" and "power." Not enough to make sense of, but if Ari went to the effort to hide it in her pack, it must be important. She didn't know why she brought it on this trip, but it was small enough to add little weight, and it made her feel as if she had a part of him with her.

As she checked the contents of her pack for any intrusion of mud, seeing the vials brought back the thought that had begun to nag at her with increasing insistence. Was it a mistake to go to The Village first? At Finn's house, she had been so close to the dodec. Half a night's walk through the tunnel, and she could be back inside. Even without a plan, if she was careful, she might be able to sneak back into the Transitionary unnoticed.

But now she was headed in the opposite direction in hope of finding allies. When Finn had explained the skills that the villagers had developed—skills as good as Finn's and better—they sounded to her like superpowers, precisely what she needed to help Ari and the others escape. But could she convince the people with those talents to help her rescue her friends? And would it be too late?

For the rest of the trip to The Village, nature withheld her fury, but apprehension tormented DC's brain like a hard rain.

They must have been quite a sight, entering the village square in shirts tattered by the mudslide debris, their cuts not yet healed, not knowing where to go or who to ask for. But everyone they came upon seemed genuinely interested in their welfare, and it wasn't long before a small group surrounded them, and all agreed that they should be taken to Great-grandmother Sophia's house.

"I need help with the garden and fix-its. You'll stay with me," Great-grandmother said to the three of them after the introductions.

It felt like home to DC from the moment she crossed the threshold, with its overstuffed couch and big picture windows, a fireplace made of river rock, a front porch shaded by the leaves of old oak trees and a back porch littered with seed pots. It seemed to her that all of nature's elements had been invited in to share this place, and she felt the comfort of their company. But no amount of comfort could shake her foreboding that back at the dodec, something was amiss.

Chapter 33

The knife flew past DC's cheek with the speed of a hawk in pursuit of its prey. Before she could duck, its tip had lodged itself in the wall behind her. When she realized the near-miss, she gasped, staring wide-eyed at the ten-year-old girl in front of her.

Darby burst out laughing, but when he saw the frown cloud the girl's face, followed by the warning glance from DC, he swallowed and fell silent.

"I'm sorry," Katina said. "I was trying to lift your spoon. Auntie Shar says I have to see the energy better in my imagination."

"I'm sure you're going to be very good at it one day. But let's finish eating right now," DC said, hoping to end the telekinetic demonstration while sharp objects were on the table.

Great-grandmother Sophia silently cut the tomato on her plate, but DC thought she noticed a twinkle in those old eyes and a hint of a smile pass the wrinkled lips. She was fascinated by this ancient being, how the veins crisscrossed her hands like sycamore roots, how her fingers shook when she held a fork, the scratchiness in her voice and the slight bend in her back, how she seemed to notice everything but say very little about it. This was old age, and DC wanted to know all of its details. This is what she had prevented at the Transitionary, and she wanted to know what had been lost.

The villagers seemed to cherish it. Everyone nodded to the white-haired folk they passed on the street. Some stopped by Great-grandmother Sophia's house to ask her advice. Others brought her pastries and tea. Everyone here was friendly to everyone else, but the elderly they treated with deference and respect. It was as if they were precious gems to be placed softly on the best satin and admired with satisfaction.

DC was beginning to understand it, as already she felt a sort of reverence for this woman who had been chosen as their host. Or had Great-grandmother Sophia chosen them? DC wondered for what reason had she and her fellow travelers been placed in that house.

The three houseguests usually said little at mealtimes, sensing that attention belonged with the youngest and eldest at the table. Their silence paid off, as Katina's blurted-out thoughts were often entertaining, and Great-grandmother's deliberate morsels of practical philosophy were occasionally offered for them to digest with the asparagus.

Great-grandmother waited until the meal was nearly finished to give them the news they'd been waiting for. "The Wisdom Council has agreed hear your purposes next week." She noticed the glances her houseguests exchanged, and then returned to her plate, knowing that they would ask their questions when they were ready.

Chapter 34

DC had been in a state of awe for three weeks, but of all the marvels she had seen in The Village, nothing had prepared her for this. Twelve white heads in a circle, and below each mane of white, eyes with deep pools of wisdom. She could not describe the feeling in the council chamber. It was as if the air was heavy with a primordial perfume that carried discernment in its scent.

Last week, she and Darby had watched the Youth Council as it made decisions for the day-to-day progress of The Village, and the atmosphere in the room was more like a spring breeze. They discussed how the seesaw at the new playground would have underground lines connected to the village's well. In this way, they could harvest the energy of children to run the water pump. They heard how lipids would now be extracted from sewage for the making of membranes to control runoff on the bio-roofs. They heard how the sap from the nearby pines could be sustainably harvested to make a strong glue. *Ari would have plenty to do here*, DC had thought.

To her, the Youth Council had seemed like the screeners for creative ideas. In contrast, the Wisdom Council appeared to be weighing issues of wider significance. Tonight, they were asked whether Dodec One should be provided with the five hundred hardwood trees it requested. Another issue was whether the forest fire in the highlands should be allowed to burn itself out, or should the weather-wooers call in rain to quench it.

It wasn't just the issues that fascinated DC, but how the council deliberated. After each question was asked, the room fell into silence for several minutes. Some on the council closed their eyes. Others stared into the distance. When they reconvened by returning their attention to the group, they had somehow reached a unanimous decision. The only discussion was after the fact, working out some detail of how the decision would be implemented.

After all of the deliberations had ended, one of the elders turned her attention to the small group of onlookers.

"Today, our guests from Dodec One are here with their traveling companion from the outlands." The council members looked at the trio. "The council offers you welcome. May your hearts dwell in peace here."

Finn, DC and Darby nodded their thanks, and the elder continued. "You may tell us your purposes, and if they are for the good, you may receive service."

DC and Darby turned their heads toward Finn, as if his life outside the dodec automatically put him first in line to address this council. He took their cue and stood.

"Thank you for your time, attention and wise counsel," he began. "My name is Finn. I've had the gift of seeing since I was a child, but my ability is neither strong nor consistent. I wish to develop it by working with a master. That is why I came here."

"For what reason do you desire this?" a council member asked.

"I believe it can save lives and help people avoid difficult situations. And because it's my primary gift, it feels like it must be put into action, as if it is yearning for expression."

"Your heart does not mislead you," the council member said. "There are many seers here in The Village. The right one knows that you are looking for him. He will find you when the time has come."

The joy from knowing he had a teacher, and the impatience at having to wait, intertwined themselves in Finn's chest as he thanked them and sat, making way for DC to present herself.

She felt awkward and small before this august group, but she used Gemini's breathing technique to keep herself steady, and she pulled up the same courage that had allowed her to make her escape from the dodec, to jump from the transport, to make the trek to The Village.

"Thank you for considering my request," she said. "I'm asking for help in getting my friends out of the dodec. I can't do it alone. Even with the help of my friend," she motioned toward Darby, "it wouldn't be enough. I don't have a strategy yet, because our course of action will depend on the talents of the people who go with us. We'll need a seer, and probably someone good at telekinetics. I'm just beginning to learn all the abilities you have here. Perhaps you can suggest who to contact to begin putting together a group with the right skills."

To DC's surprise, the council entered its silent deliberation process. When they had all opened their eyes, one elder spoke, not to her, but to Darby.

"Are you going on this quest?"

Caught off guard, Darby's words stumbled as he stood, "Well, ma'am, it's no..., if I..., it's just that..." He paused to collect his thoughts. "I hadn't planned to go, no. I have a different purpose."

DC couldn't hide her shock. She had always assumed that he would go with her. The one time she asked him outright, he had said he needed time to decide, but hadn't she implied it often enough since then? He had never raised an objection, so what was this sudden decision that seemed so solid? She struggled to hold her anger in check, for surely these wise elders would sense it.

"Please explain that purpose," the elder said to him.

"I must see the sacred ones," Darby replied. "Something in me has changed, and something new is emerging. I know that they will have the answers I seek."

So what? DC thought. *Go get your answers. What will that require? Ten minutes?*

"The sacred ones do not take an audience. That is not their purpose," one of the council members said.

DC smiled inwardly. *See? You may as well come with me. Do some good in the world for once.*

"Then I will be their first audience," Darby replied. "I saw it..." he hesitated, not wanting to go into the details of his experience beyond the doors of death, "... in a sort of dream."

"The dream world is on a different level of awareness. You saw it in a place of clarity," the councilwoman said.

How does she know that? Can she read my mind?

"Because of where you saw it from, it must eventually realize itself," the councilwoman said. "You will stand before the sacred ones. But do not wait for it. Continue your inner journey. Let what is emerging come forth so that you can discover if that is what you want."

She then turned her attention back to DC. "What you ask is not trivial. For one to risk his life for another, there must be great love. Many here have it."

Obviously not Darby, DC thought.

"Understand what you're asking," the elder continued. "You will find your companions for the journey. Just remember that you cannot make another's decision."

"What should I do to find them?" DC asked.

"Close your eyes," the councilwoman said, and DC complied. "Can you find the soft spot in your heart?"

DC found it an odd suggestion, but she followed the instruction, and in spite of her current state of ire toward Darby, it took only a few moments for her to notice that there seemed to be a place in the center of her chest that held a certain tenderness.

"Yes, I think so," she said, opening her eyes.

"If you can live there, you will know them the moment you meet them. But also know that those who go with you will not all come back."

The councilwoman now looked at the three visitors, resting her gaze on each for several seconds. "We thank you for having these experiences for us all. May our unity expand us."

With that gentle dismissal, DC sat back down. Her thoughts raced back and forth between the strange message from the elder and her anger at Darby. No matter, she would find her new companions, and they would free her friends. But the elder's last comment nagged at her. *Know that those who go with you will not all come back.*

The statement repeated itself in her mind as she left the council chambers. It would come back to her again as she lay in bed that night. It would pop up the next day when she was playing hide-and-seek with little Katina. In the weeks that followed, it would enter her brain again and again, eventually giving birth to the inevitable question. *Must I again sentence someone to death?*

But that hour in the council chambers, the elder's warning had not yet birthed the question, and DC had a different matter on her mind. Invisible steam puffed out of her ears like a two-stacked locomotive as she headed back to Great-grandmother Sophia's house.

That evening, as she forcefully pulled root vegetables from the garden for supper, Darby stood a few feet away, squeezing the tomatoes to find the ripest one.

"Be careful, you'll hurt the carrots," he said. He knew she was steaming at him, and he wanted to get it out of her so that it could be over with.

She turned to him with a fistful of carrot tops, her eyes on fire and brain boiling. "After all I've done for you, and now you won't even help me." The carrots shook like wind chimes in a gale.

"Of course I'll help you. Here's a tomato. You want me to dig a couple potatoes? I'll help bake them, too."

His playing innocent just infuriated her further. "You know exactly what I mean." Now the carrots slammed into the bucket with a thud.

"Careful! Carrots can bruise, you know." Darby pretended to calmly continue checking the tomatoes. "So, what do you think you've done for me?"

What do I think? Think? What do I know I've done for him? In her thought-stopping anger, she was ripe for the trap, and she stood and faced him, hands on hips, and in rapid-fire succession listed his debts.

"First off, I saved your life. I didn't see anyone else walking out of that morgue alive. Then I helped you escape. I got you out of that suffocating dodec and to freedom. Freedom! You're certainly not complaining about that. Then, when you fell off the bridge, I risked my life to pull you back up. Now here you are because of me. Is that enough? Is there anything else I have to do for you to get your help with the one thing that's important to me?"

Darby put his finger on his chin and tapped it, looking upward to feign thinking. "Hmmmm. I'll take three more save-my-life-even-though-I-didn't-asks, two more make-me-jump-into-a-raging-rivers, one more get-me-to-risk-my-newfound-life-walking-across-a-slippery-bridge, and maybe another mudslide just for the fun of it."

Now her eyes narrowed and she shot daggers out of them in his direction. She grabbed her bucket of carrots and stomped past him into the house, saying, "I'm serious" as she huffed past.

Darby followed her into the kitchen with his tomato and placed it in front of her on the counter.

"All right. Let's be serious, then. You did all of that for yourself. I was just your puppet to get what you wanted. I'm not saying I don't appreciate being alive and on the outside. I do appreciate it. So I'll do for you what people do in these situations. Thank you. Thank you, DC-1128, for choosing me as the one to bring back to life and help you make your escape. Thank you for pulling me up from the bridge. Thank you for bringing me here where life is good.

And I'm not just saying that because you're upset. I really do mean it."

He had spoken with passion and insistence, and now he paused and softened his tone, speaking slowly for emphasis. "But I don't owe you my life."

The air hung thick with anticipation of where the flow of emotions would take them. DC's fuse began to burn itself out and her shoulders dropped. The silence waited for Darby to break it.

"By the way, why did you choose me? Out of all the people you saw every day in the Transitionary, why did you wait until I was on the table?"

She turned to him, and he could see tears forming in her eyes. Her voice was so low that it came out almost as a whisper, "You had the spark."

"The spark?"

Darby waited until she could gather herself for the explanation, and she ended up telling him everything—what the spark was, why she used it as her choice-making tool, how long she had planned and waited, why she took a job at the Transitionary in the first place, all about The Group and their intention to bring down the Consolidate, how she had changed her mind about the overthrow once she saw that life could be lived outside the dodecs.

As she talked, she began washing and chopping the carrots while he prepared the salad vegetables. It was easier that way, not having to look at each other. She knew he was attentive from his occasional question, and as each minute passed, she felt a little bit lighter. She had never shared the story of her adult life with anyone. Ari knew it from having been her friend through the years, but no one had actually been *told* the story from beginning to end, and it felt as if the burden of many years was lifting a bit, as if Darby was sharing the weight just by listening.

When she was finished, when the carrots were steaming and the salad ready for dressing, DC wiped her hands on a dishtowel and faced him. "Whether or not you go back into the dodec with me, I'm glad you were the one with the spark." She felt a flush cross her cheeks, and she turned to the sink to hide it.

Chapter 35

DC was quiet that night at the table. Little Katina shared her adventures of the day, and Finn and Darby told Great-grandmother Sophia about the meeting with the Wisdom Council. Great-grandmother Sophia nodded and ate her lettuce, paying attention to what wasn't said and who wasn't saying it.

When Katina had gone off to play and the men had gone to the kitchen to do the dishes, Great-grandmother Sophia turned her attention to the wounds in DC that were asking for healing.

"Ours is not a better way. Ours is just another way."

These people on the outside are always saying such puzzling things, DC thought to herself. "I'm sorry, I don't understand," she said to Great-grandmother Sophia.

"The dodecians have been traumatized by the very life they were born into. Brutality comes in many forms, and the worst kind is the kind you don't even notice. You could say that they're living in shock. Here, we live in tranquility. Each way has many benefits."

"I'm sorry, I don't mean to be disrespectful, Great-grandmother, but I can't see any benefits to living the dodec life. People work all day doing things they don't like, and then they escape the pain of it by turning off their brains in the fun tunnel. Oh, I'm sorry, you don't know what that is. We have screens on our eyeglasses with moving pictures, and we can enter the picture and interact with the scenery and characters in it. It's like a drug that everyone's addicted to. In a society like ours, addiction is everywhere."

"You've been sorry thrice already."

"I'm sorry, what?"

"Four times."

It took a moment for DC to figure out what Great-grandmother Sophia meant. "Oh, I'm apologizing too much."

"For what?" Great-grandmother asked.

"It's just a manner of speech," DC replied.

"A mannerism crafted by the society in which you live. That is a valid experience. Is it what you want to continue experiencing?"

DC felt as if she was being led in circles.

"The trauma of living in the dodec has shaped you," Great-grandmother continued. "If you watch your words and actions, you'll see what shape you're in. Only then can you choose a new form."

DC remained silent for a moment to digest it. "All right, I understand that. The dodec life has distorted me. So how can that be just as good as life is here?"

"First, there's nothing wrong with the distortion," Great-grandmother said. "It's just one more experience that must be had in order for us as a whole to experience all that is possible, and you chose to be the one experiencing it. You can only judge it as bad if you see yourself as separate from the whole. The rest of us are thankful that we're not the ones having to suffer in order to make that experience available to our collective self."

Finally, DC thought, *someone has explained what's meant by, "Thank you for being the one to experience that for us all."*

She had heard it twice now, and now she finally knew what they were talking about, although she wasn't sure she agreed with the concept.

"That's enough for tonight," Great-grandmother Sophia said.

DC wanted Great-grandmother to continue explaining her opinion that life in the dodec was as good as life in The Village. The all-pervasive peace of this place had seemed surreal to DC at first. In the dodec, every person she met was emotionally stressed and self-focused, and she hadn't even noticed it until she had seen the contrast of village life. In The Village, everyone she passed on the street looked at her and smiled, and their smiles were not just politeness. She could actually feel the well-wish that came with them. Everyone to whom she talked made solid eye contact so that she felt more noticed—more seen—than she had ever felt before. It seemed as if the all-pervasive kindness of the place was beginning to gently wash away a layer of pain that she had never heeded, and she wanted nothing more than to bathe her mind in it until the ache went away. But she knew she must stay focused until her friends were here with her, because regardless of what Great-grandmother Sophia said, The Village was a better place—a much, much better place.

She wanted to press Great-grandmother to further explain her statements, but she respected her wish to end the conversation. It would have to wait until they had another moment alone. But even with the conversation unfinished, DC could feel that her reshaping had begun. It would take many such conversations for the mold of the dodec to loosen its hold, but the warmth of The Village was already softening her edges, and like Jell-o on a stove, she might eventually melt enough to pour herself anew.

Chapter 36

The knife hung motionless in the air for a moment, then slowly moved upward until its point just touched the ceiling.

"Imagine it spinning. Can you feel the whirl of it?" Auntie Shar asked.

After a moment, the blade began slowly turning, flashing each time it caught the sun coming through the window. Then faster and faster until it was a dervish.

"Good. Good. Now slow it down."

Little Katina stood as motionless as a pole anchored deep in the ground, so completely focused that not even an earthquake would shake her concentration.

"Excellent. Now bring it down into your hand."

Katina did as told and was soon holding the sharp object.

"Remember, it's only waves of energy in the form of a knife. It's just a thought made solid for a moment. Now, bend the blade."

Her little face scrunched a bit as she stared at it, and ever so slowly the metal began to curl down. When it bended so far that the tip touched the handle, the room erupted in cheers. DC hollered loudest, so proud was she of Katina's advancement in the art of telekinetics. Darby, too, was impressed. While Finn clapped, he was hoping that he had made that much progress under his tutor.

Katina beamed and her feet did a little dance of satisfaction. "Make it disappear, Auntie Shar. Show them how you do it."

"Maybe later, dear. This moment is for you."

Great-grandmother Sophia opened her arms, and Katina ran straight into the hug. It felt so soft and warm that if such an embrace was just a thought made solid, she would think it more often.

"It's really remarkable how she's come so far in just three months," DC said to Shar, remembering her near-miss with Katina's first demonstration.

"She focuses well," Shar replied. "She might one day be able to create objects straight from the void."

"Without a 3-D printer," Darby commented.

He could tell from the look on Shar's face that she wasn't familiar with the term.

"We do something in the dodecs that's similar," he explained. "We use focused manufacturing mind to create an image, which goes into a machine called a thought facsimilator, and from there it's transferred to a printer that holds all the chemicals necessary to make the thing. That's how we manufacture." He still used the term "we" when talking about the dodec, as it was still more of him than The Village.

"I can't wait to see it," Shar replied.

At first, DC didn't catch it. It seemed just an off-hand comment. But she had been in The Village long enough to know that people here didn't use words carelessly. Those tiny lies dodec people told out of politeness were not possible in a world where being authentic was as natural as breathing. Still, DC felt compelled to test the statement.

"You plan to see our manufacturing process?" she asked.

"If you'll take me back to the dodec with you," Shar said, smiling to show her delight in making the offer.

DC's heart leapt. A master telekinetic would practically ensure her success. But with the next thought, her heart fell further than the distance it had just jumped.

Shar had been coming to Great-grandmother Sophia's house almost daily for Katina's training. She and DC would often sit on the porch after the lesson had ended and talk about each others' worlds. Both were fascinated by the alien ways of another place that was so close in distance, but so far apart in convention. As they learned about their differences and sameness, their friendship deepened, until DC felt almost as close to Shar as she had to Ari's wife.

She knew Shar well enough to know she would not take the offer back. But she also knew how deeply Shar loved her family. A husband and two teenage sons were the delight of her life.

Know that those who go with you will not all come back. The words of the elder still haunted DC, and now they felt like a curse. How could she accept Shar's offer, allow her to risk losing such a life? Before she could work it out in her thoughts, she heard a rapid rapping at the door.

The boy on the porch was breathless, bent over with hands on his knees, as if he'd just sprinted some distance. Darby invited him in, but the boy shook his head, waiting to catch his breath just enough to get out the few words of his message.

"The sacred ones have asked to see you." He gulped another breath. "Right now. Come with me."

161

Chapter 37

The room itself caressed them, as if a choir of angels had sung Mozart's most uplifting aria over and over until the walls had absorbed the vibration of it and were now repeating it back silently so that it permeated all in its reach. Darby felt like the string of a guitar resonating to some sublime note.

He stared in awe at the three children hovering several feet above the floor. Eyes closed, legs crossed in a sitting position, they looked like three triangles suspended from the ceiling. He said a silent, *Thank you for seeing me,* and he knew they would hear it.

Finn closed his eyes and received, for he could feel the ocean of knowledge flooding him. He would have time to decode it later. For now, he would take in all he could hold.

DC tried to spot the see-through wires that must be attached to their shoulders. *These kids don't carry a lot of weight with me,* she chuckled to herself, planning to use the line later with Darby. *But maybe I'll suspend my disbelief until I hear what they have to say.* She appreciated her own wit and saved the second pun as well.

The words seemed to come from the air around her, as if she was in the mouth of the speaker. "DC-1128. Is that how you wish to be addressed? Or do you prefer Diana Childress?"

She was so taken aback that she almost stumbled even though standing still. This visit was not for her. And how did they know her name? She had last heard it whispered by her mother twenty years past. And that voice. It was the sound of three children talking in unison, although only the lips of the middle one moved. It produced an echo that she considered eerie.

"DC, please," she answered back.

"Your request, in ten words or less."

She counted on her fingers to ensure she'd be complying. No matter how cynical she had been moments before, she could feel the power in that threefold voice, and it commanded a serious answer.

"To free my friends and all return here safely." This, she thought, might break the curse that the elder had spoken.

"The man standing next to you, is his heart true?"

She glanced at Darby. She had spent more than four months with this man, and still she did not really know his heart. But she knew he was honest and did what he said he would do, so she answered, "Yes."

The feeling of déjà vu engulfed Darby as he remembered his vision. *I will stand before the sacred ones, and she will be my witness.*

"Darby Tate, your request."

He, too, counted on his fingers. Eleven words. Would they accept it?

"To get back to my true self without leaving this life." He had so much to ask them, but the feeling of sanctity was so pervasive that he dared not do so without an invitation.

"Go now," the voices said. "You will have what you wish, but there's one thing you must do to guarantee it."

Finn smiled. In his mind he could see the accomplishment of their tasks, and he knew he had received his request without having to ask.

The triune voice spoke its final words. "Bring us the heart of the Benefactor."

Chapter 38

It was DC's turn to play devil's advocate. She could sense Darby's consternation, and she reveled in the thought of delving into it. He was walking so fast on the path back to the house that she almost had to run to keep up. But she wouldn't miss this exchange for the world, so she matched his pace.

"I guess you'll be coming with me, then." It was hard to keep a straight face, but her years in the transpods proved a fine trainer.

"What, we're going to murder the top person in the Consolidate and cut out his heart? Are you crazy?" Darby was practically yelling. "Even if we could get to him—which is impossible, by the way—but even if we could, would you do it? Could you kill someone in cold blood and then take a knife to his chest and cut out his heart?"

"I've done it thousands of times already. Well, not the part about the heart."

He stopped abruptly to look at her, and she congratulated herself for catching him off guard.

"This is different," he said. "And this is serious. It's not something to joke about."

"All right, seriously then. We're talking about a man who has presided over the misery of millions. I can't imagine that he even has a heart. And if he does have one, I know several people who would be more than happy to cut it out of him. Anyway, if Shar is with us, it will be easy. We won't even need a hand to hold the knife."

She was not serious about using Shar for the deed, but she couldn't resist egging on his aggravation for one more moment, and she was delighted when his open mouth showed his shock.

"Well, I don't want any part of it."

"All right. The old Darby Tate is more interesting anyway."

She slowed her pace and allowed him to pull ahead. She wanted that thought to dangle in his mind for a while until it put down roots, an epiphyte clinging to the dendrites in his brain. She knew she had just taken advantage of his trust, but now, it was for his own benefit, not just hers. Those hovering humanoids wanted the Benefactor's heart in exchange for Darby's enlightenment, and she was just trying to help him get what *he* wanted.

After that day in the kitchen during which she had told him about her life, he had opened up about his own past, including how his temporary death had changed him, how he sometimes felt that his old personality was dissolving, how he had sensed a much more expansive self in that place beyond death, and it called to him with the insistence of instinct, like a robin calling her fledgling to fly from the nest.

DC had asked Great-grandmother Sophia about Darby's condition in hopes of gaining a better understanding of it. Great-grandmother had provided an answer in her typical fashion.

"What is in this?" she had asked DC, holding up an empty glass.

"Nothing, just empty space," DC had replied.

"And if I move the glass over here, where does the space go? Is it here with the glass, or over there, where the glass used to be?"

DC had paused to think for a moment. She didn't like these trick questions. "I guess it's both places, because space is everywhere." She was pretty certain she had nailed it.

"Darby has identified with the form of this glass all his life, and certainly it is his current form, but he is also the space within it," Great-grandmother had said. "When he died, he sensed his full self, because it was no longer contained by the vessel. It's hard to be chained once you have experienced freedom."

It hadn't made much sense to her, but she did start noticing that at times he was Darby Tate the lifelong rebel and independent thinker, and at other times, he behaved more like expansive space, although she preferred to tease him with the term "spaced out."

DC was going to need the rebel for the trip back into the dodec, and she felt justified in using her knowledge of his condition to manipulate him into the proper decision. *To get what he wants, he has to go back with me.* The thought made her steps more buoyant as she walked back from the sanctuary of the sacred ones to Great-grandmother Sophia's house. *He'll do it now. He would do whatever those airborne adolescents told him to.*

Chapter 39

Finn did not tell Darby and DC what he had seen during their time with the sacred ones. He had been working with his teacher for two months now, and although he had rapidly advanced, his lessons had begun not with skill building, but with ethics.

"When you see something at a distance, you can believe it. You are seeing it at this moment, and if you tell it to others, you will be speaking true," Eli had told him. "But what you see of the future, you should rarely discuss. It cannot be trusted. Nor are most people meant to know it. When you see the future, you are seeing the greatest probability from within a field of infinite possibilities. It is the most likely outcome only at that moment, and one person's thought or action could change it tomorrow so that a different probable event emerges." Eli had paused and studied his pupil to make sure he understood. "Never forget that a change of one heart can change the whole world in an instant."

"If we weren't meant to know the future, are we breaking some universal law by looking at it?" Finn had asked.

"No, because you are not really seeing the future at all, only the result of the combined intentions of every thinking being up until this moment," Eli had replied. "The future is not set until the instant it happens. So you see, it does not really exist. Time is just an infinite collection of nows, each one new, but nevertheless now."

New nows. Finn had never considered the concept. But he planned to contemplate it deeply, for everything his mentor said had layers of significance.

Today, he had much more to think about. It was as if those few minutes with the sacred ones had supercharged his budding talents, and he felt like a flower opening to the morning sun. Back at Great-grandmother Sophia's house, he went to his room to be alone, to revel in the energy of this new unfolding and to start unwrapping the gifts of information he had been given in that hallowed room. Knowledge bathed him like a warm waterfall, and he soaked in the pool beneath it.

In this new now, there was one thing he knew for certain about his own future. He would be going with DC and Darby to the dodec. What he had seen in his mind's eye while standing before the sacred ones felt like his destiny, and he would follow it. It was no longer a probability within the great field of possibilities. It was his choice.

Chapter 40

When Sharlotta learned that they would soon be leaving for the dodec, she could barely contain her excitement. This would be a grand adventure. It was an excursion into the city—something few villagers had done. She did not know why the Wisdom Council would allow it, as anything she did while inside might be construed as breaking a two-hundred-year-old treaty of non-interference, but she trusted that the council had seen that it would be for the highest good of all concerned. She relished the idea of getting a first-hand look behind those opaque polygons. It would be like traveling back in time to see the way of life before the Great Shift. But it would be more than simple sightseeing. She would participate in a mission, helping at least four people escape that giant glass cupola.

Never before had she felt such a flutter in her chest. When her boys were born, she had experienced the thrill of bringing new life into the world, and at her betrothal ceremony, she had encountered the exhilaration of romance anchored by a solemn commitment. But this feeling was new—an intoxicating frenzy of anticipation.

DC warned of the dangers they would all face, but Shar felt confident in her skills. She might be able to lift the whole dodec if she put her mind to it, so how could anyone inside of it cause her harm?

"Our lives here may be free of stress and calamity," she told DC, "but your world has such interesting variety. You have fights and reconciliations, heartbreaks and triumphs, hopes and frustrations, authenticity and deceit. How fascinating! What a wonderful backdrop of contrast. What incredible circumstances you create to learn all about yourselves. And the opportunities for developing and expressing compassion must be unlimited. It's not that I would exchange my life for it, but it's worth a bit of risk for a chance to see it."

"At the Wisdom Council, I was told that of those who went, not all would come back. I could never forgive myself if something happened to you there."

"See what I mean? I want to experience the society that gave birth to a concept like having to forgive oneself, or feeling responsible for someone else's decision. And don't worry too much about what the elders say. Their words can have many meanings."

"That sentence seemed pretty clear to me. What else could it mean?"

"Well, maybe it means that Darby will finish his transformation into his more expansive self while he's there and leave his ego-self behind."

"That would be enough to bring the Consolidate down," DC said, and they both laughed.

Chapter 41

Two specks of yellow flashed in the trees behind Darby.

"Fireflies!" DC announced, pointing to the place where the light from their campfire met the blackness of night. In her studies of the outside world, she had read about these little insects carrying their own light and was glad that the journey back to the dodec was providing the chance to see them. Her companion travelers turned in the direction she pointed, waiting for the next spark. It reappeared not as a flash but as a constant glow—two golden eyes reflected by the fire.

"Wolves," Finn whispered.

Darby knew almost nothing of forest creatures, but Finn's tone was so ominous that he instinctively grabbed the longest stick next to the fire pit and stood to face the glowing ovals, arm cocked for battle.

Finn closed his eyes to search for the probable outcome. He could see a set of long fangs sinking deep into DC's thigh and another canine jaw pulling down the arm that held Darby's stick. He also saw the four of them packing up camp the next morning, unharmed and happily chatting. Both possibilities weighed equally on the scales of future events, as those around the campfire had not yet chosen their next actions.

"The fire in the highlands," DC whispered, remembering that at the Wisdom Council meeting, they had decided to ask the weather-wooers to call in rain to quench it. "If they've come down from there, they must be hungry." As she spoke, two more sets of glowing eyes emerged from the darkness.

"I think I know what might work," Shar said, matching her friends' hushed tones. "I learned it as a child in Agàpe Class."

"Then do it in a hurry," DC huffed, sensing that every second could make the difference between life and death. These fierce animals might not take much time to study their prey.

"You have to do it with me," Shar whispered back. "Everyone close your eyes, and imagine the people you love the most. See them in your mind, and feel your love for them in your heart." She paused to give them a few seconds to follow her instructions.

This is no time for a guided meditation, DC thought, and the only thing she could feel in her heart was three beats per second. *In a moment, it won't be the Benefactor's heart that gets cut out.*

"Now, expand it out. See the feeling of love as light, expanding out like a bubble, getting larger and larger until it encompasses all the area around you. Send it into the trees, the sky, the ground, even the wolves. Let go of your fear, and send your love right into them."

Now DC was certain she was about to become dinner. She could see that Finn and Darby had their eyes closed and were doing as told. But hers were wider than ever, and every muscle was taut and ready for flight. She noticed that the glowing orbs behind Shar had disappeared, and she imagined the wolf circling round for the kill. Now the eyes behind Finn were gone. She jerked around to look behind her. Had they sized her up as the weakest animal in the herd? But all she saw was blackness. Her gaze made a circle around the surrounding trees. Only the soft glow of the fire flickered in their branches.

"They're gone," Finn said, now in a normal tone.

"How do you know?" DC demanded, still in a whisper.

"I can see it," he said. "They caught the scent of a family of badgers. Smaller prey, but at least they know what to expect."

"Are you sure?" DC rasped, still frantically searching behind her.

"Positive. They're gone. I promise."

DC's shoulders relaxed a bit as she turned back toward the fire and her friends. *So we were saved by the scent of some other animal. It wasn't the love bubble after all. Pop that theory.*

Then she remembered her particle beam pistol. How could she have forgotten it the one time it was really needed? Could fear freeze her mind to such a degree that it lost the obvious?

"Maybe they'll come back after that little snack," she said to Finn. "Can you see if they're going to do that? Maybe we're still the main course."

"They won't be back. Don't worry, we're safe."

Still, DC pulled the pistol from her pack and rested her hand on it the rest of the night.

Chapter 42

The remainder of their journey was without incident. The weather-wooers had agreed to keep their path clear of spring storms, and the animals they encountered did not stalk humans. As they walked, they formulated their plan—how they might get into the dodec unnoticed and sneak other people back out. DC was a bit disappointed that Finn could not tell them in advance what the best strategy would be.

"There are too many variables," he explained. "The field of possibilities is infinite."

It had been DC's idea to start at a trading station. She remembered the Wisdom Council weighing the Consolidate's request for hardwood trees. Products were obviously going into the dodec, and she had learned that the villages had set up several trading stations where goods could be loaded for transport to one of the tunnels that stretched between dodecs. DC was certain it was the best way in.

Now, after two days of travel, they spotted the trading station from the top of a hill. As they walked toward it, Shar explained the trading arrangement between The Village and the Consolidate. Inside the dodecs, they needed at least some of the earth's resources—timber, salt, granite, zinc and the like. There was nothing manufactured in the dodecs that the villagers really needed, but they appreciated some items for the convenience they offered. And to trade one thing for another created balance. So the Wisdom Council weighed every request against the sustainability of mining or harvesting the materials. When it agreed to supply raw goods, it asked for manufactured items in return—things the villagers did not want to make for themselves.

"Anything that creates more time for leisure, but in balance," Shar said. "In the old world, the so-called conveniences of modern life were an illusion. They ended up stealing everyone's time. People kept working harder and faster just to buy and install and repair and get rid of and replace more and more stuff."

"That's still how it is in the dodecs," Darby said.

Shar made a mental note to observe it once there. "We think about what goods would actually save more time than they steal, and we ask the Consolidate to provide that. By keeping our material goods mostly to necessities, and by living in a mild climate by a river, we've been able to cut our working time to a few hours a week."

"I think people would miss some of the high tech gadgets of the dodec," Darby said, "our wristgear and optiscreens and 3-D printers. We have everything, including all the accumulated information of humankind, available at the touch of a fingertip, and we can communicate with each other instantly. Our devices get better and better every year."

Darby had no way of knowing that technological advancement had actually slowed to a snail's pace since the dodecs were built. Subjugation stifles innovation, and what might have been developed in twenty years now took two hundred.

"All of that outer technology is needed when you're so busy working to accumulate it that you don't have the time to develop your inner skills," Shar replied. "All information is available to us, too, without gadgets. And communication is as easy as sending a thought."

Darby had seen the villagers use telepathy. The idea of someone else reading his mind had alarmed him at first, but then he learned that it was by mutual agreement. If the receiver didn't want to be intruded upon, he would simply not open his mind to another. Darby had also watched Finn pull information right out of thin air, not from the mind of another individual, but out of what Finn called "the field of infinite knowledge." Great-grandmother had said that these were some of the natural talents that all humans had to some degree, and each villager chose which to develop.

Darby could understand how using these so-called inner technologies instead of physical devices could reduce the need for labor, but he wanted to know why living in a mild climate by a river made it possible to work only a few hours a week.

"After the World Civil War, when our ancestors no longer had access to all those gadgets, they noticed that most of their labor was expended to feed themselves and stay warm in winter," Shar explained. "So the villages were built where winters are mild. Our shelters don't have to be elaborate to keep out the cold, and we can grow food year-round, eliminating the need for extra effort to preserve and store it. And casting a net in our river can fetch a week's worth of food in ten minutes."

Food and shelter—the necessities of survival that had once required struggle to obtain—were now available to all with little effort, leaving the villagers free of stress and with time to do whatever they loved most.

Darby compared it to his world. He recalled being taught that the benevolent Consolidate had been able to reduce the workweek from forty hours to thirty without people having to give up their quality of life. *An interesting expression—quality of life,* he thought. *It's been skewed to mean how many things dodecians can buy.* He had been taken in by that trick, feeling thankful that the Benefactor was so concerned for his welfare. The truth was that six hours a day plugged into the thought facsimilator still left him drained and unhappy, and that the dodec way of life had few benefits and many drawbacks for the mass of the populace. The benefits had been consolidated at the top. He was beginning to understand DC's ardor for the plan that her group had hatched. What if they could overthrow the Benefactor and the directors of the Consolidate? Would the dodecians seize their new freedom and power, he wondered, or were they so conditioned that they would ask for new rulers to take the place of the old ones? He realized that he was about to help start a revolution, if one hadn't already begun.

"DC," he said, "we've been gone for months. Do you think they've already attempted the overthrow?"

"We'll know soon enough," she said as she stepped up onto the trading station's platform. She pointed to a waiting cargo box filled with broken rock. "There," she said. "That's our ticket in."

Chapter 43

The thought of seeing Ari made DC's heart twirl like a waterspout. Perhaps this very night she would be in his arms for that short moment of a welcome-back. After four months apart, she would merit no more than a momentary hug, for in the decade since Ari's wife's death, she had never told him about her true emotions. At first, she had kept her feelings to herself out of respect for his grieving. By the time his heart had healed enough to open to someone else, it felt like the distance she had kept between them had solidified into some barrier she could not cross, as if to tell him that she was in love with him would somehow threaten the sanctity of the deep friendship they had forged through their mutual grief. To trade deep love for mere romance seemed like a sacrilege. Or perhaps that was just her excuse for not having the courage to say what she felt.

From her perch on top of the mound of broken rock, she vowed to change that. Her time on the outside had loosened the ties on her emotional straightjacket. Her arms were now free to do as they please, and her heart was ready to take the risk. And perhaps the fact that she no longer witnessed dozens of people dying every day allowed her to deserve what she wanted. No matter the reason. Her mind was made up. And it no longer mattered that Ari was ten years older than she was. In The Village, they could love each other into old age. She could now afford to imagine more than a moment enfolded by those broad shoulders.

She shifted her weight to waken the leg that was tingling from a rock edge pressing a nerve and then resettled her back against Darby's. They had folded their sleeping pads to sit on, but the cargo of jagged stones was still a torturous perch. The walls of the cargo box held so much black dirt that the travelers were using each other for backrests. They did not know how many hours they would have to sit under the cargo box's tarp. But they did know that the trading station only operated during the day, so if the truck hadn't left by sundown, they would climb back out of it to sleep on the ground, and then get back in it the next morning and wait again.

I'd wait a hundred years to get back to Ari, DC thought.

As she leaned against her transitioner's back, she felt the warmth emanating through his shirt and even a bit of a tingle. He was, after all, a handsome man. *I would have to be dead to not feel some attraction*, she thought. Her feelings for him swung like a pendulum between affection and frustration. *Just like all my feelings, yo-yoing out of control,* she thought as she tried to ignore the sensation.

Darby turned his head toward DC's ear so that only she could hear his question. Ever since they left the sacred ones, he had been aching to ask it.

"Diana Childress." The way he said it sounded like the wind's whisper. "It's a beautiful name. Why do you use your Directory of the Consolidate identification instead of your real name?"

DC sighed deeply. It had been so many years since she had been called by her birth name that it sounded almost like a foreign language to her now. And how much did she want to reveal to him of her real self? She started with the information that felt safe.

"My mother said she named me after a goddess because I was the most divine thing in her life. Diana was the goddess of the hunt in one of the old mythologies, and she was also the goddess women prayed to when they wanted to give birth. My last name, Childress—that's what they used to call a person who ran an orphanage. I always thought it was an interesting contradiction. The goddess of birth who's in charge of orphans."

She paused for a moment, not wanting to tell him the real reason she had abandoned her own name, not knowing how to explain why she didn't deserve one.

"Anyway, my initials are the same as Directory of the Consolidate. Either way, it's DC. It's just easier, I guess."

She was glad that they were back to back so that he could not see her face as she offered her explanation.

Darby asked no more questions, and DC returned to her thoughts of Ari, trying to remember if *he* had ever asked her birth name. She imagined his caress. It would be gentle yet committed, soft yet sure of itself. She knew him that well, better than anyone else, and her decision to confess her love was now certain. Not only did she love him, but he came with fringe benefits—a beautiful daughter that she would like to call her own. If she had borne another human, she would have hoped for a child as fine as Gemini, and she would be doing honor to her dead friend to fully step into the role of mother. Although at seventeen—*eighteen now,* DC corrected herself—Gemi was no longer a child, and Ari had done a fine job of raising her. Now, DC could give her a different world where she could be free from the oppression of the dodec, dance over open fields and smell the scent of fresh air and pine needles, live among people who would cherish her inner beauty—a world where she could truly breathe, and a world where she did not have to live with the anticipation of her father's impending death.

The sound of footsteps broke through her thoughts, and the cargo box's hidden inhabitants felt a slight tip as the weight of what must have been a large man was placed on the cab's sidestep. In less than a minute, they felt themselves moving forward, gaining speed and momentum. They felt the rocks beneath them slip and settle, and they adjusted their positions for what comfort they could get.

DC lifted an edge of the tarp overhead and let a shard of sunlight slip in. When the truck stopped, there would be no light. The cargo box would be backed into the blackness of a tunnel, hooked to a transport cab, and delivered to one of the entrances at Transport Control.

While DC imagined what she remembered of that cavernous room with its glass booth in the middle, Finn was seeing it for the first time in his mind's eye. He could see that when they stopped, the transport driver would leave the boxcar at the end of the tunnel without bothering to look below the tarp. He could see past the tunnel's entrance to the booth, that it would be empty within hours of their arrival, giving them a free pass into the bowels of the Transitionary. But he could not see beyond that. Too many people with too many tasks occupied the ground-level world of the Transitionary, even after-hours, and any one of their choices or actions could change the outcome. The most probable scenarios flashed before his mental screen like a multiple-exposure film clip.

DC was also thinking about the possibilities. They would wait in the boxcar until night, when fewer people occupied the first floor. But there were four of them, and how could they go unnoticed? They would have to make spur-of-the-moment decisions as they relied on Finn's skills to see just ahead and perhaps Shar's ability to move whatever object needed it, whether a locked door or security camera.

For the first time in months, fear spread through DC's chest like a spider's venom, numbing whatever it touched.

Chapter 44

As the transport slowed to a stop, its passengers remained as still as stone until they heard the driver exit the cab and detach the cargo box. For several more hours they waited, listening to the occasional sound of footsteps in the cavernous room of Transport Control and the whir of other transports as they accelerated on their magnetic tracks.

When no sound had been heard for nearly an hour, DC finally asked, "Is it safe?"

With his remote vision, Finn saw the Transport Control booth empty. He saw an exit sign over a hallway and scanned down it for movement but saw none. What he had failed to see did not move at all. Its lens was hidden in darkness at the mouth of the tunnel.

"Let's go now," he said, whispering in spite of being sure that no human was within hearing distance.

The four stowaways jumped down to the ground, leaving their sleeping pads on top of the cargo. Small backpacks carried by hand would not attract attention, but bedrolls attached to them would. DC hoped whoever found the sleeping pads would be puzzled by the strange items atop the pile of rock but not suspicious.

The gurgle of the river of renderings echoed down the hallway. DC's stomach turned, and she tightened her hold on her emotions.

Inside the elevator, the bright artificial light seemed to burn right through her, exposing her past complicity. The elevator was taking her back up to the scene of her misdeeds, and it felt like a trip to the hanging platform, where the noose would welcome her neck. She reached for the wall to steady herself as her trachea constricted. She, the executioner, who had always failed to stay the trapdoor, now felt as if she was about to fall through it.

Darby noticed her distress and looked into her widened eyes. "You're holding your breath," he whispered. "Breathe."

She obeyed, taking in the precious air and letting it fill her lungs. Her trachea was still intact, and she forced her mind to unfreeze itself. *Gemi's breaths, remember, four counts in, inhale, four counts out.*

It tickled Shar to experience such suspense. Fear had been a foreigner in her emotional life, and the newness of it was exhilarating. She felt the hair stand up on the back of her neck and a shiver run down her spine. *Reverse kundalini,* she thought, fascinated by the new sensations.

The elevator's ding announced their arrival on the main floor, and they stepped out into a foyer as empty as a hangman's heart. A hundred feet to the exit door and they were out into the safety of night.

Away from the Transitionary's entryway light, the darkness enfolded them like a cloak. It wasn't just DC who sighed a breath of relief. All four of the intruders had sensed the danger that could befall them at any step while they remained inside the Transitionary's walls, and all were happy to make it to the comparative safety outside.

DC pointed down the street that would lead them to a subway tunnel. She thought it the best way to cover the distance to Ari's house.

"When I hold my hand up to the turnstile plate, can you make the display read 'four'?" she asked Shar as they entered the subway station.

"Easy," Shar said.

DC cautiously eyed the commuters. Did any notice that two of the people in her group did not belong? To her, it seemed like the energy surrounding Shar and Finn made them as obvious as lightbulbs in a coffin. But she saw no stares aimed in their direction, and when the train spit them out at their intended station, she was confident that no one had bothered to pay attention to them. She remembered that she was back in a world in which people had learned to contract themselves, pull in their focus and mind their own business.

As they exited the subway tunnel, Shar's eyes widened at the sight of the large glass display window of Trinket Village, amazed by the sheer number of trifling objects the dodecians had created.

DC suggested that her friends go to the coffee shop while she went alone to Ari's house. She promised she would return for them before they had emptied their first cups.

Anticipation swirled through her like champagne bubbles as she ascended the front steps of Ari's house and knocked on the door. But when it opened, she could barely hold the cork. It was a woman's face that appeared before her. *A housekeeper? A girlfriend? A wife? Anything could happen in four months.*

"Is Ari in?" she asked.

"I'm sorry, you must have the wrong house. No one by that name lives here."

DC's mind imagined a dozen possibilities in a mere moment. "Forgive me. I'm looking for the past owner. I didn't realize he had moved," she said, hoping the woman would know Ari's current address.

"We bought the house directly from the Consolidate," the woman replied. "But good luck."

The door closed, leaving DC in solitude.

Her mind reeled. The woman's statement could mean many things, none of them good. Why had the Consolidate taken ownership of Ari's house? It was still several months until he turned fifty, and even if he listed early, Gemini would certainly keep the place.

She walked back toward the coffee shop with thoughts still a jumble, unable to even begin thinking what their next move might be. She had never imagined Ari wouldn't be there, never bothered to think of an alternate plan. Where would they start now?

"My old place," Darby suggested when DC explained their predicament. "It's twenty minutes on foot. It may still be empty."

Chapter 45

The floors were hard and unforgiving without their sleeping pads. It had been easy enough to break in through a basement window that was already cracked, but the home offered no comfort, barren as it was. A nearby streetlight provided just enough glow through the windows so that they didn't trip over each other.

They sat in a circle, sharing a meal of dried salmon from their packs. DC asked Finn to look for Ari with his mind's eye, and he now sat in relaxed concentration. Darby watched him closely, wondering if his own training in focused manufacturing mind might allow him to access some of these skills the villagers had.

"The room is small, white walls, concrete, high up," the words began pouring out of Finn, describing what he saw. "Tall ceiling, one light, no window, metal door, secure, he's sleeping, broad shoulders, snoring, bare feet, uncomfortable, the bed is too small."

Imprisoned. The thought hit DC like a punch to the stomach. But at least he was still breathing. "Can you see Gemi, Gemini Stockton?"

Finn took a few moments to shift his focus. A smile touched his lips. "She's happy, very happy, thinking about what has recently happened, connecting it to her future. She's happy about an imagined future."

Finn opened his eyes and looked at DC. "Just like you," he said, "Always imagining the future while remembering the past. Very strange how you dodecians think."

"You lose your power that way, not staying focused in the present moment," Shar added.

This present moment is not the time to get philosophical, DC thought to herself.

"Just see if you can figure out where she is, please," she said to Finn.

He focused on Gemini's present moment and described it. "A lot of light blue, made special just for her. Sitting cross-legged on a bed, blue comforter, blue pillowcase."

"Can you expand your view beyond the room, see where it is, a street sign or something?" DC spoke quietly, not knowing whether her words would break his concentration.

Finn went right on without a pause. "A woman in the living room. I feel a sort of numbness or sleep, but she's sitting upright. Her glasses have tubes extended to the skin around her eyes."

"A fun tunnel," DC whispered to Darby.

"And a boy," Finn continued. "Maybe a man. No, he's small. But important somehow. Important to your society. An important role, I guess. His fingers are moving in the air. Oh, wait a moment, it's a projection. He's typing on an image projected from the middle of his forehead, or maybe from his glasses."

"Has to be the glasses," Shar said. "You folks don't know how to project from your inner vision yet."

Be quiet, Shar, DC thought, transferring her feelings of frustration to her friend.

"Can't you get more than that?" she asked Finn. "A name, a street, something that will tell us where's she's at?"

"Hmmmm, yes. Ar... Or... Ori... Orine..."

"Orion!" DC almost shouted. *Of course. She's at Orion's house.*

She now knew her next move, and it allowed her to get off the mental pins she'd been sitting on. She had never been to Orion's house, but she could find his address. She would be able to see her sweet Gemi. And with Orion, she would have a friend from The Group who could tell her all that had happened. But one thought continued to needle her the rest of that night. *If Ari's in custody, why isn't Orion?*

Chapter 46

The data stick felt light in Gemini's hand. It contained a bill with half a million words meant for Director Wolfe's desk. Of all her tasks as an aide to Senator Smallman, acting as courier was near the top of her list. From office to office, she kept her ears perked and learned much of politics.

The lobbyists came and went like a tide full of kelp, leaving their proposed legislation and accompanying perks on the decision-makers' desks, returning again and again with more requests and offerings. She caught pieces of their conversations and judged which discourses worked best. She discovered which players had power. They spoke with the confidence of those who know the outcome in advance. She noticed the tricks in their arguments—what words they used to turn the decision, how they played on a senator's fear or pride or ambition. It was all so fascinating, how one man's emotion could shift a financial market, how a few words could be wielded like a carving knife, how the interplay of hundreds of humans all pulling different strands in the web of self-interests made the web move and shake without ever breaking it.

She stepped into the elevator and pressed fifty-two—the top floor of the Consolidate and the highest point under the dodec. She shifted the data stick from her right hand to her left. She knew what it contained, as she had read every word of it. And not only that, she understood its machinations. General Electronics wanted a share of the optiscreen market. It held the patent on a photoreceptor cell

197

in the human eye, and if Vision Enterprises maintained its claim that no one else could create an optilens with featherweight polycarbonate in it, then General Electronics would request changes in the Consolidate Standards Institute rules that governed how optiscreens were allowed to interact with photoreceptor cells.

On the surface, it all seemed a bit ridiculous. But Gemini understood its purpose. The art of politics was mediating such disagreements to constantly re-divvy the financial pie in a never-ending game of one-upmanship. And she knew she would one day be very good at it.

Already, Senator Smallman had taken notice of her hard work natural talent. She had pointed out to him that the Consolidate Standards Institute's director would be retiring at the same time that Senator Smallman's term was up, and its board would be looking for a replacement. The institute's board was weighted with former General Electronics executives, enough to put Senator Smallman on the shortlist for the high-paying job, as long as the bill tilted in General Electronics' favor.

The senator's eyes had narrowed when she pointed it out, and at first she thought he might be upset by her insolence in offering an uninvited opinion. But then she noticed that those two eye slits also contained a gleam, and after that day, he began giving her more important tasks.

That she would be asked to deliver a data stick to a Consolidate director's office was a statement of trust, for only the most trustworthy couriers carried the beamkey that would allow access to the upper floors, and now such a beamkey hung around her neck, even if it was just for this moment.

She stepped out of the elevator into a reception room, its mahogany walls radiating a dark richness. It was so silent in the room that she could hear her own soft steps on the thick carpet as she approached the receptionist's desk.

"A packet for Director Wolfe from Senator Smallman," Gemini said, offering the data stick.

Instead of accepting it, the receptionist motioned toward a chair. "Please be seated. You will deliver it yourself."

Chapter 47

Gemini sat. It felt as if a helium balloon had lifted the chair right up to the ceiling, and she floated there in bliss. *A chance to meet a director of the Consolidate—one of the four most powerful people under the dodec.* She couldn't believe her luck. But her next thoughts dropped her right back down to the deeply padded carpet. *I have to impress her. What can I say that will make her remember me?* Then another thought struck her. *What's so important in this bill that it has to be delivered in person?*

"You may go in now," the receptionist said, motioning to the giant mahogany door behind her desk.

To control her heart rate, Gemini used the breathing technique she had learned after her mother's death. When all of her tears had finally left, leaving a drought in her heart, she had returned to school and her daily routine. But now and then, without warning, her heart would begin fluttering like a butterfly's wings, and her mind would empty itself as the world stole her breath. Her father had taken her to a psychologist, who had taught her how to breathe through these panic attacks and bring herself back from the brink. Today was the first time in many years that she had to use the technique, and she was glad that she had practiced it so much that it was still automatic.

Gemini was surprised at how easily the door swung open for how large and heavy it was. Three people sat at a round table to the right of a large desk.

"Come in. Have a seat," said the one woman among the three, "motioning to the chair next to her."

A seat? This is no simple delivery. Gemini dropped the data stick back into her pocket. She would wait and see what game these three wanted to play before delivering anything.

"Gemini Stockton, I'm Director Wolfe," the woman said, offering her hand.

She knows my name. So this has something to do with me, not the data stick. She shook the hand firmly to show confidence, and then sat in the empty chair in front of her.

"And this is Director Malik and Director Huang," the woman said, nodding at each as she spoke their names.

The men did not stand up for a handshake, so Gemini remained seated as well and used a slight nod as a greeting, forcing her lips not to smile. A smile showed a need for approval. It was a weakness, and in this room, she must show only strength. Her breathing technique automatically kicked back in. *All three directors! Oh my God, what is this about?*

"Senator Smallman says you're very talented," Director Wolfe began. "It must be difficult to know your father's in custody and still be so dedicated in your work."

"Not at all," Gemini replied, certain no hint of red had flushed her cheeks. "My father may have been misguided, but he was doing what he thought was right, and I'm doing the same. Senator Smallman's work is important to us all."

She detected a slight rise in Director Wolfe's right eyebrow. *Surprised or amused?* Gemini wondered.

"You may be doing the same work one day," Director Wolfe said. "Many aides become senators themselves. And your trait test shows it would be a good fit."

Gemini already knew all of that. *Get to the point*, she thought. "It is my intent," she said. She no longer needed her breathing technique. She was alert and powerful, more alive than she had ever felt.

"What can you tell us about this?" the director asked, sliding over a piece of paper encased in plastic.

Gemini looked at the molecular diagram. She had passed her chemistry class, but she did not share her father's passion for the field, and although she understood the letters marking each hexagon on that piece of paper, they did not make a whole sentence that she was able to read.

"It looks like my father's handwriting, but I can't tell you what it's for. I could get a bill passed easier than deciphering a chemical signature."

Director Wolfe pulled the paper back as Gemini congratulated herself for her cleverness. This was going just right. They hadn't thrown her yet, and by now they had noticed her shrewdness and would be standing back to reassess.

"You've asked the senator's help in locating DC-1128?"

A feint. It made Gemini's mind blink, but she would not be distracted by it.

"Yes, she's been missing quite a while." *Keep it noncommittal. Wait for the real attack.*

"Actually, she left the dodec." Director Wolfe paused, watching for the wound to bleed. But for more than ten years, Gemini had been polishing her inner shield, and she used it now to break the blow. Later, she would tend to the shock that had passed through her, but right now, she must appear invincible. She forced her face into an expression of curiosity and remained silent, unable to craft a verbal response.

"We expect she'll be back," Director Wolfe said, "and she's most likely to get in contact with you. Will you let us know when that happens?"

It isn't a question, Gemini thought as she nodded yes.

"You may keep your beamkey. Come right to my office as soon as she contacts you."

"Of course," Gemini replied. "Would you like the data stick?"

Now it was Director Wolfe who was caught off guard, if the slight dilation of her pupils was any indication. She held out her hand to receive it.

Clumsy of her, Gemini thought. *Once the fish is caught, get your lure out of the water.* The lobbyists she had watched these past few months knew more than that.

With the transfer of the data stick, Gemini Stockton's first sparring match with Director Wolfe was over. As she rode the elevator back down to her congressman's office, she felt disappointment, not at DC-1128 for leaving the dodec, or even at her father for concocting some chemical that was obviously intended for nothing good. It was Director Wolfe who had failed her expectations. If an eighteen-year-old aide could outfox the Wolfe, what was the world coming to?

Back at the mahogany table, Director Malik was summarizing the meeting's results. "She'll think you're safe now," he said. "She thinks she's more clever than you. She'll even think you need her. Congratulations, Director Wolfe. You may have just saved the Consolidate."

Chapter 48

By the time the first slants of morning light slipped through the windows, Darby had rescued his hidden treasure from beneath the floorboards. He had convinced himself that it was the real reason he had come back to the dodec, not to kill some high official, but to retrieve the only objects that mattered to him.

The two blue stones sat in his palm, speaking to him of his mother. He remembered her lullabies when he was young and had a fever or stomach ache, her caress when he cried from being bullied, her tender ministrations when he skinned a knee or sprained an ankle. He remembered her friendship when he had become a young man, how she treated him as an equal, fostering his sense of respect for himself. And he remembered the day of her Listing, how she had entrusted him with these two small objects as if they were precious gems. And the riddle she had left him: "One day, you will know what to do with these. Trust your heart."

But what could be their purpose? What could he do with two small stones? Was there some magic in them like *Jack and the Beanstalk* seeds? He did not care at the moment. It only mattered that he had them.

He slipped the stones into his pocket and scanned the room's walls. Except for his mother, his life had been as empty as this room was now. What had he done with it? He had used his mind to manufacture products, that was all. He had no children, no spouse, few friends. In fact, it seemed like his life had not really begun until the day that he died.

And what a beginning it was. He had escaped the dodec through a ball of flame, survived a raging river and a landslide, learned that there was an entire society on the outside, and been granted an audience with the sacred ones—enough excitement for fifty years all wrapped up into four short months. And now, he was on some crazy mission to cut out another man's heart. No, not just another man, but the most important man in the government.

He watched the emotions that accompanied these thoughts, and they flowed like a raging river, transitioning from longing to possessiveness to self-pity to pride to awe to apprehension, all in a matter of moments. *What a wild ride we humans take on the rapids of our egos,* he thought to himself. It amused him, and he started to laugh.

Of course she would walk in at that moment, when he was again chuckling at what appeared to be nothing. And that amused him even more, so he laughed even harder.

"What's so funny?" DC asked. She was still shaking off sleep and in no mood for silliness.

"Never mind," he said, diminishing his mirth to a few last chuckles. "Look at these." His eyes widened like a child making a new discovery, and he held the stones out in front of her.

She glanced at the board next to the opening in the floor. "Is that why you wanted to come back? For a couple of pebbles?"

He looked at the stones and feigned a frown, then seriousness. "Oh, these aren't just any rocks, my dear, they have special powers. I think they can aid your mission."

Though he didn't show it, he was still feeling merry, and she deserved a bit of mocking. He knew she would want to believe that the stones had some magic. He also knew she would never admit it, that she needed the safety that cynicism gave her.

"Oh, really? What do they do? Make you invisible, I hope."

He ignored the insult, intent on winning this one. "Remember the blue fire in the tunnel?" he asked.

She pictured the brimstone burning behind them, remembered the acrid smell of sulfur. He made a motion as if he was throwing the stones to the ground, and as his mouth made a noise like an explosion, he threw his arms wide in the air to describe its size.

She rolled her eyes at him. "If you're done playing with your toys, we've got some planning to do."

Darby followed her, laughing, into the living room, where Finn and Shar were already discussing the preferred future.

The plan sounded simple enough. They would contact The Manufacturing District Group, which would provide a hiding place until their mission was accomplished. DC would go get Gemini, Orion and Vostro. Gemini might know where her father was being held. With Finn's vision and Shar's ability to wield objects at a distance, they should be able to free Ari from his cell, and The Manufacturing District Group could provide transportation back to the safety of their hiding place.

Then they would use Orion's knowledge of Consolidate security, combined with Finn's and Shar's skills, to get access to the Benefactor. They would ask for a volunteer from The Manufacturing District Group to do the bloody deed, and they would also offer to take any members of the Manufacturing District and Old Town groups back out to freedom with them.

"Do you realize we're planning an assassination?" Shar asked in a tone of voice that one would use in anticipation of some wonderful new experience.

"It's on the orders of the sacred ones," DC reminded her, just in case she was having second thoughts. She would have been shocked to know that Shar fully trusted the murderous instruction because of its source.

DC, for all her bravado, was repulsed by the idea of cutting out a person's heart, but her mission was so important to her that she was willing to pay a high price. The intentional killing of another human, no matter how evil that person, was wrong. She knew that now, and she no longer wanted to be merciless. She hoped that someone in The Manufacturing District Group would see it as justice and jump at the chance for retribution. They would know soon enough, as getting in contact with that group was their next step.

"Four people attract more attention than two," DC said. "Shar, I might need your help getting to The Manufacturing District Group leader. Will you come with me?"

"Delighted," Shar said, and got up from the floor, ready for the next adventure.

DC had never interacted with her group's counterparts in the other districts. But she knew a name, Simeon Sing, and that was all she would need to find him.

Chapter 49

From outside the door, the glass of the peephole magnified the eye so that the pupil looked like a black yarmulke atop a big blue dome. A male voice came out of the speaker on the wall. "Who is it?"

"I'm looking for Simeon Sing," DC said. "My name is DC-1128. I'm a friend of Ari Stockton."

DC and Shar stood at the door in silence for half a minute. When it finally opened, they could barely keep from staring at the shock of curly orange hair above the sapphire-blue eyes. Dark brown eyebrows accentuated the incongruity. He looked like a portrait done by three diverse artists.

"You were supposed to have escaped," he said to DC while sending a quick glance in Shar's direction. "You're already a folk hero among us. A lot of people will be disappointed if they learn that you never made it out."

"I did get out," DC said, and then nodded toward her friend. "This is Sharlotta Octavia. She's from one of the villages on the outside."

Simeon looked at Shar and raised his inconsonant brows.

"Yes, there are people on the outside, many of them, perhaps as many as in the dodecs," DC said. "Can we come in and talk?"

Simeon stared at them in silence. When he turned to lead them into the house, DC could see the particle-beam pistol tucked under his shirt. He had reason to be suspicious, and it would take time to earn his confidence.

After DC satisfied Simeon's questions, she learned of Ari's fate, and that Vostro was in custody, too. When she heard about Gemini and Orion, she was thankful that she had visited Simeon before contacting the remaining members of her own group. The news of Orion and Gemini would require a change in plans.

"They might be compromised," Simeon said. "Orion has not tried to contact us, so at the very least, he's being watched. But if you must risk a visit, don't trust them."

DC's mind twisted itself in consternation. Gemini was now entangled in a treasonous mess. Even if Gemini still didn't know what was going on, she would have a target on her back. The Consolidate left no loose ends.

As their conversation continued into the afternoon, Shar remained mostly quiet, while Simeon's daughter Elva came and went like a bee bringing pollen back to the hive. Simeon always paused to fulfill his daughter's requests—a sandwich, a fun tunnel channel, and could he help her find her giraffe? Nothing, not even the overthrow of the Consolidate, was more important to him than this little being, and she provided a needed respite from the flood of ardent information that passed back and forth between the conspirators.

DC learned that the overthrow plans had been slowed but not thwarted. Vostro had provided the necessary bomb parts before his arrest. Now the devices were ready. They were only waiting for a foundation-repair project to begin at Consolidate Headquarters. Two of their people had been hired for the construction team. Without Orion's help, they had not yet found a way to place the bombs for the Transitionary, but this might be their only chance to hit the primary target, and they planned to take it.

"But you said that Ari is in that building," DC said.

"Yes, and Vostro, too," he replied. "We all knew we might have to give our lives for the mission to succeed."

It wasn't until Elva went down for a nap that Simeon revealed why he was willing to give his own life for the project. He blamed the Consolidate for the death of his wife. She had been rushed to the hospital after a warehouse accident. If not for the pecking order under the dodec, with distribution workers at a lowly Level Eight, she would have received the care she needed in time to save her life. DC could see revenge burning in him like a flickering fuse, and in its smoldering, she saw her best executioner candidate. His particle beam pistol could cut out the Benefactor's heart like a precision laser. But would he be willing to make it a priority?

It would be a supremely difficult feat to gain access to the Benefactor. To coordinate that with the bombing—nearly impossible. Might she be able to convince him that killing only the Benefactor was a better scheme than bringing down a building with the Benefactor and all three directors in it?

She crafted her arguments to shift him toward her plan. First, the destruction of the figurehead would be very symbolic, and it spared the life of innocent people in that building. Furthermore, Shar's skills would be made available to help him pull off the Benefactor's assassination. But most of all, Elva would be able to grow up free and unfettered by the dodec's oppression, because regardless of whether the dodecians rose up to complete the revolution, he and Elva could return to The Village with them.

Shar had been sitting quietly in utter fascination at how the people of the dodec interacted. Even when they told the truth, they had hidden intentions, trying to sway circumstances to their favor. It was as pointless as trying to reroute a river, and she couldn't imagine how they had fooled themselves into thinking that they controlled their own fates, let alone the choices of others.

"Shar, will you give Simeon a demonstration of your gift?"

She was happy to share when asked, and she lifted the kitchen table and all three chairs upon which they sat. Simeon gripped his seat and his blue eyes widened under his incongruous brows.

"You can see why the Consolidate leaves them alone," DC said. "And that's just one power."

"Skill," Shar corrected.

"They have weather-wooers who can make it rain or turn the direction of a storm," DC continued. "They have people who can see in advance what is likely to happen. One of them is here with us. They have elders who give wise counsel to anyone who asks. They have people who talk to the trees and plants and can coax them to grow or flower. They have people who can send their awareness anywhere in the universe. And the place is more beautiful than you could imagine. There's a river that sparkles in the afternoon sun and trees so tall that they would nearly reach the top of the dodec."

She could see that her picture was pulling Simeon toward it.

"Everyone spends their time doing what they're passionate about, and they only work one or two hours a day to take care of the necessities. Some of them don't even have to eat. They've learned to pull in energy from the sun. And there are no incurable diseases. They've all become so good at maintaining their bodies that the healers are only needed when there's been an accident."

She emphasized the last word, hoping he'd connect it to his wife.

"There's no need to kill innocent people here," she continued. "Rid the dodec of the one person at the top who maintains a society in which innocent people suffer and die. Then come with us. Give Elva a life of freedom."

Simeon sat silent for a moment, scratching the reddish stubble on his chin. "I don't think it's enough to kill just the Benefactor. He sits atop a three-legged stool—the directors. One of them will just rise to take his place.

"Great-grandmother Sophia would say that the dodecians have chosen domination, and we cannot choose for them. We can only choose for ourselves."

Simeon squinted to show he wasn't convinced, and DC gathered all her learning from her time in The Village to craft her next argument.

"You see, the villagers see all of life as one great unified thing. They believe that this unified whole needs to experience all that is possible, and that before we're born, each of us chooses a different aspect of life to experience. I know, it sounds like a strange concept, but after you're with them for a while, it starts to make sense. They say that when we, as a unity, are done checking out discord and strife and injustice, no one will choose such a life. But until then, there's nothing we can do about it, that we should be thankful that someone else is experiencing those things for us."

"Meanwhile, the sacred ones hold the balance," Shar offered.

DC's thoughts split in two directions at the unexpected comment. She didn't want to get off topic when the fish was nearing the net. At the same time, Shar's comment answered a question that DC had meant to ask, and she took a moment to consider it. *So that's the purpose of the floating kiddos.* She made a mental note to question Shar in greater detail later. For now, her concern was that Simeon had not fully swallowed her hook.

"What need is there to remove the Benefactor if it will make no difference in the lives of the people?" he asked.

What need indeed, DC thought to herself. *Why do those meditating munchkins want his heart?* She remembered Great-grandmother Sophia's response to their assignment from the sacred ones. Killing the person at the top will not change the lives of the people below him, she had said, explaining that the discordance in the dodec was endemic to their entire society, every human within it.

DC understood now that the Consolidate got its power from the people—their silent collaboration. It was the lending officer who signed papers for a loan that would likely default, just so that he would get his commission. It was the clerk who would not solve a customer's problem unless he made another purchase, because following the scripted response to a complaint brought a paycheck. All were complicit. The greed at the top was no different than that at the bottom. A pauper cuts in line because he cares about no other. A rich man hoards his cash for the same reason. "So it is not the people at the top who must change, but all of us," DC had said to Great-grandmother Sophia to show her understanding. "As long as our society believes in lack, in dog-eat-dog, in survival of the fittest, any person who makes it to the top will act the same."

She had learned that the ancestors of the villagers had simply shifted from "me first" to "we first," and that made all the difference. Or as Great-grandmother Sophia had put it, "No change is possible without a change of heart. They must first decide who they want to be."

But how could she convince Simeon of these things when he had never had a chance to see first-hand how the acceptance of a few new ideas could lead to a utopia? She could see that he was still intent on carrying out his plot.

"At least give us time to get Ari and Vostro out before you bomb the building," she said to him.

"You better hurry," he replied. "The construction project starts in a week."

Chapter 50

The envelope had arrived at Senator Smallman's office, not addressed to the lawmaker but to his favorite aide.

"Meet me at seven p.m. at the coffee shop next to Trinket Village," the note inside had said. It held no signature or return address, and no one had seen who delivered it. It was as if it had somehow floated through the door all by itself and landed on Gemini's desk.

She was getting used to intrigue, and she enjoyed it. A meeting in a public place would be safe, no matter who the sender. The invitation itself meant that someone had concluded that she would be rapidly climbing the Consolidate's ladder. And whoever it was did their research—enough to know that she had passed that coffee shop a thousand times on her way to her father's office.

Gemini wore her best expression of nonchalance as she stepped in through the coffee shop door with the logo, "Relax and Rev." She had been learning the art of doublespeak, and she smiled at the example in the name of a simple coffee shop. In the last few months, she had memorized at least a hundred lobbyists' names and faces, and as she walked through the labyrinth-like room of partitioned coffee tables surrounded by overstuffed seating, she scanned it for anyone familiar.

A hand reached out as she passed behind a high-backed chair, and the touch was so gentle that she barely noticed it. Before she could walk around to the front of the chair, DC stood and faced her, with arms slightly raised to invite an embrace.

"There's the fairest girl in all the land," she said softly.

DC had always loved this girl, but now, more than ever. Her time in The Village had dissolved some of the scars from her heart, and it felt unprotected enough to open to its full width, wide enough to contain a mother's love, vulnerable enough to be damaged.

"DC-1128," the teen-age aide said, and sat without showing any sign of surprise or acknowledging the arms' offer.

All right, she's mad at me for leaving. We'll get past that.

They sat for a moment just staring at each other, DC trying to decide how to start, and Gemini waiting, knowing that the chess player who makes the first move is more likely to lose. A trickle of old emotions escaped her hold, and she pushed them back into place. She had once respected this woman. No, it was more than that. *The longing of a child,* she thought to herself, *but it no longer serves me.*

"I've missed you, Gemi."

DC waited for a reply, but Gemini needed more than that if she was going to reposition a pawn.

"Have you seen your father?"

Now Gemini knew the game they'd be playing. DC-1128 knew her father was in custody. It was safe to engage.

"Every week," she said. "He'll be pleased you're back."

Pleased? DC hoped he'd feel more than that. In DC's expression, Gemini noted the weakness, and now she knew where to place her queen.

"How is he? I'd like to see him," DC said. "Where is he being held?"

"In a room at Consolidate Headquarters." *Show some trust to gain the same.* She had learned the game well, and she would use it to her advantage. "They don't have a facility for insurgents. It's not exactly a common problem." She paused to observe whether DC identified with the label but could see that the woman's only concern was the man now imprisoned. "You would risk getting caught just to see him? You'd be guilty by association, you know." Her voice came out with a bit of an edge, and she scolded herself for letting her emotion show.

"Oh, Gemi, don't be mad at me. I just wanted freedom. But I came back for you. I came back to get you and your father out. I would never leave you."

"Were you part of the insurgency?" Gemini asked, her face now still as stone.

DC could see that Gemi's shell was no longer cracking. "What does it matter? What matters is that there's life on the outside—a wonderful life beyond what you've ever imagined. I want that for you and your father."

Gemini could feel the pieces of her shell scattering on the floor as the pain that had been held in check for so long tried to surface. *What you want,* she thought. *Did you ever think to ask what I want?* Her mind raced back to DC-1128's comment about life on the outside. *Why are you lying? What are you trying to trick me into?* Her face did not follow her thoughts. She forced it into the expression she wanted DC to see, for this was, after all, not a reunion, but an assignment from the directors of the Consolidate.

"But it will never happen now, will it? My father's in custody. How would you propose to get him out?"

DC remembered Simeon's warning and held back her rook. "We'll find a way, Gemi. I promise. Nothing is impossible."

The pause hung heavy between them.

"How's Orion? Are they treating you well?"

If she knows I'm staying at Orion's, she's in contact with at least one of my father's co-conspirators. Check, Gemini said to herself, and moved a knight into position to capture the king.

"My fiancé is fine," she said to DC, and held up her hand to show the ring.

DC congratulated her almost-daughter, trying to hide her shock behind a facade of happiness. Gemini thought it made her look like a court jester.

"I'm happy for you, really."

"But you think I'm too young." Gemini finished the unspoken retort silently. *We're waiting a year, but why should I have to tell you that? You're not my mother.*

Out loud, she said, "I'm old enough to be an aide for a senator. I'm full-time now. A professional."

If the news of Gemini's engagement to Orion had been a blow, knowing that she was working for the Consolidate took DC down to her emotional knees. She tried to keep her face blank, tried to remember how she had done it in the transpods, but that seemed another lifetime.

Gemini, meanwhile, had decided to move her rook all the way across the board, making DC-1128 think that she would be amenable to escape. She needed information for

Director Wolfe, and she didn't want to leave the coffee shop without it.

"If you really think you could get us out, Orion would have to come with us. But I still can't imagine how you'd be able to free my father. Until I know it's possible, there's no need to discuss it."

"There is a way. I can't give you the details yet, but I may need your help. And of course, Orion can come with us."

Checkmate, Gemini announced to herself, and she imagined herself no longer in Senator Smallman's office, but ten floors up, as an aide to Director Wolfe.

"I have to go now. I can't stay long in a public place. You understand. But I'll be in contact soon. I promise." DC stood and waited for Gemini to do the same.

This time, the teen-ager offered the hug, but it was stiff and held no warmth.

Oh, Gemi, what have they done do you? DC thought as she walked out the coffee shop door.

The moment she was safely around the corner, she let the tears come, and she felt a new hole in her heart that no scar could cover. She realized that this might be the last she would ever see of the girl who would have been her daughter.

Chapter 51

"Let the images come and go as they please. Just watch them. Notice them appear and disappear." Shar's voice was soft and steady as she guided Darby's trance.

She waited several minutes for Darby to go deeper into the imaginal realm. She settled back into one of the overstuffed chairs that Simeon had provided for them. The air in the warehouse basement smelled a bit dank, but she was happy to be off the hard floor at Darby's old house.

"Now, notice what's beyond the images. What have they been emerging out of and dissolving back into? Shift your focus to that. Can you move into it? Can you follow one of the images as it dissolves back in?"

Darby's head had dropped forward so that his chin nearly touched his chest. His hands lay still in his lap. Only his chest moved, slowly expanding and contracting as the breath moved steadily past his slack jaw. Suddenly, his head jerked upright and his eyes shot wide open.

Shar laughed. She gave him a moment to refocus into the third-dimensional here and now.

"That's not an uncommon reaction when my students first visit the void," she said. "But they're my advanced students. I really didn't think you would get that far."

"It felt like annihilation, like I better get out fast," Darby said, almost breathless. He fingered the blue stones in his pocket as if they would anchor him back into this world. "It was like the absence of existence."

"Of course it was," Shar replied. "It's infinity—the great void from which everything came."

"But how can something come from nothing?"

"You'll have to ask it on your next visit," she said, a merry twinkle in her eye.

"That's where you go when you manifest?" Darby asked.

"That's where I start. I still have to create whatever it is and bring it back through the layers. Holding onto it while it accumulates density is the hard part. But I think you could learn to do it. You have some ability already."

It fascinated her that a man who was fifty did not yet know his talent and purpose. In The Village, parents usually knew their children's primary skills by the time they were five. And by ten, children were beginning to explore how they might use their gifts to serve others. Shar's primary gift was telekinesis, but it was so closely akin to manifesting that she had some skill in that area as well, much like a violinist who can pick up a cello and play with some degree of competence.

"What's the largest thing you've manifested?" Darby asked.

"I think it has less to do with size than need," Shar said. "And complexity. I don't know if I could manifest one of your optiscreens, but this pen was easy, especially because we needed it at the moment." She pointed to the pen on the coffee table. She had pulled it out of the void as a demonstration, partly for their entertainment as they waited for DC to return, and partly because they needed it.

"Your focus is excellent," Shar said. "Is it a natural talent, or did you learn it for your work?"

"I don't know," Darby said. "I had to spend six hours every day in intense focus. But I think it was my death in the Transitionary that made it easier to go where you were leading me."

With the topic shifted to Darby's death experience, Finn joined the conversation. Both of the villagers were interested in every detail of his transition—where he had gone, who he had met, what he had learned and brought back. Right after it happened, he had been reluctant to talk about it. If he had remained in the dodec, he might have kept it to himself forever. Dodecians already thought he was different, and they would have considered him crazy if he had told what he'd experienced in the transpod. But for village people, it was not an unusual conversation at all. They saw life and death as a smooth continuum. It was more like *this* part of life and then *that* part of life, as simple as the transition from childhood to adulthood. And so for Darby, talking about it with Shar and Finn was like being a kid who had once magically become an adult for a day, and now he was telling his friends what that had been like.

"I had the most incredible sense of freedom and bliss," he told them. "Ever since then, I've had a longing to go back to the peace of it, the expansiveness. And sometimes I can feel it, but it evaporates as quickly as it came. I both want it and don't want it, because it scares me a bit. It can feel like the emptiness of the void I was just in."

Shar remembered what DC had told her about Darby's sense that he was losing hold of his personal identity. She was familiar with the feeling of vastness from her own trips to the void, and she knew that Darby's mind, in its desperate attempt to understand its experience, was simply interpreting infinite space as nothingness.

"I think I can understand what you're struggling with," she said. "What are you, after all? You've been living in a body all these years, and then one day, your body is gone. Yet you discovered you still existed. And what were you then, without a body?"

Darby thought about it before replying. "At first, I was still me, but without form, still an individual. I was still a collection of all the experiences I'd ever had, and all my emotions about them."

"And what held that collection together?"

Darby had to stop and think again. These were not the typical schoolbook questions in a dodecian's education.

"Only my will to do so," he finally said. "But that's just it. It felt as if all those experiences had been nothing more than a strange but brief dream. And it was natural to let go of it—as natural as when you wake up in the morning and start your day and forget about your last dream. Even though it seems so real while you're in it, you don't try to hang onto the dream once you're awake, because now you're, well, in the actual... in the more real..."

He paused, frustrated by the lack of words to explain his experience. Shar and Finn waited, giving their friend the respect of silence. The only way Darby could find to get close to describing it was through metaphor.

"Let's say you had been dreaming you were a snail, and you woke up as the human you'd always been. You would think, 'That was a strange dream. I thought I was a snail.' You might reflect on the dream for a few minutes, because it was fascinating. It was interesting to feel encased by a shell and vulnerable underneath. It was interesting to have a brain that couldn't really think. It was interesting to be so slow and limited in movement. But after a few moments of going back over the dream in your mind, you would get on with your day. You wouldn't regret having dreamt about it, but you certainly wouldn't try to go back to being that limited little snail, because it was actually awful to be that limited compared to what you really are."

"But what if you felt like sleeping in that morning?" Shar asked. "Maybe you would want to explore more of what it's like to be a snail, just for the fun of it, just for a few more minutes, because it is, after all, just a dream. And maybe if you became lucid in that dream, it would be even more interesting to explore snailness."

"That's the thing. It feels like I'm the snail again. It's as if I now know that I'm in a dream, but I'm not sure I want to let go of the dream, because when I do, I won't exist. And isn't that true? The snail will no longer exist. But at the same time, I feel a longing for the expansiveness of the person who woke up."

"I can tell you what Great-grandmother Sophia would say."

"What's that?" Darby asked.

"She would say that you have eternity to experience your awakened self. So why not enjoy the dream while you're in it, even if it is limited? After all, it only lasts a few minutes, and isn't it a fascinating dream?"

"It certainly will be in the next few days," Darby said, and they all laughed, the thought of the task ahead pulling them completely back into the present moment.

"Well, we better get back to our planning if we're as limited as snails in this dimension," Shar said, and they returned their attention to the paper on the coffee table between them.

Earlier that day, Finn had remotely viewed the fiftieth floor of Consolidate Headquarters to sketch out the floor plan, thus the need for the paper and pen that Shar had manifested. Moving his inner vision to the future, he had seen where the floor's occupants would most likely be throughout the day. He could sense the purpose of floor fifty: interrogation enhanced by technology. Its rooms were not meant to be holding cells, but Ari and Vostro had now occupied two separate rooms on that floor for more than three months, and each was guarded twenty-four hours a day by an armed sentry. The Directors themselves wanted access to the conspirators, and they weren't about to travel all the way to the jail for it.

The trio of new conspirators sitting in a warehouse basement in the manufacturing district began outlining how to free the captives. Once on the fiftieth floor, they would recognize the holding cells as the only two rooms with security guards standing outside. Finn had seen that three times each day, the prisoners were escorted to the restroom, and twice more, the doors opened to bring them food. Shar could easily take care of the guards. The hard part would be getting the prisoners down fifty floors and out the door.

Shar had manifested a credit disk so that they could buy what they needed for their plan. Creating a beamkey programmed for upper-floor access had been a challenge, but with a detailed description of how the thing worked, she thought she had managed to do it. Finn moved his awareness forward in time to find out. "Eighty-five percent probability, yes, it will work."

Finn had also viewed the location of the security cameras and sketched them out on the floor plans. Shar said she would be able to create a repetitive loop when the time came so that only an empty hallway would show up on the monitoring screens.

The thing Finn couldn't see was the flight down the stairwell. There would be too many people making split-second decisions. No probability gelled itself out of the field. The outcome would remain uncertain.

"Once you're in the stairwell, Shar can lock all the stairwell doors. If they're after you, it will slow them down a bit, but you'll have to move fast," Finn said to Darby. "And you'll be completely exposed between the exit and the flyvan. It's those few moments when you'll be the most vulnerable. But if you can…"

He stopped abruptly at the sound of footsteps in the stairwell, and they all turned in the direction of the sound. The warehouse basement had been their hiding place for less than a day, and the unlockable door leading down to it did not foster much of a sense of security, but Simeon had assured them that they would find no safer place under the dodec.

The figure that emerged from the darkness of the stairwell was DC's. The pace and energy of her was recognizable even in shadow. But Darby noticed that her shoulders were more sloped than usual, and her step not as sure of itself. When she emerged into the light, they could see the redness in her eyes.

"It didn't go well," Shar said.

"I think I've lost her," DC replied, and she slumped into a chair. "The Consolidate owns her now."

Darby sat next to her and put a hand on her shoulder. "She's young, DC. At that age, things can change so fast. It could all be different by tomorrow."

"By tomorrow, the Consolidate will know that we're here," she replied. She looked at each of her friends to make sure they understood the importance of what she was saying. "I hope you've spent the evening making plans. I stopped at Simeon's and told him to be ready first thing tomorrow morning. If we don't get them out now, we'll never have another chance."

Chapter 52

"I have information that Director Wolfe requested," Gemini told the receptionist. "I believe she'll want it as soon as possible."

"She's in a meeting, and no, she cannot be interrupted," the receptionist said. "Have a seat, if you like."

Gemini thought the receptionist's tone was a bit condescending. *She probably thinks I'm too young to be important. She better mind herself. One day she may be* my *receptionist.*

As each minute passed, Gemini felt more on edge. Last night, she had sized up DC-1128 with a new astuteness, not with the eyes of a child, but with the expanded vision of someone who has walked the halls of power and observed the maneuvers of the best political players. From this new perspective, she had sensed in DC-1128 some things that she had never before noticed—a tactical cleverness and a sense of certainty. It gave Gemini reason to be wary. Perhaps she had won the first game last night, but this was a tournament, and she sensed that DC-1128 knew something that made her believe that she would be the one capturing the grand prize.

She has an advantage that the Consolidate doesn't, and I don't know what it is, Gemini thought. *And now, time is my handicap.*

Gemini had lost more than twelve hours. She had to wait until morning to request a meeting with the director. She had arrived in the mahogany room at one minute to eight, but now, every second was playing to DC-1128's favor.

The nervousness in her stomach was telling her something, and she paid attention. She had noticed that the top players on the political scene were not those who manipulated best or who presented the most convincing arguments, but rather, those who had honed their instincts. Sometimes, a corporation sent its chief executive instead of a lobbyist into the halls of lawmaking, and they were fascinating to watch. Powerful jaguars in the jungle, they knew exactly when to stay still and when to pounce. As a result, she had started paying attention to her own intuition, and she sensed that whatever was about to happen was not in her best interests.

The door to Director Wolfe's office opened, and two suits walked out. Gemini recognized the chairman and vice-chairman of General Electronics. They closed the director's office door behind them and left the reception room. Gemini waited no more than a moment before standing to prod the receptionist to make the call.

"Gemini Stockton is here. She doesn't have an appointment. Your eight-fifteen should be here shortly."

The director's response went directly into the receptionist's ear, so Gemini could not hear it, but she immediately knew what it was, because the massive door swung open, and the director herself beckoned her in.

"News?" she asked, before they had even sat.

"DC-1128 is back. I met with her last night. I think she's going to try to get my father out."

"Oh?"

"Yes. My instinct tells me she won't wait. She'll make a move before we're ready for it."

Director Wolfe pushed a few numbers on the keyboard that was projected onto her desk. The wall behind her became the backdrop for a dozen holographs—mostly still images of rooms and sections of hallway. A few of the holographic tubes of light showed people working at their desks. In one, the towering frame of Vostro was unmistakable, pacing back and forth across his holding cell. Another held the form that Gemini would recognize from any angle. It was her father, sitting on the edge of his cot and writing on a tablet.

Director Wolfe watched for a moment and then touched the hologram that held Ari in its light. She moved both hands outward to zoom in for a closer look. It was not the words that Ari was scribbling, but the motion of the pen that caught her attention. As he continued writing, his hand did not move down the page. Rather, it went back to the beginning of the same line, writing it over and over.

The director swung to her desk and punched a number on the keyboard. "Security breach on fifty!" she rasped. "Lock down now! I want WASPs at every exit and security in my office in less than thirty seconds."

When the director looked up from her desk, Gemini saw ice in her stare and imagined fangs exposed by a drawn-back lip. Two blue suits burst through the door as if expecting to find a fire.

Director Wolfe nodded toward Gemini. "Take her to the basement. Put her in the cage."

Chapter 53

Finn had seen that the guards took Ari and Vostro to the restroom at the start of each morning shift, so DC and Darby had arrived on the fiftieth floor at one minute past eight on the dot, providing just enough time for the guards to retrieve the prisoners from their rooms.

As DC and Darby exited the elevator and entered the hallway, they could see the guards down the hallway escorting the prisoner toward the restroom—not one guard per prisoner, but two. Had Finn's vision been wrong, or had the guard been doubled overnight? Either way, it meant trouble. *It probably won't be the last thing that doesn't go as planned,* DC thought.

They started down the hallway and stepped through the nearest door on the east side of the building. The room they slipped into was empty, as Finn had said it would be.

Finn was a block away in the backseat of the flyvan, narrating what he saw to Shar. "You're going to have to disarm four guards, not two. Can you do it?"

"Of course," she said, her face gleaming like a child at play.

Simeon sat in the driver's seat, watching the fiftieth floor windows like a hawk seeking a field mouse. "There!" he said, pointing to DC's hand waving a signal out the window. He handed the particle-beam pistol to Shar, who floated it up and out of the flyvan. Shar's right hand motioned forward, and the pistol flew toward the building and into DC's reach.

DC fingered the pistol nervously. Her heart was beating in staccato, but she was too focused on the task at hand to try to calm it by counting her breaths. The almost imperceptible buzz of an overhead light entered her heightened awareness, and she imagined a hive of wasps ready to protect their nest.

She and Darby walked to the door and peeked down the hallway. Previously, when each prisoner had only one guard, the guards would go into the restroom with the prisoners, leaving the hallway empty. But today, while two of the guards did indeed go into the restroom with the prisoners, the two additional guards stayed outside in the hallway.

"I hope Finn is seeing this," DC whispered to Darby. *This may not be the last time that we're going to have to improvise,* she said to herself.

"Maybe we should wait and rethink this," Darby whispered back.

"No, we go now," she said and opened the door. He had no choice but to follow.

Fifty feet from the guards, her heart began pounding in her throat. Twenty feet, and it was thumping in her skull. *Shar, what are you waiting for?*

The guards' weapon belts unlatched and flew to the ceiling. Their faces flashed confusion before they noticed that the woman set in a ready stance in front of them had a pistol aimed in their direction.

"Inside," she commanded in a low tone, motioning at the door with the pistol.

The guards hesitated, glancing up at their weapons on the ceiling. She shot a quick beam at the ceiling, and it sliced the plaster like a carpenter's knife.

"You're next," DC growled. "Now get in there."

As the first guard opened the restroom door, he yelled into the room, "Code eight!" But the guards on the inside were already disarmed, their weapons stuck to the ceiling like stalactites. The weapons outside the door followed them in, sliding across the ceiling and into the restroom like upside-down lizards.

Vostro had exited the restroom stall, and seeing the guards jumping up to try to retrieve their guns, he made his move, tackling one into the wall. Ari came barreling out and followed Vostro's lead, his broad shoulders giving him as much advantage as Vostro's height. But before the two prisoners could pin their opponents, the guards followed their weapons into the air. Ari and Vostro stood back in amazement, wondering how gravity had reversed itself, but the real shock came through the door carrying a pistol.

"DC!" Ari gasped.

She was too focused to pay attention to him. "Finn, can you hear me? Tell Shar to drop them now."

The four guards fell to the floor with a thud. DC fired a quick particle beam shot on the floor between them as a reminder of what would happen if they tried to make a move. She let the pack drop off her back and handed it to Darby, who pulled several lengths of rope out of it and threw them to Ari and Vostro.

"Tie them up," he instructed.

When all four guards were bound and gagged, the weapons descended from the ceiling. Ari's eyes widened, but this was no time for questions. Darby threw the weapons into the backpack.

The escapees exited the restroom and ran down the hallway with DC in the lead. She burst through the door to the stairwell like a cannonball leaving its cylinder. Ari and Vostro followed, with Darby on their heels, carrying the pack full of confiscated weapons. Its strap caught on the door lever, and the pack jerked out of his hand. From halfway down the first flight, DC saw him hesitate.

"Leave it!" she screamed. "Get that door closed!"

The moment it clicked shut, the deadbolts of fifty stairwell doors engaged in unison. *Thank you, Shar,* DC thought, as the sound of the locks echoed through the stairwell.

It felt as if her feet weren't even touching the stairs, so fast were they flying down them. A blur of gray flashed around her—gray brick, gray railing, gray concrete steps. The sound of her own breathing filled her ears, her lungs pumping not with air, but fear.

Her foot caught the edge of a step just before the landing, and she gripped the railing to stop herself from stumbling. In that pause, she heard the rattle of the door lever. *Cuts through aluminum but not steel,* she remembered from the pistol manual. *The doors are steel, they can't cut through.* The sound of the rattling lever meant Shar's lockdown was holding.

It also meant the Consolidate knew the escapees were there, trapped in a stairwell that now felt like some descending tomb. Even at this speed, it would take several minutes to get to ground level, and by then, a thousand security personnel could be in position.

I pray you're as good as you say, Shar, DC thought.

Chapter 54

"Twenty-sixth floor! They're on twenty five! Twenty-four!" Finn sat in the flyvan's backseat, narrating what he saw in the stairwell with such intensity that Shar thought he might as well be in there with them. He scanned forward to the lower floors. "There's some sort of square device just outside the door at eleven. It'll blow the door! Shar, get it out of there!"

From where they hovered—about thirty stories up and half a block away—they could see the sidewalk and street where the escapees would be exiting. Teams in black helmets and beam-proof vests were scurrying into position.

"Shar, on the roof," Simeon said, pointing to three black figures on top of the building. But Shar had her eyes closed for the moment in order to imagine the box-like device on floor eleven. She tossed it backwards with all her mental might. On the screen of Finn's mind, he watched it erupt in a shower of fire and black smoke.

Shar opened her eyes and looked to where Simeon was pointing. She was already tracking a dozen weaponized artificial-intelligence security personnel—WASPs for short—near the ground-floor exit, along with their human counterparts. The group on the roof meant she would have to handle both levels at once.

"Drone! Get rid of it!" Simeon yelled. He pointed with one hand to the helicopter-like device above them and clenched the steering wheel with the other.

"Not yet. We wait until the last second for as much as we can," Shar said. "Can't let them know what we're up to."

She had no idea if she could disarm so many men and machines all at once. She had never imagined such a feat, let alone tried it. But she remained as unruffled as a hen on its roost.

The drone dropped down right in front of the flyvan. Simeon turned toward Finn in the back seat to obscure his face. "Open your eyes!" he whispered. "Make it look like we're having a conversation."

Finn did as instructed. "I need to close my eyes to see what's going on in there. Shar, you're going to have to get rid of that thing."

From her perch in the front passenger seat, Sharlotta smiled and waved at the drone, not with intent to move it, but to fool it. During their planning, they had discussed the possibility of drones, and Shar knew they contained both cameras and weapons. She primped her hair and then blew a kiss and waved again in its direction. The drone lifted and zoomed off to check another vehicle in the vicinity. *There's more than one way to disarm a drone,* she thought.

Simeon returned to scanning the street. Finn returned to his closed-eye vision.

"Tenth floor!" Finn gasped. "Ninth... eighth... seventh..."

Six black sedans squealed into place on each side of the street. Four black flycars appeared from the parking garage across the street. They hovered over the sedans for an air blockade.

"Sixth... fifth..."

Shar's hands began flying through the air as if she was conducting a symphony in allegro. The weapons flew out of the hands of the security team on the roof. The air-blockade flycars tipped so that their noses pointed straight up to the sky.

"Fourth floor!" Finn shouted. "Third!... Second!"

Thirty WASPs on the ground all lost their footing in the same instant and landed on their backs. Their weapons rose ten feet into the air and floated there like the sacred ones. The sedans on the street started spinning like tops.

"First floor!" Finn shouted.

The ground-floor exit door popped open an inch. A blast pulverized the sidewalk next to it.

"The drone!" Simeon yelled. He sped the flyvan toward the smoke and dust that now blanketed the area of the exit.

Shar separated the drone from its rotating blades. It plunged to the street, its weapons exploding on impact like fireworks. The flyvan rocked sideways from the energy of the blasts. Shards of metal lodged themselves into the flyvan's doors.

DC and company jumped back behind the building's ground-floor door for cover as the WASPs got back to their feet. Shar scattered them to the four directions.

Simeon brought the van right up to the exit, and the escapees emerged from the cloud of smoke and dust like firemen abandoning a building. Two black figures ran at them, and DC fired her pistol, slicing through their ankles.

Finn flung open the back double-door, and the escapees scrambled in. As Ari pulled one door shut, the upper corner of the second door sliced off.

"Shar, a particle beam! Can you see where it's coming from?" Finn yelled.

"I can't in all this smoke. You'll have to find it for me."

He closed his eyes and zoomed in on the figure moving toward the flyvan.

"Behind us! Thirty feet!"

Everything in the vicinity flew into the air—parked cars, drone parts, WASPs—it all rose above the ball of smoke like bits of lava thrust higher than a volcano's cloud of ash. Shar was taking no chances.

Simeon maneuvered the flyvan up above the conflagration as bits of burning debris flew past. "More drones!" he yelled as he watched the rocket launch directly toward them. Shar saw it just in time, and it burst into flames a few feet from the windshield, rocking the van backward. She saw the next missile in time to turn it, and it plowed back into the drone that had fired it, exploding it into bits. She stuck her head out the window and looked up to two more drones descending from the top of Consolidate Headquarters.

"Reroute the missiles to hit the dodec! Make them think twice!" Simeon shouted.

Shar waited for the launch—two at once—and sent the missiles straight up. The impact echoed back to them, vibrating everything as if they were inside a bongo drum. A million drops of fire rained down toward them. Simeon punched the lifter, and the van zoomed upward toward the drones. They withheld their missiles, and Simeon knew his strategy had worked.

He hit the forward accelerator and slipped into a flycar garage, zooming straight through it and exiting the far side into regular air traffic.

"Shar, behind us!" Finn bellowed, pointing to the two black sedans that seemed to appear out of nowhere.

DC was in the backseat with Finn and had opened a side window. Now, she was ready with her pistol. She shot a beam toward one of the sedans, but it dropped out of sight, and the beam sliced off the top of an innocent car. "Sorry," she mouthed to the shocked woman in the front seat. She leaned out the window to look for her target.

"Leave it to me," Shar yelled. "You're going to kill someone."

Shar brought the flying sedans to a dead stop, and one was rammed by the flycar behind it.

"Don't they get it yet?" Simeon asked no one in particular.

He spotted the subway entrance and steered the van down into it. Commuters screamed and scattered as he zoomed through the station and into the tunnel.

He sped down the main tunnel, zipping into a cross-tunnel just in time to miss an oncoming train. He continued down the main tunnel and then brought the van to rest at an empty platform still being built.

Stacks of construction materials littered the concrete floor. Simeon scanned the walls to make sure security cameras had not yet been installed. Satisfied that they were undetected, he dug into the duffel bag next to him and handed each team their hats and hooded sweatshirts.

He consulted his wrist assistant. "Next train, forty seconds. You'll go with Darby and Finn," he said to Vostro, nodding toward the two men that Vostro had never met. "Get off at the next station, Second Avenue."

He turned to Ari. "You're with DC. You'll be getting off at Pelican Street."

Vostro and Ari knew by now that their escape had been well planned and they'd best just do as instructed. There would be time to ask questions later.

"They'll be watching every station by now, so have your hats and hoods on by the time you exit the train. We'll create a diversion, but get up to the street as fast as you can." Simeon glanced from Ari to Vostro. "Your team leaders know the plan. Just follow their lead."

Simeon and Shar stayed in the flyvan, while their five compatriots got out and stood on the platform, looking like ordinary commuters waiting for their train. Simeon pulled the flyvan behind a stack of construction supplies. When the train approached, Shar slowed it to a stop. Without a human conductor, the unplanned stop would register only as a small blip on a screen somewhere, and it might easily be overlooked. Shar remotely opened the train's doors so that the five new passengers could enter.

Now it was time for Simeon to create the diversions that would allow Darby, Finn and Vostro to reach Second Avenue without detection, and Ari and DC to exit the subway at Pelican Street. The final feat would be getting himself and Shar out to the street without being captured.

Shar moved the train backward so that Simeon could pull the flyvan in front of it. He sped down the tunnel and careened recklessly onto the Second Avenue platform, panicking the pedestrians who instinctively ran for the exits. When the train arrived, its doors opened to chaos. Some of the passengers clung to their seats, frozen in fear. But dozens of others scurried out of the train to follow the crowd, with Finn and the two escapees among them.

The train left the station on its programmed schedule as if nothing had happened, still carrying DC and Ari and a handful of wide-eyed passengers.

Simeon pulled the flyvan back onto the tracks and followed the train. It deposited DC and Ari at the Pelican Street Station, where they casually exited, just two more commuters reaching their destination.

Simeon hovered in the darkness of the tunnel, waiting several minutes more so that a new group of commuters could fill the Pelican Street platform. He and Shar got out on the tracks, and Shar lifted the now-empty van onto the platform, making it spin and skid, again scattering the people waiting for the next train.

In the midst of the mayhem, Shar and Simeon climbed onto the platform and ran to the escalator, clamoring like the others to get away from the danger.

At the top of the escalator, Simeon removed his hood and Shar tossed her hat in a garbage bin, just to look a bit different than the two who had jumped onto the platform from the tracks. From the station below, they heard the flyvan's horn honking and the screech of its tires. Shar glanced at Simeon and winked. "They'll think someone's still in it."

Shar and Simeon turned right onto Pelican Street. DC and Ari had exited the same station and turned left a few minutes earlier. Each pair circled half way around the block. By the time Shar and Simeon slipped into the front seats of the car parked on Seagull Street, DC and Ari were already in the back. As Simeon maneuvered the car toward the manufacturing district, in the rearview mirror, he could see the flashing lights of Security Division cars heading for Pelican Street.

Chapter 55

How do you make a man who is nearly seven feet tall less conspicuous, Darby wondered, as the trio sauntered down Second Avenue toward Old Town. Three blocks from where the subway tunnel had spewed its human contents onto the street, they saw the sign for E-Repair, and Darby no longer had to worry about their exposure.

A bell jingled as they walked through the door and up to the counter. The man behind it was gaunt and moved like an insect, the magnifying glass attached to his eyewear creating a bulbous cornea. The pincers in his hand held a tiny chipset that he had just removed from an optiscreen lens.

"Two weeks wait for anything other than batteries," the man said without looking up.

"Nice day for a stroll through Old Town." Darby articulated the memorized line and waited for recognition of it.

The man looked up, his magnified eye so pronounced that it grabbed all of their attention. "Karthik Koh," he said, thrusting out his hand. "You're here for the overstock?"

Darby shook the man's hand and nodded.

"Follow me."

They passed shelves stacked with boxes overflowing with wires, chips, lenses, capacitors, pins, jumpers and a thousand other parts that no one but Karthik Koh recognized, and then climbed up the steps at the back of the shop into a living room that only a bachelor techie could love, with three holograph projectors on the coffee table and a keyboard console on every armrest.

"May as well make yourselves comfortable," Karthik Koh said, motioning to the couch and chairs. "The delivery isn't scheduled 'til ten." The room was unaccustomed to guests, as was Karthik Koh. "Well, then," he said, and turned and scuttled back down the stairs, leaving them to find their own comfort.

It wasn't the only formality that had been left unheeded. Vostro had never met Darby or Finn, and they now had a chance to introduce themselves.

"You live on the outside?" Vostro stared at Finn in disbelief. But he had a more pressing matter. "I need to get to my family, if it's not already too late."

"Don't worry," Darby said. "We've got them. They're safe. You'll see them in just a couple of hours."

Darby explained to Vostro that they had split into their separate groups in the subway because a band of seven people would be conspicuous, and also because if the Consolidate had caught onto the movement of one group, the others might still make it to safety. Darby's job was now to get his group back to the warehouse via a delivery truck that Simeon had arranged for them. They had picked up Vostro's wife and two girls the night before, and with extra donations of furniture from The Manufacturing District Group, the warehouse basement could now comfortably house them all.

Vostro remained quiet, envisioning what his first visit with his wife since his capture would be like. She could be as tender as a Jersey's teat or as tough as an overcooked flank steak. She would either be so thankful that he was all right that she'd smother him in kisses, or she'd berate him so far up one side that he'd feel three feet tall by the time she got down the other. There was no in between with Mari Salano.

After imagining his immediate fate, he began to wonder what awaited him and his family over the long run. Did the jailbreak mean The Group was ready for the bombing? He would not ask until he was in the company of the man he trusted most in this world. He would also wait until he saw Ari to divulge what he had learned during his questioning when he was first taken into custody. If it was true, he had to stop The Group from carrying out their plan. Otherwise, their plot would turn into their trap.

Chapter 56

Orion's synapses fired like a turbocharged ping-pong ball, and the anger shook his small frame like a sapling in a cyclone. How could they arrest his fiance? Hadn't he done everything they asked? Hadn't he convinced Gemi of exactly what they wanted him to?

"The insurgents recruited your father by making the Consolidate the scapegoat for your mother's death," Orion had lied to her. "The Consolidate sees him as a decent man who was just misled and needs to rethink things. Why do you think he's still alive? Why do you think they're helping you with a job and a place to stay?"

The argument had seemed to work. Gemini had to admit that neither she nor her father had suffered the consequences one would expect for an insurgent and his offspring.

"The best thing you can do is show them where your loyalties lie," Orion had told her. "Show them that your father raised a good patriot in spite of his own failings. Decide which side you're on, and act accordingly."

Perhaps it was her inclination toward politics. Perhaps it was pride. Perhaps every daughter needs a way to break the bond with her father. Perhaps in some hidden part of her, she, too, blamed her father for her mother's death. Orion wasn't sure why she had bought his argument, but she had. And it was he, Orion, who had lied to her in order to convince her, just as they had requested.

And now they think they can take her away? How dare they?

He imagined all the things he should do to them. He should crash their central registry. He should erase their core data. He should renumber every birth certificate and throw the Transitionary into chaos. He should insert a virus into the Benefactor's systems-support program. He should put Director Wolfe's name on the List.

As he paced his living room, his mind breathing dragon-fire, the hacked message from Director Wolfe to the vice president of security flashed onto his optiscreen. "Terminate rebel group with extreme prejudice. Collateral casualties acceptable."

At that moment, Orion knew exactly what he would do.

Chapter 57

Director Merideth Wolfe cursed the day she had decided to give Gemini Stockton the benefit of the doubt.

That little double-crosser, she thought. At the same time, she almost admired the girl. She was impressed that an eighteen-year-old could pull off such a feat, convincing everyone, even her fiancé, that she had turned against her own father, and then having the chutzpah to play decoy, right there in the director's office, in order to give her co-conspirators time to free her father.

What audacity, she thought. *No one has caught me off guard in at least a decade. Too bad she has to be eliminated. She reminds me of myself at that age.*

Perhaps that's why she let the girl fool her. Like Gemini, Merideth Wolfe had risen at a young age to a position above her own father. And now, Merideth's father, the rightful heir to the Benefactor's chair, would never go beyond being a senator. It was Director Wolfe, not her father, who was now first in line to take her grandfather's place at the top of the Consolidate. Soon, she would hold the title of Benefactor. She just had to get that old man out of the way.

In Gemini, she saw the same ambition, or thought she had seen it. Now she realized that the girl had a weakness that she would never allow in herself. Gemini loved her father. *I admit she has grit, but it's the only thing we have in common.*

Of course, the girl hadn't had the benefit of the director's upbringing—military training beginning at age eight. The ability—and willingness—to kill a full-grown man with her bare hands by age twelve. Counter-intelligence expertise at fourteen. Her education rounded out with doctoral-level studies in history, politics, finance and physics. Her trainers and tutors had literally raised her, so she knew what it felt like to be motherless. Her mother wasn't dead, but she may as well have been for how often Merideth saw her. When she did get to visit, the woman was as cold and untouchable as dry ice, ever the dutiful mother and wife, pushing her husband and child to the very top.

Director Wolfe had never had children of her own. She had better things to do. A few husbands had been in her past, either because they were a rung on the ladder, or because they could hold their own in bed. She had taken the last name of one of them to remind herself of what she had become. It was, after all, who she *wanted* to be. And the surname Smallman simply would not do for a woman rising rapidly to the pinnacle of power.

"Director Wolfe, the security vice president is here to see you," the receptionist's voice came over the speaker.

The girl Gemini was in the cage, and she'd deal with her later. At the moment, she had a crisis to manage. She punched a number on her projected keyboard. "Let him in."

The vice president of security looked somewhat like Orion, she thought, just with twenty extra years and a bit of a gut. He walked in carrying a backpack and placed it on her desk.

"The contents are intact, just as you requested," he said. "We swept it but otherwise haven't checked what's in it. For your own safety, will you reconsider?"

"Status update?" she said, not giving him the courtesy of an answer.

"DNA matching from the flyvan points to a warehouseman, Simeon Sing, Level Eight. The two people in the van with him were not identifiable by facial recognition, and either they didn't leave any genetic material behind, which is hard to believe, or they aren't in our database, which is even less likely. But if they're with the warehouseman, we should have them all before the day's over."

"I want updates every hour, Sorensen."

With that, he was dismissed. He left her office like a dog with its tail between its legs, and Director Wolfe turned her attention to DC-1128's pack.

Frayed at the straps and pieces of mud stuck in the seams, it looked like it had seen combat. The director slowly opened the main pouch and removed the weapons that the escapees had confiscated from the guards. She turned it upside down and shook it, but only a sprinkling of dried dirt fell out. A small inner side pocket hung down, and she pressed her fingers on either side of it, feeling the cylindrical objects. She unzipped the pocket and pulled out the two vials of clear liquid. Unfolding the small note, she read the few decipherable words: "shamans used... dimethyl... beyond the veil... power." From her desk drawer, she grabbed the paper from Ari's office with the chemical signatures and compared the handwriting.

"So that's how they did it" she said quietly to herself. "Chemically-enhanced telekinesis."

She held one of the vials up to the light and admired its clarity, its potency. "Well, there's one way to find out."

She removed the cap and carefully tapped two drops into the glass of water on her desk. She drank it down, and her breathing remained steady as she waited to find out where it would take her.

Chapter 58

The moment Vostro emerged from the stairwell into the warehouse basement, Mari was around his neck. He had caught her when she jumped, and now her feet dangled two feet off the floor. A scream of "Daddy!" had pierced the air when he entered, and now the space at the bottom of his legs was occupied by two little girls, each hugging one of his legs. He resembled some ancient tree draped with thick mosses.

Mari hid her face in his neck and sobbed. He was out of the woods for now, but he knew a scolding would come later, and he was already cringing at the thought of it. Sometimes he thought he should just loose his wife on the Consolidate, for surely it would crumble.

He glanced around the room. It looked like an eclectic flophouse, spartan but roomy. With the extra donations of furniture from The Manufacturing District Group, the warehouse basement could now house all eleven of them—rebels and refugees—Vostro, DC and Ari, Darby Tate and the two villagers, the Vostro clan, and Simeon Sing and his daughter. For Simeon, it was no longer safe above ground.

When Vostro's family finally let go of him, Ari rose to greet him. DC and Simeon were in a corner, too engaged in a heated discussion to pay attention to what was happening beyond them.

"That's the exit they'd expect us to take," DC was saying to Simeon. "It'll be a death trap."

"They don't know we're planning to leave the dodec. If anything, they think we're planning a bombing, not an escape," Simeon replied. He leaned forward in his chair to take the pressure of the particle beam pistol off his back. Held in place by his belt, it was cold against his skin. "The transport tunnel will be no more guarded than it was the first time you got out."

"They're going to beef up security everywhere," she retorted.

"They beefed it up after your escape, but you still got back in," he countered.

"That's different," DC said. "The Consolidate knows the villagers are peaceful. It doesn't need to watch for intruders. No, it's too risky. We have to create our own exit."

"I just watched missiles bounce off the dodec like harmless flies hitting a window. It's impenetrable," Simeon replied.

"Then we'll go under it," DC said. "It's no longer just a few of us. There are too many people to get them all out through a transport tunnel."

That gave Simeon pause. Word of the existence of villages had spread quickly throughout The Group members, and many wanted to leave the dodec. Some had only wanted freedom in the first place. Others saw an opportunity to better fight the Consolidate from the outside. Simeon guessed that they'd have to get at least fifty people out. He knew that DC was right. Taking that many through a transport tunnel all at once was too much of a risk. They would have to either find a different route out of the dodec or limit the number of escapees.

His mind sifted through the options, and he chose the only one that would not choke off their already narrow chance of making it out.

"The Consolidate doesn't know who the rest of The Group members are. It's only targeting us. We can get the others out later," he said. "Perhaps the villagers can help. Maybe we can negotiate their release. I don't know how we'll do it, but we'll find a way. You said The Village has a wisdom council. We'll take it to them. They'll know what to do."

Now it was DC's turn to pause for thought. It would be selfish to escape with only the people she cared about and leave the others to an uncertain fate. But what fate would she create for them if there were too many people to make the escape all at once? If the other Group members all left now, they might die in their flight to freedom. If they stayed, they might be stranded in the enslavement of the dodec forever. How could she make such a choice for people she didn't even know?

"What's so important over here that you can't greet an old friend?" Vostro's deep voice broke through the intensity of DC's thoughts, and she rose to give him a hug. She had come to love this behemoth like a brother, and she felt protected next to his herculean frame.

The room erupted into conversation as congratulations followed all around. They had just pulled off a colossal feat, and each wanted to recount what they had experienced.

"You should have seen your face when you saw the guns stuck to the ceiling," DC said to Vostro. "I don't think I've ever seen you shocked."

"Nice job neutralizing that woman's car," Ari ribbed DC about her particle beam slicing the top of a bystander's vehicle. "I don't know what we would have done if she had caught up to us," he chided.

They continued to laugh and chat, needing respite from the intensity of the escape. Vostro wanted to know more about Shar. How did she do all those things?

"It's no different than learning to ride a bike," Shar explained. "Anyone can do it. You just have to love it enough to practice."

Of everyone in the room, only Darby remained outside the circle of conversation. He sat quietly in a chair and watched the others chatter as if they were at a cocktail party. He reached into his pocket, as he had done a dozen times a day since retrieving the blue stones from under the floorboard. They had become his touchstones, his gauge to measure how grounded he was in this reality. They made him feel safe, like a boy in his mother's arms.

But he knew the feeling of security would soon be gone. He knew that they must now act quickly if they were to make it out of this mess alive. He knew that removing two prisoners from the fiftieth floor was child's play compared to removing The Benefactor's heart. They had caught the Consolidate off guard, but they no longer had that advantage. And he did not need Finn's level of skill to sense the dark cloud approaching from the distance.

Chapter 59

Merideth Wolfe retched into her trash can, her stomach holding onto its convulsion as if it was a python. She tumbled out of her chair to the floor below her desk and clung to the trash can like a lifejacket but soon could not hold onto it. As she slumped to the floor, her shoulder hit a leg of the desk, and the vial of liquid fell off the desktop and rolled next to her open hand. Perspiration escaped every pour, and a shiver overtook her whole body.

It felt as if her skin was increasing its depth, and she, a snake, was loose within it. She writhed and turned within her outer membrane. A roar overtook her, and she became the vibration of it.

This must be death, she told herself.

All became still. She floated in blackness and noticed the feeling of utter freedom.

In an instant, she was standing in a hallway at the back of a queue of people waiting their turn to see a man behind a desk. The walls around her sparkled. She could feel their aliveness. She looked at the floor, and it, too, emanated an awareness. She touched the shoulder of the man in front of her. He turned his head to look at her and scowled.

This is no hallucination, she thought to herself. *It feels more real than anything I've ever experienced.* And yet she was aware of her body back on the floor of her office. *Curious,* she thought, and examined her surroundings more closely. And then it was her turn at the desk.

"Oh, you're a preemie," the man said. "I'll call someone to take you back."

"No, I want to stay!" she exclaimed. She had surprised herself with the intensity of her own voice. Such a large charge of emotion had risen within her, as if without skin, she had no way to contain it.

Suddenly, she was in a large round room, domed at the top. Hundreds of people sat on benches or shuffled here and there, their eyes as blank as darkened screens. One reached toward her. Suddenly, without her own volition, Merideth Wolfe found herself rising into the air.

"You don't want to let them touch you," said a voice from behind her.

She felt hands under her elbows, lifting her. But it wasn't the touch that grabbed her attention, but the feeling of love emanating from it. It penetrated her entire being to depths she did not know she possessed. It felt like a substance in which she could swim, like a current of electrified water in the most ancient river, flowing through every cell, every tissue. Her response was automatic and the only one possible. "I love you, too," she thought back. It escaped her mind before she could stop it.

Together, she and the one holding her flew to the top of the dome, and then right through it. She felt a kind of static as they pierced the roof. They ended up in the darkest of night, and she thought she saw the twinkling of faraway stars. As they moved through the blackness, scenes appeared around her in rapid succession—a forest rich with deer and rabbit, a woman with multiple arms extending out from her shoulders, a city made of crystal, a white-bearded man on a throne, a million people bathing in liquid fire.

"The belief-system regions," said a voice in her head. It was not really a voice but a knowing, yet still a communication. Vision after vision flowed through her awareness, some pleasant, some atrocious, each accompanied by an understanding of what it was. The tour of heavens and hells might have lasted an eternity or a moment. Here, time did not exist.

In the next instant, she was high above the Transitionary, and she watched as souls left it, moving like shooting stars through the night sky. A wave of understanding encompassed her as she watched the streaming lights being pulled like metal shavings toward the magnet of what they expected to find after death. Then, from each of these magnetic regions, she could see brighter lights leaving, moving on to she knew not what.

Suddenly, she was standing in an old house. She knew, without knowing how she knew, that she was on the third floor. A ladder ascended into an attic, and yellow light filled the hatchway. She climbed up into it and found a circle of people sitting along its perimeter.

She walked up to one and knew what to ask. "Do you have a message for me?"

The man solemnly shook his head.

She asked the next and the next and the next, but each remained silent as stone.

Finally, a woman stood and said, "Yes. I do have a message for you." Her voice sounded like moonlight. "Love is all that matters. Be kind to one another."

A chorus of voices took up the refrain and repeated it over and over. "Love is all that matters. Be kind to one another." The most beautiful music she had ever heard, it flowed through her like warm honey.

Again she was in blackness, but the choir of golden voices followed her as she felt herself moving. No matter the distance, the singing went with her.

And then she felt the hard floor below her. The voices were no more. Curled like a baby in a womb, she lay there still and silent, trying to remember all that had happened.

It felt as if she was pulling the memories back through molasses, and anything she did not bring back now would soon be lost. Already, she could not recall the tune of the song, as if it didn't belong here—was too beautiful for this place. But the words of the song were etched in her mind forever. When she had retrieved all that she could hold, she slowly uncurled herself.

And for the first time in her life, Merideth Wolfe was born.

Chapter 60

The stairwell magnified the voice like a megaphone. "Helloooo."

The reveling rebels froze. Only one person from The Manufacturing District Group had been authorized as their liaison, his twice-daily visits their only contact with the world above, and he was given a specific knock to use before entering. So who was this intruder announcing his arrival?

"Hellooooo," the voice came again, now accompanied by footsteps. "It's me, Orion."

Ari recognized the voice, but he did not trust it. "Could be a trap," he whispered to the others.

DC grabbed her pistol from under a couch cushion and pointed it squarely at the dark rectangle that framed the stairwell. Darby placed himself in front of Shar, wanting to protect their most effective weapon.

That's who I saw with her, Finn thought, as the insufficient frame of Orion stepped into the light of the room.

Seeing DC's pistol, Orion flung his arms in the air, and the smile left his mouth.

"Whoa. It's me. I come in peace."

His joke fell flat, and the room remained heavy in silence. It was Ari who broke it, and the growl in his voice set Orion's bones to rattling.

"Are you alone? And before you answer, you should know that we have someone here who can tell if you're lying. If you lie, you die. That simple. Now, is anyone else with you?"

"No." The voice was so small it was almost a squeak.

"Does anyone else know you're here?"

"No."

DC had never seen such intensity in Ari. He seemed to expand to the size of bear, and his words were cold and deliberate, cutting through the air like arrows of ice.

"How did you find us?"

"I've been tracking the other Group members." Orion noticed Ari's jaw tense even more, and he quickly added, "Don't worry, I blocked it from the Security Division. No one else knows. I promise."

"Why are you here?" Ari demanded.

"They've taken Gemini into custody."

"Liar!" Ari shouted. He moved toward Orion, but Vostro grabbed his arm.

"Wait," Vostro said. "Let's hear him out."

With the immediate threat held at bay, Orion began talking rapidly, explaining how he had learned months ago that the The Uptown Group members were about to be arrested and how he claimed to be an infiltrator in order to remain free so that he could help them.

"You mean help yourself," Ari interrupted, his scowl so pronounced that Orion could barely look at him.

"I thought it was the best thing to do," Orion pleaded. "How else could I help look after Gemi?"

"Or turn her against me," Ari snarled.

"You have to believe me. I did what I had to do. These were difficult circumstances. And I'm here now to help. Look," he said, pulling his glasses from his face. "I have the

268

only untraceable optiscreen in the entire city. You're going to need me."

"If that's true," Simeon said, looking at Ari, but before he could finish his sentence, DC chimed in.

"Finn, can you tell if he's telling the truth?"

Finn closed his eyes. It was much easier to see the past than the future. "He hasn't told the Consolidate anything that would lead them here. And his probable future actions appear to be helpful to us."

Very diplomatic, DC thought, and she noticed the level of tension of everyone in the room drop off—all except Ari, who still looked ready to pounce.

"Listen, that's all we need to know right now," DC said. "We have to finish planning. If we don't make our move soon, Orion's intentions won't matter."

Chapter 61

Finn could not see where Gemini was being held. While the others began solidifying the escape plan, Finn went into his deepest meditation, but he still could not see her. When he returned to the group, to keep Ari calm, he began his explanation with, "Not being able to see someone has nothing to do with whether they're alive. I don't know what the problem is. I just can't find her."

The crease in Ari's forehead deepened, and he glared at Orion. "If anything's happened to her, I swear..."

"The Faraday cage!" Orion exclaimed. "That's it! They must have her in the cage."

The basement of Consolidate Headquarters had a room shielded from electromagnetic waves, Orion explained. Built before the dodecs, it was a safe refuge for the Consolidate directors during electrical storms. Now, the dodec provided sufficient protection, and the Faraday cage in the basement was used only for equipment calibration.

"Thoughts are electromagnetic," Darby said. "Finn wouldn't be able to see into a Faraday cage. That's why they put her there. That would mean they know we have a seer with us."

"Or they're just being cautious. It must've been obvious that we've got a telekinetic," DC added, then turned to Orion. "What does the Consolidate know about these skills?"

"I have no idea," Orion answered. "I've never seen any chatter about it."

"The Consolidate knew about our plans for the bombing," Vostro piped in. "When I was questioned, they asked how we planned to plant the bombs. They knew about it and would have used it as a trap. It may be a moot point now, but it shows that we have to assume they know everything."

They all agreed to proceed on that base assumption. The rest of the planning was a matter of compromise. Simeon was the only one who wanted to kill the three directors. Darby was the only one who needed the Benefactor's heart.

Shar sat back and enjoyed watching the scheme take shape while Mari kept the children occupied in the opposite corner. Shar's skills were a strong enough trump card that DC thought they might be able to negotiate their way out of the dodec, with the Benefactor as hostage.

"The directors want us gone," DC said. "They don't care if we're alive or dead, as long as we're not disrupting their hold on power. We negotiate first, see how far we can get with them. And they may be thankful we want to take the Benefactor with us. That way, one of them can take his place."

DC wanted to bring the man, heart and all, to the sacred ones, let them do the cutting.

In the end, they agreed to try her strategy. But if it didn't work, they had a Plan B, which would lead them through bedlam before they got out.

Chapter 62

The next day, they prepared for the carrying out of their plans, both A and B. Ari and Simeon had made a list of the materials they needed. Shar would manifest the simple chemicals while their liaison located the more technical devices.

The wait gave DC a chance to catch Ari alone and away from the others.

She placed a hand on his arm. "Don't worry. We'll get her out. I promise." She saw his worry lines soften as he gave her a tender smile.

"Thank you. But getting her out of that cage won't bring her back to me. Every week when she visited, I could see her receding farther and farther. All the skills of the villagers combined might not be enough to bring her back."

"She's a smart girl, Ari. She may have been playing both sides. She would have known that your visits were watched. Maybe she was just doing what she had to do to convince them she was on their side, just like Orion."

A flash of anger flitted across Ari's eyes at the sound of Orion's name. "I know my daughter," he said. "We'll have to drag her kicking and screaming out of the dodec if we want to get her out."

"Then we'll drag her kicking and screaming."

Ari shook his head, and DC paused to decide if the moment was right.

"Ari, she's like a daughter to me, too."

"I know that. I'm so thankful she's had you. I don't know what she would have done without you all these years."

"And you?" DC held her breath. She had finally asked, and there was no turning back.

Ari reached out and grabbed her shoulders. He bent his knees so that he could look her straight in the eyes. Beyond the tears that were forming, DC saw the emotional tug-of-war deep within him. He pulled her to him and wrapped her in his gentle arms. His lips touched her ear, and he whispered, "I can't leave without her. And I won't force her to go."

DC hid in his hug for several moments. The protective layers had fallen from her heart during her time in The Village, and now it sliced wide open. Ari had made his decision. She had seen love in his eyes a moment ago, but it was not enough to convince him to come with her. He loved his daughter more. And how could she blame him, for she, too, was sure of her choice. She would leave the dodec without him, because more than anything else, even more than she needed him, she needed her freedom.

As they slowly separated, she knew her heart would never again be whole. A piece of it would stay in the dodec forever. It didn't matter what happened now—Plan A or Plan B—it was all the same. Even if the Consolidate agreed to their terms and let them walk free, it wouldn't be long before Ari was on the List.

"I understand, really," she said to him, forcing herself to not look away, while silently she thought, *Goodbye, Ari Stockton, I will always love you.*

Chapter 63

From the moment Finn had seen Gemini in his inner vision, his breathing had seemed different, as if he had to remember to coax every breath. The sacred ones had shown him the future, and it felt inevitable. It wasn't just attraction to the girl's beauty, although she certainly was a pretty sight. Nor was it compassion for the pain he saw buried deeper than a vein of ore, so stuck in solid rock that it might never come out. It wasn't even the capacity of love that her heart could hold once it had grown and bloomed. It was something more that he couldn't quite touch. Destiny was his best description for it, but it felt more like a must. Was it a command from the sacred ones? Were they the directors of his fate?

In that brief time with the all-knowing oracles, a cornucopia of information had been planted in his brain. When he had time to sit with it—to pull out its contents one by one and examine them—he had been thrilled, amused, distraught, saddened. *No one should know the future,* he had said to himself. *It's too much of a burden.* And now it was his burden—a weight to carry alone—for he would wish it on no one else. For those he cared about, he wanted life to unfold moment by moment.

And yet this new knowledge from the sacred ones was also a gift, for he would not have to live his life questioning every choice. He now knew some things that were fixed, so neither apprehension nor uncertainty would visit him at every turn.

At the time, he had taken a mental preview of the dodec, and it had shown him the heart of the society within it. It was filled with fear and longing, both emotions numbed by distraction. This was the fate of not just the masses, but also those who controlled them. He had seen that The Group had broken the bonds of manipulation, and with that initial taste of freedom, no yoke would hold them. He had watched their struggle unfolding and had seen its future conclusion.

And now, on the day before he was to meet his destiny, he knew that many fates were about to come together in one life-defining moment. He knew that tomorrow, DC would kill for the first time so that she could learn the difference between that and what she had done as transition witness. He knew that Shar would meet her match, and the man would not have a pure heart like hers. He knew the Benefactor would not be leaving the dodec. And he knew that he, too, would be staying, for his future lay under that great glass arc.

Chapter 64

DC could hear each of them breathing. She watched Director Malik's chest rise and fall, rise and fall, his steady respiration sounding like waves brushing upon the sand. Director Huang's belly hung over his belt, pushing itself into the table with every inhale. DC had to listen closely to hear Director Wolfe's breath, so much did she control herself, but there it was, making her the same as everyone else. No matter how high they rose, the directors would always have this simple commonality with the rest of the populace. And one day, their breath, too, would stop.

It might be today, DC thought. But she hoped that within the hour, she would have successfully carried out Plan A— negotiation—avoiding the need for death.

"You'd rather not have to deal with us at all," she was saying to the directors. "Trust me, the feeling is mutual. The solution I'm offering will rid you of the rebels forever. All we ask in return is safe passage out. We will never return and we will not plot against you from the outside."

"And you can vouch for the future actions of more than a hundred other people?"

Orion had warned DC of Director Wolfe's craftiness, that she should ignore the surface question and look for the one hidden beneath it. *She wants me to correct her if there are fewer people in The Group. They don't know how many we are! Well, two people can play the game of double meanings.*

"I can tell you that by leaving the dodec, they will have achieved their goal. There's no reason for violence when they can attain their objective safely."

"You assume they share your desire for freedom. Revenge can be a stronger motivator."

Ah, a tit for a tat. A hidden threat in return for the one I just offered, DC thought. *They see the need to avenge the breach of security.*

"If we leave peacefully, you can spin it as a punishment—an expulsion into a dangerous place that holds certain death. If we're forced to fight our way out, it will take much more than a sound bite to convince the rest of the herd that there's no cliff out there. Some might start thinking like the rebels and want to see for themselves."

As DC spoke, she removed the vial from her pocket and pressed the sticky side of it to the bottom of the conference table. It was her compromise with Simeon. A means to kill the directors would be put in place, but the remote detonator to release the poison gas would remain in her pocket—her assurance that it would not be used if the directors agreed to give The Group free passage out.

"It's too late for negotiation," Director Malick said. "The treaty has already been broken."

The slight rise in DC's eyebrows told the directors one of the things they wanted to know. They could draw her toward their trap.

"You didn't consider the broader implications of your actions," Director Malick continued. "The non-interference agreement with the villages became null and void the moment you brought two villagers in with you."

So they know about Shar and Finn. DC would not let a surprise revelation trip her up again, and she answered without pause. "Then you know the advantage we have, and that I'm here as a courtesy."

"Do you think we haven't bothered to develop our own people with those skills?" Director Wolfe chimed back in.

Director Wolfe's departure from the script made Director Malik squint at her with a sideways glance. And now they all paused to consider the new path they were taking. DC thought about the night in the woods when the wolves surrounded their camp. She imagined the directors with glowing yellow eyes. What had Shar suggested? Send them love? No, she still could not manage that. Every fiber in her was urging her to flee, but now she knew she would have to fight. Now that she knew their intention, further conversation was a waste of breath. Only one more question needed to be asked.

"Do you have a counter offer?"

"Do we need one?" Director Wolfe asked.

"Not if you're the ones holding the trump card." She let it hang there like a question, letting them know that there were still things that they did not know, and it was no ruse, for within moments, Simeon and Darby would be in the Benefactor's office, holding either his arms or his heart in their hands.

Chapter 65

"There are no guards. But there are three deadbolts in the door's steel framing," Finn was saying to Shar from their hiding place in the basement of Consolidate Headquarters. He kept his eyes closed as his mind traveled to the Benefactor's office fifty-two floors up.

"An alarm wire is attached to each deadbolt, and just beyond the door, I see several laser trip wires near the floor. You'll have to lift them up and over the lasers for the first four feet past the threshold."

The day before, Shar had lifted a beamkey from someone working on the fifty-second floor. It had gotten Darby and Simeon to the entrance of the Benefactor's office, and now they waited for the clicks of the deadbolts.

Click. Click. Click. The door swung open, and they found themselves lifted a foot in the air. But the shock they felt resulted not from the sudden weightlessness, but from what they saw in front of them. As Shar moved them toward it, they grimaced at its grotesqueness.

A severed head sat atop a Plexiglas column. Deep wrinkles folded the forehead like an accordion. Patches of white hair littered the scalp. A pair of optiscreen glasses rested on the bridge of the nose.

The eyes sprang open, and if Shar had not been holding Darby and Simeon in her mental grip, they would have fallen backward. It was alive! And not only that, it could command an entire army with a single glance.

Simeon lurched forward and pulled the optiscreen from the Benefactor's face to relieve him of his command. The man's teeth snapped at him, and Simeon jerked his hand back.

Darby recovered his wits as Shar set him gently down in front of the freakish thing. He started to laugh, so absurd was the thought of an entire society ruled by a disembodied chief. *He's just a figurehead,* Darby thought. The pun made him laugh even harder, and he would have continued his merriment had he not noticed what was in the column. As he continued to look at it, his laugh tapered off to a chuckle, then stopped altogether. He approached it slowly, curiously.

"You're dead men!" the face barked. "You can't get away with this."

Darby was now close enough to see it clearly. On a Plexiglas shelf a foot below the head were two black stones, smooth and shiny, each with one flat and one rounded surface. The size of sparrow eggs, they sat in two small metal cups, a wire protruding from each.

Darby bent down, and his eyes followed the wires to where they disappeared into the base of the column. Then he followed the wires up to two small sockets at the base of the neck. He looked over the entire Plexiglas structure for a means of access. He reached for the head and grabbed it with both hands. The Benefactor growled and snapped like a cornered animal. Lifting and holding the head with one hand, he unplugged the wires with the other. It appeared to have no effect, other than the head began screaming epithets and threats. Darby shoved the head at Simeon, who held up his hands and used several gestures that meant "no."

"Take it," Darby insisted. "Just for a minute."

Simeon's instinct was to pull the particle-beam pistol from his belt and blast the thing to smithereens. But he held himself in check and reluctantly followed Darby's instruction. He grabbed the clacking skull by a patch of hair and held it at arm's length to keep from being bitten. He recoiled from its ugliness and glanced around the room to find anything else to focus on.

Across from the Plexiglas column was a video camera and sound recording system for the Benefactor's weekly address. Next to that was the makeup table. Brushes and rouge and eyeliner pencils littered its surface, along with jars of beige substances—thick liquids to fill in the crevices in that wrinkled face. A piece of prosthetic rubber to create a smooth neck. A wig of thick, dark hair to cover the balding scalp.

All day long, this man looks at the tools of his illusion, Simeon thought as he glanced back over at the Benefactor's perch.

Darby was lifting the top off the column. He reached inside to remove the black stones. From his pocket he pulled his mother's last gift and put the two blue stones inside the tiny cups on the Plexiglas shelf.

"Bring it here." Darby nodded Simeon toward the column, and Simeon rushed over, wanting nothing more than to be done holding the monstrosity. "Hold it while I plug it back in."

Now the head was screaming. "Guards! Guards! Security breach! Guards!" But it was to no avail. Shar had already deactivated the voice command microphone.

As Darby placed the head back on its perch, Simeon fought the urge to pull out his pistol and destroy it.

"How do we take his heart? He doesn't have one."

Darby pulled the black stones from his pocket, holding them so Simeon could see them. "I think we have what we need."

They turned to leave, stopping four feet before the door so that Shar could lift them over the lasers.

"You will regret this day," the head yelled after them. "You haven't seen the last of it."

Chapter 66

The Consolidate Headquarters basement felt like a place of secrets. It looked innocuous enough, with cages filled with stacks of old equipment, a janitorial supply room with mops and cleaners, ladders and hand tools, a room with a chute in the ceiling for trash to fall into a giant compactor, a generator room with a hydrogen boiler, its dozens of water lines extending up and piercing the basement ceiling like stiff copper fingers reaching up through some tomb.

Other than the twenty-foot metal box in one corner, it held nothing unusual, so it must have been the crawlspace that made Vostro nervous. The light from the basement illuminated the crawlspace entrance and then slowly faded into darkness. Soon, he would have to go through it, for it came out underneath the Transitionary, and their escape would be there, through a transport tunnel. The very thought of the four-foot height of the crawlspace made Vostro claustrophobic. He imagined it filled with a million whispers—stories that could only be told in shadows. Or perhaps it was the basso hum of the boiler, like some underground monk chanting one extended aum, that kept him on edge. Whatever it was, it felt to Vostro as if he was about to be buried there. He pulled his two girls in closer to him and glanced at his wife, who sat next to him holding Simeon's daughter.

The only voices were occasional exchanges between Shar and Finn, the latter describing what he saw five hundred feet above them, the former moving her hands in the air, as if playing some invisible harp. Vostro wondered if everyone in The Village would act with such strangeness. He hoped he would get there to see it.

Orion stood nearby, using only his eye movements and his optiscreen to shift the cameras and sensors of the building's security system.

That's not so different than what Shar and Finn are doing, Vostro thought as he watched Orion.

He wondered how Ari was faring. Shar had opened the door of the Faraday cage—a solid silver box—and Ari was now inside of it with his daughter, pleading with her to leave with them. If she refused, Ari's heart would shatter, and Vostro would not be able to stay with his friend to help pick up its pieces.

Finn's voice captured Vostro's attention. "They've got the heart," he was saying to Shar. "They're waiting for you to lift them back over the laser beams."

Shar raised her hand, palm up, and moved it sideways, and then asked, "What's happening with DC?"

Finn's eyes moved beneath his closed lids like a dreamer in sleep. The images flashed in black-and-white as his vision roamed the fifty-second floor. The chair in which DC had been sitting in Director Wolfe's office was empty. The office lobby held only the receptionist. He looked down the hallway and saw Simeon and Orion exiting the Benefactor's room and running toward the elevator. His mind zoomed down the hallway to the elevator shaft. He found the elevator car at floor twenty with no one in it. He checked the stairwell, his mind racing up and down at the speed of thought. *Where is she? I've lost her!*

"Finn, where's DC? Have you lost her?" Shar echoed his thoughts.

"Just a minute, I'll find her." His mind began scanning each floor, searching quickly but methodically. "Of course, the fiftieth floor. Security Division," he said, mostly to himself. And there, in a small room, he found her.

He zoomed his vision in. Leather straps held her arms to a chair, and a headpiece covered her scalp like a shower cap with dozens of circular indentations. He described what he saw. "Orion, what is it?" he asked.

"I think it's an image extractor," Orion said. "Let me see if I can disengage it."

"No, that'll take too long," Finn said. "Shar, can you get it off her? And remove the wrist straps, too."

"What about security personnel? Let's take care of them first," Shar said.

Finn scanned the room and the hallway outside. "Strange. There's a technician in the room, but no guards anywhere."

"None?"

"No, none. Just get her out of there." Finn's voice was starting to sound frantic.

Shar held her hand with fingers pointed downward and palm rounded and then pulled slightly up. The skullcap lifted from DC's head. Shar remotely unfastened the wrist straps, and DC began to stand, but before she was fully upright, she slammed back into the chair, and the straps secured themselves around her wrists.

With his remote vision, Finn glanced at the technician, who leaned casually against the far wall, a smirk on his lips.

"Shar, she's back in chair. Undo the straps!"

287

"I already did."

"I know, but they're back on her wrists. Get her out of there!"

"What are you talking about?"

"Just do it!"

Shar moved her fingers again, and again the straps unlatched. Again DC began to rise, and again her body slammed back into the chair.

"They have a telekinetic!" Finn yelled, and just then, the elevator door to the basement opened, and Darby and Simeon rushed in.

It was Orion who addressed them. "They've used an image extractor on DC. They probably know we're here. You've got to get out of here. Right now."

"Where's DC?" Darby asked.

"Fiftieth floor," Finn said. "They've got a telekinetic. He won't let her go." He closed his eyes again and watched as the two puppeteers—one on the fiftieth floor, the other in the basement—continued to pull DC's strings in opposite directions. "Stop, Shar, you'll pull her apart!"

"Listen," Orion said to the others. "This may be your only chance. We'll find a way to get her out later. But the rest of you go now or you may never get out. Go!"

Vostro had never seen such vehemence from the little man. He stood and joined the others, while Simeon, who had retrieved his daughter, stood back several feet, as if that distance would protect Elva from the panic that now filled the room.

"I can't go without her," Darby said.

"I'm in it until the last minute," Shar chimed in.

"Me, too," Finn said.

"Simeon and Vostro should go, at least get their families out," Darby said. He turned toward the two rebels. "Get a head start. We'll try to catch up."

"No," Vostro said. "We stay together. It's all or none."

"Where's Ari?" Darby asked.

Vostro pointed to the silver box. "In the Faraday cage with his daughter."

"All right," Darby said. "Everyone calm down. Maybe they don't know we're here. Now, how do we get DC out? We need to..."

The elevator's ding silenced him, and they all stood frozen, staring at the opening doors.

Darby wondered if the elevator car had some trap door from which they sprang, as it seemed like a never-ending stream of security guards rushing out.

As each one approached, Shar flipped them on their backs and made their weapons fly into the air.

Then it looked as if someone had hit the rewind button, and the security guards were back on their feet, their weapons in hand.

Shar flipped them again, and they flipped back up.

Now it was Shar who flew into the air. Pushed backward and up at the speed of a bullet, she slammed into one of the storage cages. The force of it knocked out her breath, and with wild eyes she hung there, watching a lone man walk out from the back of the elevator car.

The doors closed behind him, and his eyes slowly took in the room. His smirk turned into a sneer as he casually walked past the security guards. He glanced at Simeon's drawn weapon and locked the trigger finger into stillness. Then he surveyed his rebel catch.

Suddenly, his shoulder jerked backward, not of its own accord, and he shot an angry glance at Shar. Her eyes widened, and a choking sound came from her mouth.

"Stop it!" Darby yelled and charged at the man. Vostro was right behind him, but they both ended up sprawled on the floor.

The elevator door opened again, and out walked Director Wolfe, her air of confidence filling the room like some poisonous gas. Every security guard sensed it, and even the Consolidate's telekinetic felt the message it carried: *You dare not.*

"Let her down," Director Wolfe said.

Shar dropped to the floor and sat there in a heap, gasping for breath. Finn rushed over to her and helped her sit up.

"Not bad," the wolf said. She paced back and forth in front of the prisoners, looking from person to person, sizing each one up. Her eyes paused on Vostro's children. "Oh, and little ones, too."

Darby grabbed Vostro's arm to keep him from making a mistake.

"Well, you're all quite clever, aren't you? We've never had the excitement of dealing with anything like this." She paused and looked straight at Darby. "You almost gave the Benefactor a heart attack."

Darby thought he saw her wink but chalked it up to stress playing on his imagination.

She walked to the silver cage and opened its door. At the back of its twenty-foot length sat Gemini, arms crossed and scowling, her father beside her.

"You can come out now, my little worm," Director Wolfe said.

Gemini stood and walked out with a huff, showing no fear of the Consolidate's second-in-command.

"Be thankful," Director Wolfe said to her as she passed. "The bait usually ends up in the prey's stomach."

She pulled the door wide open and gestured toward the inside of the box. "Your accommodations," she said, looking at the defeated group.

Finn helped Shar to her feet, and they followed the others into the box. Vostro could see his friend Ari at the back, looking like his light had gone out. The door began shutting behind them but suddenly stopped.

"Oh, I almost forgot to give you this," Director Wolfe said. She reached in through the opening with a closed hand. Simeon was closest to the door and held out his palm to receive it. "Someone left this in my office." She dropped the silver tube of poison gas into his hand. With her other hand, she held up the dime-sized detonator. "I think I'll keep this."

The door shut and the light switched off. And they were in darkness.

Chapter 67

"Do you enjoy pitting daughter against father?" Gemini asked as the elevator ascended toward the top of Consolidate Headquarters.

"It won't be your last sacrifice," Director Wolfe said, as she removed her contact lenses from her eyes. She pulled a small case from her pocket, inserted the lenses, and handed it to Gemini. "These will sync with your optiscreen. But don't put them on until tomorrow, or you'll lose everything you still hold dear."

Gemini's obdurate look was softened by curiosity.

"You will have the quickest rise to power in Consolidate history," Director Wolfe continued. "You're too young to be wise, but at least be wary. You will have many enemies, not the least of which is yourself."

The elevator's digital display showed they had reached the fifty-second floor, but when the doors opened, the director did not get out.

"My receptionist has a box for you," the director said. "It's your father's last gift. One day, the world will no longer make sense to you. That's when you should open it."

The doors slid shut, and Gemini Stockton stood alone in the reception room outside of Director Wolfe's office.

Chapter 68

Inside the Faraday cage, seven people contemplated their impending deaths. What regrets haunted them as they breathed their last breaths? What hopes inspired peace in their hearts? What fears would follow them through that opaque veil?

Simeon Sing pulled off his shirt and ripped it into strips. Folding one piece into a double thickness, he tied it around his daughter's head to cover her nose and mouth and then made a similar mask for himself. The third strip he wound round and round the deadly little canister. He knew it would be ineffective, but he did it nonetheless.

We're going to see Mommy soon. He told her silently, because how could he make such a promise out loud? He held his daughter on his lap and began humming a lullaby. Sound, love, light. Nothing could leave that impenetrable box. The music flowed from him like a river, hit the walls and travelled back, flooding the room with its sweetness.

Mari Salano snuggled deep into her husband's shoulder until it felt as if she was merging into him. Vostro enclosed her, as if his bulk could protect her from anything.

"If the only thing I did right in this life was loving you, then that will have been enough," Vostro whispered to her.

"Stay with us," Mari replied. "On the other side, don't go gallivanting around without us. You're not going to have that big body of yours for me to keep track of. So keep us by your side. Promise me."

"I promise." He pulled her in tighter. She felt the soft plink of a tear landing on top of her scalp.

Ari Stockton rested his head in his hands. *Where did I go wrong, Sarafina?* he asked his dead wife. *She grew up so fast. I tried to be enough. What didn't I see?* His mind raced to the future. How would Gemi end up? Past and future, future and past. Even at the last moment of his life, he would be pulled to the two times that did not exist.

Orion Soloman's synapses lit up like fireflies illuminating the night in surprising places. He rapidly calculated the odds of half a dozen possibilities of escape, while other areas of his brain flashed on his mother and his future wife. Gemi was the only thing he ever really wanted. And with a simple ring, he finally had her within his grasp. His brain finished its escape calculations. *A five percent chance, at best.* "Gemi," he said, as the light from the last synapse faded.

Sharlotta Octavia calmed her mind and travelled into it, deeper now, and even deeper, navigating the black depths like some seafarer on a winter's night. She had watched several elders begin their final voyage, and she knew how to prepare for it. She was not worried about her family's loss, nor did she mind leaving this world for the next. She would soon be able to do much more than move objects. If she wanted, she could create entire cities in an instant with that finer substance that she would find on the other side of death. How easy it would be to manipulate and mold mind-stuff instead of matter. *What a grand adventure,* she said to herself.

Darby Tate had been there before. He knew what to expect and was not afraid of it. His life had now run its course, and he had fulfilled his last purpose by replacing the Benefactor's heart. *Mother, how did you know?* He felt the black stones in his pocket. *I'll see her soon enough to ask.* There was no longer a decision to make—whether to remain an individual or become his larger self. Soon, he would have no choice but to merge back into the infinite, and he had only one regret. *I wish I had known you all of my life, DC-1128.*

Finn Sylvan's mind was calm. He simply waited. He knew the door would soon open, and Director Wolfe would lead them to freedom.

Chapter 69

Light precedes every transition. Whether at the end of a tunnel, through a crack in the door or the flash of an idea, it is always there, heralding a new beginning. Two dark frames were silhouetted against the bright background as the heavy door swung open. Simeon squinted as his eyes adjusted to the light, until he could make out the faces of Merideth Wolfe and DC-1128. The pistol was in his hand in an instant, pointed squarely at the director's forehead. His forefinger felt the finality of the trigger.

"Simeon, no!" DC's voice was urgent. "She's going to get us out."

The two women entered, and DC closed the door behind them.

Director Wolfe held up the detonator so all could see it, and then she reached toward DC and dropped it into her hand. Simeon kept the pistol aimed at the director as she strode through the cage's twenty-foot length. Its occupants made way for her like the sea parting for the chosen one. She ended at Ari, who still sat on the bench at the back of the box.

"Get up," she commanded.

She pulled the seat up and toward her, and like a hide-a-bed, it opened. The bottom third of the wall was now an entrance, and Merideth Wolfe lowered herself into it.

"Come on, let's go," she spoke through the opening. "Do you want to get out of here or not? Hand me the children first."

And so they descended into the tunnel, its blackness lit by the director's single light tube.

"If this is a trick, I'm taking you with us," Simeon whispered as he climbed in and past Merideth Wolfe.

"Keep moving," she replied. "Once we're out of the cage, the telepaths will be able to pick us up. Carry the children. We can't let them slow us down."

When they were all in the tunnel, Merideth set the pace at a jog. Consolidate Headquarters was near the center of the city, and they would have at least two miles to run.

As DC ran, she listened to the breathing of her friends as it increased in speed and intensity, their lungs demanding what they needed. She could hear her own breath echoing in her head. After a mile, the sound of panting was all she heard, and by the second mile, it had put her into a trance and seemed to be growing in a slow crescendo.

"Stop!" Merideth called out. "Listen!"

The group came to a halt, but they could barely hear over their own rasping breaths. They tried to quiet themselves, and the loudness of their breathing diminished somewhat. In the quieted air, they could hear the dull thuds of feet hitting the earth.

"Hurry," Merideth commanded, and they took off in the quickest sprint that their legs and lungs could handle.

A beam pierced the wall behind them, slicing a deep slash. If not for the curve of the tunnel, it would have cut them in half. Fear pushed their legs forward, and they flew down the tunnel to outrun their deaths.

Another section of wall disintegrated into dust behind them. As the curve straightened, they could see the light where the tunnel opened. They were no more than a hundred feet from freedom, but in that last length of tunnel, their pursuers would have a straight shot.

Simeon held out his daughter to the runner next to him. "Take her," he gasped.

DC caught the girl in one arm without missing a step.

Simeon turned back toward the darkness of the tunnel. He pulled the small metal tube from his pocket, unwrapped the material he had wound around it, and threw it.

"Detonate now!" he yelled behind him to DC.

She understood, and she did not hesitate.

Simeon fell to the ground and rolled to the tunnel's edge. Pulling out the pistol, he waited. Two seconds later, when the vibration from their feet thundered through his chest, he fired a steady beam. He could hear bodies crashing into bodies. Two cries rang down the tunnel. He fired again.

Before the poison gas could enter his lungs, his head lopped off.

Chapter 70

As they sprinted beyond the tunnel and out into the clear air of freedom, DC said to herself, *He's still with me.* For Ari had run with them, and now she could see him just a few feet in front of her. But her attention was pulled to Elva's screams.

"Daddy! Daddy!" The girl reached over DC's shoulders toward the tunnel as if her little arms could stretch all the way back into it to retrieve him. DC held tighter, for there was nothing more she could do.

The group sprinted another fifty meters before Merideth's shouting had stopped them.

"Wait!" she yelled. "You're safe."

They all looked back. No one was at the mouth of the tunnel.

"I think your poison gas did its job. But no matter, the treaty forbids any violence beyond the dodec," Merideth said between heaving breaths.

"But the treaty was already broken, wasn't it?" Darby asked. "Finn and Shar interfered inside the dodec."

"And if the Consolidate responds in kind, it will no longer have the upper hand in claiming betrayal," Merideth said. "There are bigger objectives than killing a few rebels."

"And a director who escapes with them? How big is that?" DC's question hung in the air unanswered.

"Where's Simeon?" Ari asked.

"The gas," DC said. "It was his choice... for her." She nodded toward the girl in her arms, who was now whimpering.

"And Finn?"

In the rush and confusion inside the dark tunnel, they hadn't noticed that he wasn't with them.

"He stayed behind," Shar said. "He told me that he had seen his destiny, and he had to follow it."

"His destiny inside the dodec? Is he crazy?" DC surprised even herself with her intensity. How could she have let this happen? "We can't let him stay there. He's just a boy, really, and his skills are no match for the Consolidate—not alone, anyway. We have to..."

Ari stopped her with a hand on her shoulder. "Let it be. Just like Simeon, he's made his decision. When I get back in, I'll do what I can to watch after him."

"Oh, the rebel fugitive and the village intruder. I'm sure you'll be very effective together." Her tone had been sharp, as beneath it, her heart was again under the knife. Ari had just confirmed that he would be true to his word. He would not remain outside the dodec without his daughter.

He cradled DC's face in one hand. She tried to absorb the feeling of it, knowing this could be his last touch.

"My dear DC-1128, you'll understand one day. You have the same responsibility now."

DC had spent her entire career on death, yet at that moment, she had no idea what words to say to the little girl about it. She moved Elva's head onto her shoulder and whispered into her ear, "It will be all right."

304

Now, she was so focused on the girl, that she barely heard Orion's announcement that he, too, would be returning to the dodec for his fiancé.

Why did I even bother to go back? Ari, Gemini, Orion, Finn. Four of the people she cared about most in the world were choosing to remain in the dodec, to give up their freedom, their *lives.* It all seemed so senseless. But she knew the futility of trying to change their minds, for how could she challenge the strongest powers on Earth? It wasn't the Consolidate that held them captive. It was simple emotion. Love, pride, desire. These were the determiners of their fates.

"I'm going to the Sylvan home," she announced. "Finn's grandmother deserves to know what happened."

She could hear the faint echo of the mighty river in the distance, and she knew that if she followed it, she would reach her destination.

Those who go with you will not all come back. She had been warned, but still she had gone. The elder's words haunted her every step of the way to the warm-hearthed home.

Grandma Sylvan, in her typical fashion, made what DC labeled a tragedy seem more like a blessing. "If he follows his heart, his journey will be perfect for him and all in his path," she said with such simple conviction that DC couldn't help but believe it.

But she could not muster Grandma Sylvan's acceptance of circumstance when it came to the people who were closest to her heart. Ari's and Gemini's paths had diverged from hers, and as she weighed the value of her freedom, she was not fully convinced it was worth the price.

V

Chapter 71

Darby oozed from his bed like balm squeezed from a tube. The tapping at the door was soft, as if to say it was all right to ignore the knock at this early hour. But he had been waiting two months for an invitation, and he would not risk missing its delivery. He pulled a robe over his bare skin. There would be no need to make himself fully presentable. Those who see beauty in every person don't care if your hair is combed.

The sweet smell of fresh air whooshed in as the door to his new home opened to the boy on the porch. Darby remembered being his age—a teenager leaving behind the vulnerability of childhood. Back then, he could feel the intoxication of life surging through him, sense the mastery his mind and muscles gave him. Indestructible and innocent, unobstructed and strong, he had entered the age of responsibility with clarity and zest. That was another gift his mother had given him. She had protected him from the brutality of the world long enough to grow his emotional bones into a strong framework, and it would hold him steady and solid for his entire life.

He wished he could talk to her now that he knew her story. Why had she never told him? Did she fear he would risk too much if he knew of the communities outside of the dodec? Did she think he would try to escape to his true home? His mother had been born here in this village, raised in this place of tranquility. Why would she choose to leave it for the confinement of the dodec, and then never tell him about it? When he had asked Great-grandmother Sophia, she simply said, "It was her calling."

He smiled at the boy at the door to let him know it was all right to have woken him up at six a.m. The last time the boy had come to fetch him, the lad had been bent over, propping himself up with his hands on his knees, trying to catch his breath. This time, the messenger of the sacred ones must have traveled at an easy pace, for his message was not delivered between rapid breaths.

"They will see you today. Bring both women with you."

Chapter 72

DC heard the tiny voice through the crack in her bedroom door. The vibration came into her ears, and then it travelled straight to her heart, where it transformed itself into a gentle smile.

"Eat these leaves. You have to grow up tall so you can see over the top of all the trees. The trees are really, really, really, *really* tall here, so you have to eat a lot."

DC listened to the little girl playing with the two giraffes that Shar's son had carved. That would be the mommy giraffe speaking to the little one. *The mommy giraffe.* Elva Sing had designated the larger of the two animals not as a father, but as a mother, and DC cherished the meaning it held.

A child's heart can heal so fast, she thought.

She tiptoed to the door and peeked out into the living room. The mop of red curls bobbed up and down as Elva trotted the two giraffes side by side toward the twigs that she had wedged into a crack in the floorboards to keep them upright. The mommy giraffe bent a twig down with her neck, and chomping sounds came out of Elva's mouth as the head of the little giraffe disappeared into the leaves.

DC quietly laughed. She had forgotten the joy of such innocence. And she had never before known her own gentleness. These months of caring for Elva had taught her that it's not the love taken in, but the love traveling out from the heart that softens its scars.

Great-grandmother Sophia shuffled into the living room in well-worn slippers, each step brushing the floor with a sound like labored breath.

"Hello, little one."

"Grape-grama Sophia!" Elva jumped up, toppling trees and animals, and rushed to the woman who could only bend so far for a hug. Two little arms encircled the ancient neck.

"Come, now. Let's make some breakfast. Do you want to help?"

"Yes!" Elva jumped up and down to make her answer even more evident and followed Great-grandmother Sophia into the kitchen.

DC slipped back into the warmth and comfort of her feather bed. This is how all of life felt now, even without Ari. Warmth, comfort, serenity. She was blanketed between a child and a crone, and the varieties of love therein contained a spectrum broad enough to satisfy her deepest longing.

Chapter 73

The cold morning air misted Vostro's breath as he leaned against the cow's warm skin, its full udder pressing against his arm. Milk squirted into the silver bucket in thin white jets. He felt the rhythm of it—squeeze, swish, squeeze, swish, swish. At first, the Jersey's eyes had widened as she turned her broad neck to get a glimpse of him, but now she was used to him, and she munched the tray of dried grasses, happy to be emptied of her liquid burden. Her tail flicked a fly, automatic in its intended purpose.

Vostro's hands remembered how to do this work, and he could not imagine hooking a machine to this fine beast. The milking rhythm lulled his mind into stillness, and he seemed to merge right into the cow, the stall, the morning air. All was one great flow that made him complete.

Both man and animal soon sensed the satisfaction of an empty udder. Vostro stood and lifted the bucket, patting Betsy's neck and silently thanking her for her simple gift. He had never before had a cow with a name. And not since his childhood had he had the pleasure of sensing a cow's personality. Betsy was gentle but independent, pretending she didn't care much what he was doing, aloof in her love.

"Sturdy legs," he said to her as he bent and felt her knees. Betsy and ten other cows were now under his care and protection, not as a commodity that produced a profit, but as sentient beings with their own vital strand in the web of life, their own contribution to the community they shared with humans.

Chapter 74

"You couldn't wait until the sun was up?" As they walked the path to the sanctuary, DC dissected Darby's decision to see the sacred ones immediately. "They don't care what hour it is. They're going to be hanging out—or should I just say 'hanging'—in the same place whether it's six a.m. or midnight. And you've had those stones for two months. Suddenly you need to turn them over right this minute?"

Merideth Wolfe walked two paces in front of DC and Darby. She had known them for only a short time, but already she knew to avoid the landmine of stepping between these two combatants. More than that, there was no time to focus on the triviality of DC's complaint. In minutes they would be standing before the sacred ones, and she could barely wait to see the face of true power. As a director of the Consolidate, she had heard of them, of course. She had once referred to them as "the little twits of The Village." She had thought that they were the figureheads of a new religion the Wisdom Council had created to control the hearts and minds of the people. *Strange how we assume other people share our motives*, she thought.

Now that she had lived in The Village for two months, she had learned a few things about them. They were children who had been born without forgetting. They retained the wisdom of the ages, and with that, they possessed all of the villagers' mental skills rolled into one. Seers, empaths, healers, telekinetics—their purpose was to counterbalance the darkness in the world, their resonance canceling out the lowest notes on the human scale. And they had a second purpose—to make themselves expendable.

"On the day that all beings on Mother Earth are thriving, as it was meant to be, they will no longer be needed," Great-grandmother Sophia had explained. "They work to bring that world about."

As Merideth approached the sanctuary of the sacred ones, habit took hold of her, and she began preparing herself with deadpan face and sharpened mind in order to win at this meeting. She chuckled at her old indoctrination. How useless her skills would be compared to the sacred ones' abilities and pure intent.

As they stepped up to the sanctuary's door, DC was still complaining. "You're the one with the stones, so I don't know why they need me to be here."

"It's certainly not for your charming company," Darby retorted. "Can you just go with someone else's plan for once?"

DC let out a final huff as they stepped through the carved wooden door.

The sacred ones floated serenely, their high vibration giving them the weight of particles of light. In the same way that white is not the absence of color but that which contains all the wavelengths of the visible spectrum, the silence in the room seemed to hold every voice ever spoken. The man and two women stood in front of them, waiting to be addressed.

"Did you bring the Benefactor's heart?" As before, the middle one spoke in the threefold voice.

"Yes," Darby said, removing the two black stones from his pocket and placing them on the floor. "May I ask a question?"

The sacred one in the middle nodded once.

"I don't understand. What difference will this make? He's just a figurehead. It's the directors of the Consolidate who are in control."

"The power lies with he who holds the heart of the people. Or she," the threefold voice replied.

Merideth stared at the most evolved humans on earth, and she had to disagree. From them, she could sense true power emanating, and it had nothing to do with influence over other people.

"And this is the Benefactor's granddaughter?"

Merideth snapped to attention, but it was Darby who replied. "Yes, this is Merideth Wolfe."

"Her initials are fitting, for she is the midwife," the voice said. The sacred one in the middle moved his countenance slightly to face Merideth Wolfe directly. "You will help birth a new awareness for the people of the dodecahedron. But you will be only the midwife, for it will come through another—the one to whom you left a gift."

Merideth remained silent, knowing they would offer an explanation if it would be of benefit. Instead, the sacred one in the middle opened his eyes and turned his face toward DC.

"Diana Childress, you are also a midwife."

"I am?" DC was not disrespectful but casual, as if chatting with an old acquaintance.

"Do you not know how to birth people into the next world?"

"Well, I, uh, I used to..." she stammered, "I was once a transition witness."

"You need look no further for your purpose."

DC felt incredulous if not indignant. "But that's all behind me. I have a little girl to care for now."

"Use all of your gifts."

The sacred one closed his eyes, and the three people who stood before him knew the visit was over.

Chapter 75

As they stepped out into the encircling trees of the sanctuary, silence followed them. Each remained wrapped in separate thoughts. Darby was beginning to sense his decision. Merideth was contemplating the source of true power. And DC was protesting her new assignment.

Darby Tate recalled how he had twice passed through the gates of death, and there he had felt the spaciousness of being without a physical self. From his discussions with the villagers, he had come to the conclusion that being born into a body on a planet creates the illusion of an individual self, which then accumulates the experiences that form the personality dubbed as ego. If he continued to let go of this separate self, he could live in the joy of that spaciousness.

Ever since his first death, the sheer bliss of that state had tugged at him. He sensed that the sacred ones existed in a similar state in order to serve their purpose. But that was not his purpose. He had all of eternity to experience the ecstasy of the infinite. While here on earth, he would live as a human, sharing his individual body, mind and spirit with other humans contained in their limiting skins.

Darby glanced over at the two women with him, beautiful in their introspection, and he knew he had made the right decision.

As she walked the path, Merideth Wolfe began forming words around her new knowledge about power. She had watched her grandfather cling to power as if it was as precious as breath. Even when old age dimmed the sharpness of his mind and his organs began to fail, he refused to let go his reign. All measures were taken, until finally, it was only his face and brain that remained—enough to be a figurehead, but not enough to defend his throne. The directors of the Consolidate now saw him as an impotent puppet, kept alive only because the people seemed to adore him, his only role to keep the populace calm.

Merideth now knew that whoever held the heart of the people had the real power under the dodec, and she assumed her grandfather knew it, too, for after all, he had been the one to choose her grooming, to decide what knowledge would be instilled and withheld. She wondered if he knew that he had created the monster who had planned kill him one day to usurp his power. It no longer mattered. Now, two people the Benefactor had never even met—a chemist and a transition witness—had altered his fate, altered *her* fate so completely that no vestige of her past power remained.

As she walked away from the sanctuary of the sacred ones, she concluded that true power comes from neither charisma of personality, nor brilliance of mind, nor strength of force. It was not the ability to lead or the authority to command. She sensed that it had to do with a simple willingness to exist in service to others, to merge with the great flow of life and accept its destination. *True power is internal. It does not need an external expression*, she thought.

Next to her, DC was still arguing with the sacred ones in her head. *What do they mean, 'Birth people into the next world'? All I did was sit there waiting for their last breaths and made sure they were dead. The last thing I want to be is a transition witness.* She thought about how she had hated herself for carrying the sickle of death. Its heaviness weighed her down so much that she might have applied it to her own throat if not for Ari.

Ari Stockton, her light in the darkness, her strength in the storm. Where was he now? Would today be his turn at the Transitionary? Would his last vision be the face of some other transition witness?

At least I won't have to be the one to witness it, she thought. *Become a transition witness again? Over my dead body.*

Her frown turned into a smile, and she began chuckling at the pun. Now it was Darby's turn to look at *her* askance, and that made her laugh. Darby's questioning expression become more extreme, and DC laughed even harder. Then, in the way that mirth can take over a soul and overwhelm it with merriment, DC began laughing at her own laughter, until finally she was doubled over and could no longer walk.

"What's so..." Darby started to chuckle, intermittently at first, but then DC's guffaws infected him like a virus, and soon they were both sitting on the ground, laughing with abandon.

Merideth stopped and turned to smile at the scene behind her. *Must be some private joke I don't yet know about.* She continued down the path, leaving them to their silliness. She would find out soon enough what that had been all about. At some later time, she would ask her new friend and fellow midwife. And there was one more thing she wanted to know from DC-1128. Why did she still use her Directory of the Consolidate initials as her name? Merideth Wolfe made a mental note to find out.

Chapter 76

The two giraffes zoomed through the air as Elva ran after them squealing with delight. Katina sat on the living room floor, focusing on making it fun for her younger friend, and she kept the animals just out of reach.

The girls ignored DC as she entered the front door and made her way to the kitchen, where Great-grandmother Sophia was finishing her breakfast. DC cherished her quiet talks with this woman who had become her mentor and confidante. She could share her deepest feelings, and Great-grandmother would take them in and somehow transform them so that they no longer carried such weight. She offered neither sympathy nor judgment but gave the gift of acceptance of every single thing that DC told her about. Great-grandmother sometimes just nodded, saying nothing in reply. But when she did respond with words, it sometimes took DC days or weeks to unwrap the wisdom they contained.

DC had not been gone long that morning, but Great-grandmother Sophia sensed it had been a significant meeting, and she knew that the most momentous events in a person's life happen in mere moments. As always, she waited for DC to begin releasing her burden.

"Darby asked them what difference it would make to have replaced the Benefactor's heart," she began. "They didn't really answer."

Great-grandmother waited in silence while DC mustered an attempt to evade the issue that mattered most.

She began rambling about everything except her new assignment.

"I'd really like to know why it matters if the stones are blue or black. I don't get the technology of it. Shar says that every single thing has its own vibration, and that's what she taps into to move it, so maybe there's some kind of energy they provide—a different energy in each stone. But how did Darby's mother know that, and where did she get the blue stones in the first place? I can't imagine she just happened to find them by the river. Darby said that his mother used to tell him stories about the sacred ones, but he thought they were just fairy tales—something to entertain him. There are so many questions still, and the buoyant bambinos didn't answer any of them."

She paused, having run out of evasive thoughts. She had seen Great-grandmother Sophia's eyes twinkle at her description of the levitating children. But now, Great-grandmother seemed deep in her own thoughts, and it was DC who would have to wait for Great-grandmother to choose her words.

"It was the sacred ones who gave Darby's mother the stones. They asked her to take them into the dodec. She was barely more than a girl, but she already had many talents. She was telekinetic like Shar. And she could also see, like Finn."

Great-grandmother anticipated DC's question and gave the answer. "I don't know how she got into the dodec. I never saw my daughter after the day she left."

The revelation gave DC a shock, and she jerked back as if stung by a bee. It took her a moment to calculate the family tree.

"That means... Are you saying Darby is your grandson? And that would mean Shar is his... cousin?" She waited a moment for Great-grandmother to nod her verification.

"Why haven't you told him?"

"I didn't know when you first came to The Village. It wasn't until you returned from your adventure and told the story of the blue stones. Then I knew. But I have taken some time to take counsel with myself regarding when and how to tell him, because my deathday is so near. You dodecians grieve so deeply over the death of a loved one."

The words felt like a physical blow to DC's stomach, and it took her a moment to catch her breath. Darby, Great-grandmother Sophia's grandson? And Great-grandmother nearing her 'deathday'?

DC had heard the term before. While those in the dodec observed birthdays, here in The Village, deathdays were also a reason to celebrate. But what was Great-grandmother talking about? Her deathday so near?

DC resisted the urge to run from the room. Sorrow and questioning flooded her eyes. She thought about how the villagers die with volition. After traveling as far as they wanted into old age, they either sensed or simply decided what day they would die. On that day, they would sit in a room, and family and friends would come to visit one by one. When all who wanted had shared a final moment, the old one would simply close her eyes and release her spirit back to the infinite.

DC did not understand how that was possible, no more than she understood how simple stones could change the destiny of the dodec. But she knew that it was how death happened here. It had been explained to her that this was an ancient way—the original people of the land had made their transitions in the same manner.

"Will you be my final witness?"

As if two blows were not enough, Great-grandmother Sophia's question hit her like a knock-out punch. Now the tears filled her eyes, and she felt her throat constrict.

"When?" It was the only word she could get out.

"In two weeks' time."

Great-grandmother Sophia reached across the table and enfolded DC's hands in her own. "It is a joy, not a sorrow."

DC could feel nothing but loss, but her love for this woman had grown so much that she removed her focus from her own pain to offer what Great-grandmother had requested.

"Of course," she said. "You birthed Darby's mother into this world. I will help birth you into the next."

Chapter 77

As the two weeks passed, DC could think of little other than Great-grandmother Sophia's pending death. She thought of all the people she had watched die during her time in the Transitionary, and she knew that not one carried the wisdom of this village crone. *That's the real reason the Consolidate kills them at fifty,* she mused. According to Consolidate indoctrination, in a closed-loop world, too many people would overwhelm the system, resulting in death for everyone, so the Transitionary was a necessary sacrifice that each person made for the good of all. DC knew now that it was a lie. *People with the wisdom that comes from long years of experience—that's the real threat to a totalitarian state.*

For two weeks, she did not leave the house except to pick vegetables from the garden, so precious was every moment with the old crone. There was so much more she wanted to ask, so many more things to be illuminated under the light of Great-grandmother Sophia's wisdom.

One day, she asked, "What makes a rebel?" She had never understood that part of herself that seemed so different than most others. Or perhaps she needed to know why the rest of the dodecians didn't share her passion for something better. What had created their complacency? Of all the people under the dodec, why were only a few engaged in the work of making change for the rest? Why did DC's neighbors see benevolence where DC saw malevolence? Why were dodecians satisfied by the distractions of empty entertainment or other addictive offerings? How were they blinded to the manipulations that kept them enslaved? How could they be fooled by the redefinition of patriotism as agreement with the status quo, or the representation of a good life as accumulation of material things?

"Innocence," was Great-grandmother Sophia's answer. It was not because they were too stupid or too lazy to see the truth, she explained. "Humans are simply innocent. They trust. They believe what they are told. Isn't that a beautiful thing about us?"

"But your ancestors weren't innocent. They saw through the subterfuge. They wanted change, and they fought for it."

"Oh, my dear, they didn't fight. They only survived the onslaught. And most of them didn't understand the depth of their deception. Of the thousands of lies they had been told, they had realized the falsity of only one. But that was enough."

"Really? Just one? What one truth could break the stranglehold that the power elite had held on the populace for so many years?"

"That we are all the same being," Great-grandmother Sophia said.

DC remembered Grandma Sylvan saying something to that effect, but she didn't understand it at the time.

"You've heard the term, 'divide and conquer'," Great-grandmother Sophia said. "It was not just a primary tactic in warfare, but also the primary method for maintaining control over society. If you can cause people to fear and hate others, not only will they allow themselves to be enslaved, they will demand it. And so the people in power emphasized false divisions—conservative, liberal, rich, poor, gay, straight, black, white, Christian, Muslim."

"Anarchist, patriot," DC chimed in, remembering the history lesson from Finn.

"Yes, and many, many more. But eventually, the truth began to shine through. One by one, we began to realize that we are no different than our neighbors, no matter which of those labels they carry. We are all one more cell in the great body of the planet, one more thought in the great mind of God. Our scientists had understood that for a century. Their explorations into the tiniest bits of substance had shown the interconnectedness of all things. They had proven the oneness of all that is. But that was one more division at the time—science versus religion—one more duality that kept us separate. For our ancestors, realization of their oneness created compassion for all people—for friends and enemies, for acquaintances and strangers, in fact, for all of life everywhere. Now, we don't know how we had missed it. We are all part of one great thing. Our scientists used to call it The Field. Our religionists called it God. Some people called it nature. Some people called it cosmic mind. Now, we just call it Life."

Great-grandmother Sophia remained silent, allowing DC to soak in the new information.

"Just keep thinking about it. It usually begins as an intellectual curiosity. Then it becomes a new understanding. Eventually, it dissolves the old belief in separation and becomes a way of being. Then, love for all other people is automatic, for you are the same being."

329

DC was enthralled by the history lesson and sat in rapt attention. "But how did the villagers come to this understanding?" she asked.

"When you know that nothing is separate, that you are a part of the one great mind, you can learn to tap into any part of it, future, past, here, elsewhere, science, art. All information is available."

"So they overcame the belief in separateness. And that was enough to defeat the old ways of power and manipulation?"

"The power of love is much stronger than the love of power."

"I don't understand. They just loved each other into a utopia?"

Great-grandmother Sophia smiled softly. It had been many decades since she had an opportunity to discuss the lessons of love, so ingrained were they in her society.

"Imagine that your hand feels fine, but your foot hurts."

DC went along with the game, hungry for the understanding it might provide.

"Now imagine that your hand becomes aware of itself. Imagine it grows its own little forebrain. It says to itself, 'I exist.' And your foot has its own little brain, too. It becomes aware of itself. Both are aware of themselves, but they can't see beyond their own boundaries. The hand can't see beyond the wrist. The foot can't see beyond the ankle. They think of themselves as separate. Can you imagine that?"

"Yes, I can."

"So what does the hand do about the foot's pain?"

DC gave it a moment of thought. "Well, if it cares about the foot, it will try to relieve it, maybe rub some balm on it."

"And does it care?"

"I suppose not, if it can't see past its ankle."

"Now, imagine that the hand comes to realize that it and the foot are both part of the same body. Now what does the hand think about the foot's pain?"

DC understood. Of course the hand would want the foot's pain relieved, would do everything it could to relieve it. She nodded to show her understanding. But she still wanted to know how it could relate to rebels and the dodec. "What if the foot is harming the body? Shouldn't the hand do something to stop it?"

"Maybe it should blow up a few toes with explosives," Great-grandmother Sophia teased.

"Of course it wouldn't do that," DC said. "Not if it knew it was part of the same body."

"Maybe it should leave—sever itself from the rest of the body in order to escape the foot's malice?"

DC knew that the last sentence was inflected as a question to force her to think. This was what she had done— severed herself from the Consolidate. The rest of The Group had wanted to destroy it. But she didn't have the stomach for the violence that would entail. So she chose what she thought was the only other option—to flee the oppression of the dodec. Fight or flight. The two instincts of a human when facing a threat. Another duality. Another veil obscuring the full range of possibilities.

"Isn't separation what the entire village has done?" DC asked. "We're here in The Village. They're there under the dodec."

"And we're still all part of the same body," Great-grandmother said. "Just as a body might encase a foreign invader in a cyst, so the Consolidate has encased itself in the dodec. And so our collective body has a tumor. We need to neither attack nor sever it. Be patient, my child, for our body is composed of love, and everything in nature heals itself."

Chapter 78

Ari Stockton fingered the aluminum cuff on his wrist. They had somehow fused it with his skin, and he could not imagine the chemical bonding that would make such a thing possible. This was the type of advance usually developed by his lab. How could he have not known about it? It would not be possible to remove the tracking device, but at least he was free, at least for one more day. The transition takers had been there an hour before, and tomorrow, he would be led by two transition assistants to a transpod, where he would take his last breath.

This day would not be like any other, for it would be the first time that he criticized his daughter for whom she had become. He did not want to hurt her, but he knew that gentle cajoling would not be enough. He must stop her from continuing her fall into an empty life full of deceit and manipulation. She had been seduced by the delusion of power, and he had only one opportunity to break the spell. It was the reason he had returned to the dodec—because it might give him this one last chance.

Gemini had insisted on meeting in her office where she could feel her authority. *Her office*. She was no longer working for Senator Smallman. Now, she had her own staff. Ari could not fathom how she had risen so quickly to a place on her party's ticket. In a society that lives only to age fifty, it was not unheard of for eighteen-year-olds to run for the Senate, but unlike other young hopefuls, she had grown up without political connections. Perhaps it was her pending marriage to a department head in the Security Division that had given her the edge.

That was something else he would try to stop. Orion was a free man, having convinced the vice president of security that he had once again played double agent and infiltrated The Group to foil its plot. Was he friend or foe? Ari no longer knew. But he knew that this slippery eel was not right for his daughter.

He entered the elevator and pushed forty-four. His daughter was already that close to the top of the Consolidate. The car seemed to rise quickly, and with the sound of the ding at each floor, his heart dropped another notch.

A group of four people stood in the outer office speaking in toned-down voices. As Ari approached the receptionist's desk, his glance doubled back to the group, and he had to work to contain his shock. Standing there among them was the boy he had met in the warehouse basement—the villager named Finn—the one who had stayed behind. Ari looked at Finn's wrists for an aluminum cuff. Wouldn't he at least be monitored? But he saw no band of silver. When he looked back up to the boy's face, Finn nodded toward him and a soft smile passed over his lips. It carried a message, but Ari could only decipher its friendliness.

Ari did not offer his name to the receptionist. "I'm here to see my daughter," was all he said. He would at least claim his relationship to her and the authority it gave him.

"She'll be with you in a minute. You may have a seat."

Ari remained standing. He would do nothing right now that was passive. This was his last chance for action.

Gemini's office was much larger than he had expected and richly furnished with two leather high-backed chairs facing a cherrywood desk. A small cherrywood conference table sat next to a huge window looking out to the city. Gemini remained seated behind her desk, and Ari recognized her need for a layer of protection between them. She removed her optiscreen glasses and gestured to the chair, but he walked right around the desk.

"What, no hug for your father?" He opened his arms, and she saw the flash of silver on his wrist.

"I have to maintain a certain decorum now. It's nothing personal."

Already so cold. How did you get here, Gemi? Wasn't my love enough?

"At least let's sit at the table," he said, walking over to the conference table and pulling out a chair. He could see her reluctance, but she followed him to the table, and when she chose a chair across from him, he got up and moved to the one next to her.

He gazed at her face and waited until she looked directly at him. Something about her eyes seemed different. He thought the color was off just a bit, but he put the concern aside as trivial.

"Whatever you think of me, I'm still your father. And even if you were the Benefactor himself, I would still say what I have to say now."

He saw her stiffen slightly and knew she was bracing herself. *Ah, so I can still have an impact,* he thought to himself, and prepared to unload his full arsenal.

"I'm on the List." He saw her swallow. "Today is my last day on this earth, and I'll leave it with only one regret. I

335

have raised a daughter who has closed her heart and let power seduce her." He saw a slight wince. "A daughter who is planning to marry a devious man for nothing more than political gain." He noticed her jaw clench. Each expression was a fortification of her defenses, and as he watched each one increase the distance between them, his own defenses came crashing down. All the things he had planned to say crumbled into dust, and he could only express what was in his heart.

"Oh Gemi, I would love you no matter what you did. But what will you benefit if you gain the whole world but lose your own soul?"

He could see one layer of protection dissolve, but her spine remained stiff, and she spoke with an unwavering voice.

"First of all, I want you to know that I will miss you. Every trip to the Transitionary is a sacrifice for the good of all, and I thank you for making it. It's how it has to be. Second, Orion is not just a political expedience. He is a brilliant man and will make a good partner. And any power I gain from my marriage to him will benefit the masses. In six months, I will be a senator, and I plan to be the best one the Consolidate has ever had. I don't need you to be proud of me. I am proud of myself."

And that could be your downfall, Ari thought. But now he was done trying to convince her. He felt his defeat, and he didn't try to hide it. "You're so sure of your victory?"

"And you're so innocent? You think that the people choose their representatives? It's already been decided. My opponent will be well-compensated for playing his role, but nothing more. Your daughter has been chosen to become Senator Stockton."

Ari was not surprised that elections were rigged, and he no longer cared. He remembered seeing Finn in the outer office, and a tiny light of hope lit his heart

"I noticed a boy in your reception area who had been in the basement with us that day. Part of your staff?"

"Best election adviser anyone ever had."

"And after the election is over and you no longer need him? Isn't he considered an outlaw?"

"Oh, I will always need someone with his skills."

Ari had known the boy for only a day, but in him he had seen an abiding integrity and purity of spirit. "And what is the Consolidate planning to do about the recent events that he was involved with?"

Gemini was too astute to let any state secrets slip, but Ari hoped he might get an idea of whether the Consolidate knew about the rebels who still remained in the dodec.

"The treaty has been broken, and that can't be ignored. The rest of you are no longer a threat."

He heard the accusation in the pronoun and let it go. He didn't know if her reply meant that once outside the dodec, the escapees were considered innocuous. It could mean many other things. It no longer seemed to matter. Fate would flow where it wanted, and it would take his daughter with it like a piece of driftwood held by the current.

Ari Stockton had nothing left to do but surrender, but he did so with a heart open as wide as the sky, and in that was his victory.

Gemini did get up to hug him goodbye. He felt her hold tight for a brief moment, and in her ear he whispered, "Always listen to your heart."

He was the first to let go. And as he turned and walked out of her office, his own heart fell into limitless depths.

Chapter 79

Great-grandmother Sophia sat in her comfy recliner, wearing her finest dress. The line outside her door stretched all the way to the village square, so many were the people who loved this old sage. As each sat next to her for their turn to say goodbye, she gave each a gem of wisdom or a bit of her heart. Whether blood relative or mere acquaintance, she gave equally to every soul who approached, just what was needed, nothing more, nothing less.

DC brought her tea and water. There was no need to prepare food, as the visitors brought their best pies and treats, and great-grandmother took at least one bite of each. *She's going to die of a sugar high,* DC thought, but she kept her concern to herself. She watched as the people came and went, came and went, giving their words of gratitude or honor, soothing their mentor in the way a tide attends to its wide beach.

It was long after dark that the line of people had finally receded. DC sat down next to the woman who had become her dear friend and mentor. She could see the tiredness in those old eyes. Great-grandmother Sophia reached over and grabbed both of DC's hands, and the tiredness lifted from her face as she gazed at the younger woman.

"I have been ready for this for a long time," she said. "It's time for these old bones to return to dust."

A long pause deepened the stillness as the two sat together in silence. The old woman closed her eyes, and her breathing was slow and steady, in and out with the rhythm of an ocean.

DC closed her eyes, too. She was tired from the long day of being in attendance for endless visitors arriving and departing as reliably as breath. Her mind rested and drifted, first back to the days at the Transitionary, then sitting at Ari's dining room table, then back in the raging river, rolling, tumbling, somersaulting in pink currents.

Her eyes sprung open like the door of a cuckoo clock. She remembered! After the jump from the tunnel. Those moments in the river. Or was it an eternity she had spent there? The colors! The joy! The magnificence of existence! The memories flooded her, engulfing her like the river had done. How could she ever forget the splendor of death? Now, she remembered. But she would unravel all of it later. At the moment, Great-grandmother needed her.

DC gazed at the old woman and could tell she had one last bit of sagacity to impart.

"Pay attention to what is being born in you, and what is dying."

DC smiled and a tear slid down her cheek. She removed her hands from under Great-grandmother's clasp and placed them on top of the wrinkled fingers.

"So many people have offered you their love this day, but none is greater than mine," DC whispered.

She looked for Great-grandmother's understanding, but the old eyes were focused over her shoulder now, staring into some distant world that was out of DC's reach. A look of wonder took hold of the ancient face.

"It's beautiful," Great-grandmother said. And with one final sigh, she closed her eyes and stepped out of this life.

DC wept. She laid her head on Great-grandmother's chest and cried for her loss of a friend and mentor. She cried for her own life, burdened with guilt. She cried for all of the people of the dodec who merely existed without really living. She cried for Ari, who had lost a daughter to something worse than death. She cried for Gemini, who had lost her way to her own heart. She cried for Elva, who would never again know her father. She cried for Simeon, who had given his life for his friends. Great sobs of grief wracked her chest. And when she was finally empty, she rested, her head still lying above Great-grandmother Sophia's sacred heart.

Chapter 80

Darby Tate waited. He sat in semi-darkness, the bulb on the porch illuminating a small circle around it. Everyone else had gone. They had all been there for Great-grandmother Sophia, but Darby was here for DC-1128.

During the last two weeks, he had spent almost all of his time with Great-grandmother Sophia—*his* grandmother—and had gleaned all the information he needed about his mother. He had taken the time to say his goodbye, and now, he was not saddened by his grandmother's death. He had once been where she was going, and he knew that they would one day have a joyful reunion there.

But he also knew how this transition would affect DC. It would bring the recollection of her past identity back to her in full force, and he worried that it would knock her to her knees. He remembered when they had first returned to the dodec, she had nearly fainted in the elevator on the way to the Transitionary, so debilitating was the memory of whom she had been.

And so he waited for the woman who had saved him from a transitioner's fate. As patient as a cat waiting for a trap to be released, he waited for the door to open.

It suddenly swung wide, and DC stepped out into the night air. Darby moved toward her, and as she entered the circle of light shining down from the small bulb above them, he could see her eyes were swollen. He enfolded her in his arms, wanting to be her comfort, willing to hold her for as long as she needed, yearning to find the words that would soothe her.

She returned the embrace, and they remained in each other's arms, heart to heart, exchanging the silent words that only hearts can say.

Finally, he spoke, quietly in her ear. "DC, DC, DC." His breath carried love in its current. "What you did for Great-grandmother was a gift. What happened in the Transitionary was not your fault."

He stopped the next words before they could travel the distance from heart to lips, for this moment belonged to grief. But he tightened his grip and again repeated her name, "DC, DC."

She broke the embrace and stood at arm's distance. Her eyes held the clarity of pure water, and her voice came out like the flow of a mighty river.

"My name is Diana Childress, and I am a transition witness."

About the Author

Thank God for Mrs. Hibbard. She wrote my poem out in big letters on a one-foot-by-two-foot card and tacked it up on the blackboard with a big gold star. And thus, a poet was born in the first grade.

But who can make a living on that? Common sense sidetracked me into the world of journalism, which was great for my ego, because I won dozens of writing and editing awards and ended up as the head honcho of a daily newspaper on the California coast.

When you're a newspaper publisher, everyone wants you on their boards and committees, because they think that will get them better media coverage (wrong), but that illusion allowed me to add a lot of directorships to my resumé.

A perfect life, some would say, but I could never quench the deep yearning to use words creatively—not just to inform, but to inspire, to entertain, to move you. That yearning finally had to be satisfied, and so here you have it, *The Transition Witness*. I hope it has captivated you.

I'd love to hear from you. You can e-mail me at transitionwitness@yahoo.com, or tweet me at @ttsalaky. Let me know if you want to be notified when the next book in the series comes out.

Final Words

For a new author, reviews and spreading the word through social media are lifeblood. So if *The Transition Witness* touched your heart, mind or soul in any way, please write a review on Amazon and also post to Facebook or Twitter.

If you're on Goodreads or Shelfari, consider posting a review there as well. I promise to read all reviews and use your comments to continually improve what I write. My dream of making a living at this art is in your hands.

With gratitude,
Teresa